BEHIND THE VEIL

E. J. Dawson

Literary Wanderlust | Denver, Colorado

Behind the Veil is a work of fiction. Names, characters, places, and incidents are the products of the author's imagination and have been used fictitiously. Any resemblance to actual events, locales, or persons, living or dead, is entirely coincidental.

Content Warning: This book contains dark adult themes, a full list of possible triggers can be found on page 286.

Published in the United States by Literary Wanderlust LLC, Denver, Colorado.

https//www.LiteraryWanderlust.com

ISBN Print: 978-1-942856-88-7
ISBN Digital: 978-1-942856-93-1

Printed in the United States of America

Dedication

To my mother, and the deep corners of her bookshelves,
I never knew how far it would take me, thank you.

And to Hart, you were right, it wasn't a short story
after all...

Chapter 1

Michael's time was short. Breath wheezed over his dry tongue and down his phlegm-filled throat, squeezing into his lungs with spikes of breathlessness. Dulled under the doctor's ministrations, the seizures were increasing. They couldn't stop swift attacks or save his life.

But they ensured he wasn't in any pain—he couldn't feel anything at all. Not even where his wife held his hand between palms that gave no warmth. Heat came instead from the great roaring fireplace, which kept the snow-flaked chill at bay. He'd asked for the curtains to be left open so he could see the snow fall.

The children loved snow.

Their blue eyes were wide with trembling tears as they stood at the end of the bed. They ignored the snow to stare at him. Swamped with sadness, they did not understand, and Michael ached to reassure them. He smiled, remembering how they'd been last year, bursting with wonder and cheeky delight at the wrapped packages under the tree. This was no time of the year to die in front of one's offspring. Michael's one regret.

"Please," his mother begged, "don't go, don't leave us, it can't be you. You're all I have left." She held his other hand, hers clawed with age but gentle. Her weathered face bore the marks of tragedy: a lost husband, two lost sons. At least the others had been in the line of duty as honorable deaths in the Great War.

Michael couldn't imagine going to greet them in the beyond because he'd caught a chill.

"Don't fret," he mouthed the words, unable to give them sound with the breath left in his body. "I'll tell them you love them."

He tried to promise her, but she sobbed harder at his voiceless assurances. The children darted their eyes between him and their grandmother. When her wails became too much, his wife signaled a maid to usher the silent children away. Michael didn't want them to go. He needed them to be the last sight his dying eyes withheld. Their blond heads turned away, white bedgowns fading to blurs in his weakening vision.

Michael tried to call their names, but his utterance turned into a cough that left him gasping and he shuddered, agony rising to the surface again.

"Doctor," his wife murmured, "please ease his suffering."

The doctor and nurses struggled to hold him as the seizure took him. Excruciating seconds dragged on as they jabbed the syringe into his arm, which pierced him like a blade. It hurt. It hurt. It hurt.

Yet not as much as the pain in his chest and throat that climbed to his tongue and teeth. God, even his teeth ached.

The drug slithered through his system, and Michael was so used to its soporific effect that it was a welcome balm. He'd die soon, essence and thoughts slipping away as his vision narrowed on his wife.

Her pale face was masked by the fine coating of powder clinging to her skin, eyes brimming not with sorrow but relief.

He knew her so well, for the years she'd done a wife's duty, bore his children, and taken care of his home. But she was young, younger than him. It was at her insistence he walk home that rainy day and she hadn't called a doctor when sickness claimed him. She'd always thought him weak, and now she'd inherit it all on behalf of his son.

He didn't fear for himself any longer, but he wished he wasn't leaving his children with her.

Even as the light faded, all he could think of was their enormous, innocent eyes compared to the cool indifference of his wife...

Letitia inhaled, coming out of her reverie as she avoided the final moment of Michael's death. His spirit slipped through the veil beyond, and she a solitary witness to his passing, which had not been without regret. He'd carried the ache to protect his children, but he could stay no longer.

They would have to fend for themselves.

"He died on Christmas day," she said whisper-soft, her own throat raw. "How sad for you." Letitia uttered it without thought and regretted being so careless.

"My son." The black-clad woman at the table wept, bringing Letitia back to the candlelit room. Her head spun with the vision's aftereffects. Placing her hand flat on the table she grounded herself, touching the cool walnut surface, concentrating on the whorls in the wood and ignoring the other things on the table. Her gaze drifted to the carpet—thick wool, threaded in a Turkish pattern of cream vines swirling on a black background, red blossoms adorning their branches— and across to a candelabra of wrought iron, holding aloft six fat white candles; a measure of lost time given how far they'd burned down. It shouldn't have been such a long session, but the man's death had dragged on for days, though Letitia's experience flashed by in a mere twenty minutes.

Too long, Letitia thought, before focusing on the sobbing patron.

The older woman was Michael's mother, Mrs. Peabody, and Letitia could see what made him a devoted son. The gray hair in a severe bun, the hands clawed from arthritis and some other muscular tension, the dark eyes so piercing in her pale face. But his mother brimmed with kindness and love and was bereft without her family.

It was the dainty woman beside Mrs. Peabody who was the viper here.

Cold blue eyes stared at Letitia, who could read the disdain in the wife's face just as she could sense the edge of her emotions. Letitia's abilities allowed her to experience the wife's personality in the form of elemental conditions—a crisp breeze on her face, icy and unpleasant. Letitia focused instead on the reddened eyes of the mother.

"I saw him, in a bed, the fire was going but Michael wanted the window open to see the snow fall." Letitia used the room's description to confirm her vision. "You have three grandchildren, two girls and one boy. Blue eyes like their mother, but they have their father's blond hair. He had pneumonia and passed away last Christmas. Michael wished he hadn't died in such a fashion, not compared to his brothers or his father. He wanted to be brave like them."

Her verdict set off Mrs. Peabody. The old woman's grief flooded Letitia in the profound sense of rain, falling without cease. The wife's unsympathetic gaze narrowed again, and Letitia ignored it. Whether the watchfulness came from suspecting Letitia's perception of the wife's unhappy marriage or disbelieving of Letitia's gift, it didn't matter.

Letitia cared first for her patron, Mrs. Peabody.

"Ma'am," Letitia said, using the American preferred manner of address, "please don't distress yourself. Your son may have died before his time, but his last thoughts were of his family. He has gone to join the rest beyond the veil, and he passed with no real regrets but that he left the children behind." A small lie that omitted his fear of his wife's intentions, but it didn't matter if it would comfort Mrs. Peabody. Letitia laid a gloved hand on the older woman's, and the mother accepted, squeezing it as much as she could with her fingers the way they were, crooked and disconcerting with their long nails.

"Could you please look for my husband?" she pleaded, "or even my other sons?"

"I am sorry," Letitia said, drawing her hand back, "but reading the veil between life and death exhausts me. You may book another session if you wish."

She let the invitation drift, not reaching for her appointment book. They'd had to wait a week to see her, even though she'd arrived in Los Angeles months before. Despite the few other spiritualists lurking within the city, Letitia's reputation was taking care of itself. But she would have to take care to avoid the kind of trouble she'd found in England. She was no charlatan with parlor tricks or a spiritualist with little training who would lead them astray.

"Please, whenever you can fit us in, money is no issue," Mrs. Peabody begged as the wife pouted. "Ease the pain of my grief. All I have of the world is my grandchildren and this beautiful woman my son called wife."

Letitia picked up her ledger, ignoring the protest forming on the wife's parting lips, and noted down a time next Tuesday evening. Mrs. Peabody accepted, and Letitia penciled in the time, date, and name.

"Thank you so much," Mrs. Peabody said, repeating thanks as Letitia ushered them out. The wife still bore a delicate scowl on her sculpted brow, pausing as though about to say something. Letitia met her gaze, unperturbed, and the wife appeared to think better of it and helped her mother-in-law down the stairs.

Letitia closed the door behind them.

With a sigh, she snapped on the electric lights, grateful the city was more civilized than the poorer parts of London.

Taking the stifling veil off, she straightened the black lace that rendered her face unrecognizable. Patrons could see vague features through the gauze but little else, and Letitia preferred it that way. It kept an element of mystery about her, and she was less identifiable should she run into a client. The marks of her past were distinctive enough to be recognizable. She welcomed the anonymity of the veil and the distance it gave her from her client's distress.

It was her words that mattered, the authority of her voice and the conviction of truth in what she said. Anything else would perhaps cause clients to think she was a fraud. She was the very essence protecting them from false spiritualists like the one that had led her down this dark path.

A medium who convinced grieving war widows and mothers she could commune with their dead husbands and sons. Dying in glorious battle, serving their country, they returned home in a box, nothing but a placating piece of paper and a scrap metal medal to mark their contribution.

It sickened her.

Letitia brought the families a peace she would never see.

Hanging the veil on the back of the apartment door, a prompt so she didn't forget to put it on for her next session, Letitia took off her gloves and prepared to pack away the tools of her visions. The first had to be the scrying bowl. Made of black glass, it was full to the brim with crystal clear water, a similar glass dish underneath catching any spillage. Letitia took a brass elongated spoon and disturbed the oiled surface of the water. The swirls fractured, breaking apart to reform and change shape, and she ignored the pictures within when she picked up the bowl. Nudging aside the curtain with her knee, she held the bowl and the dish with one hand so she could undo the latch and open the window.

Cold air blew over her face, the chill shivering away any lingering fog from the session. With great care, Letitia emptied the bowl into the garden a story below. Oil-infused water sprinkled onto the kitchen's sage bush, and Letitia knew the shrub would cleanse any taint staining the water.

Without closing the window, she let the breeze flow into the apartment to remove the musky scent of dragon's blood incense. Letitia bought it from the local Chinese market.

She may be a stranger to them, but they knew her craft. It lay in the bowl in her hands she was careful to dry with soft cotton and put back in its special witch hazel box. She took a key from the pocket of the black brocade dress she always wore for such sessions and locked the box where it sat on a cupboard. The bowl was her most prized and dangerous possession, and the bitter memories of when she was without it swirled in her mind before she banished them. It didn't stop hairs pricking up on the back of her neck, a shudder sent skittering over her skin. With the window open, she hadn't sensed that the cool draft's source came not from the window but the door.

A man stood on the landing, top hat low over his shadowed face. His broad shoulders, covered by a gentleman's cape, filled the doorway. He waited for her, unmoving in his perusal. The intrusion outraged Letitia, as did the silent scrutiny and the indecency of opening her door without invitation.

"How dare you? Please leave." She crossed the room, intent on slamming the door shut.

"I hear your skills are...legitimate." The baritone of his voice only added to his ominous presence, but whatever fear he meant to instill in her fell flat in the face of her ire.

"And you, *sir*"—she gave the address with derision—"need no introduction to state your bad manners."

"Forgive me," he bowed low, but not enough to take his eyes off her, "I didn't know this was an apartment and not an office. I wanted to see what you would do after they left."

Letitia guessed he wanted to see her face, as she always wore a veil. Either when she went out with her hat, an acceptable social norm, or when she was with her patrons.

Her patrons were wealthy—they had to be to afford her

8 | E. J. DAWSON

services—but she had to supply believable results, ones that would give closure to their grief. Letitia's familiarity with sorrow ran so deep there was seldom a misstep when she spoke to her patrons, voice full of consoling sympathy. Some, however, could become irate, forcing her to revert to the steely tone she'd once used as a schoolteacher. The same sternness returned now as she stared at the stranger.

Long, narrow face, less handsome than it was striking. Eyes soft green as new spring leaves, but with a severity that contradicted any gentleness in him, along with thin lips and raised brow.

A glance at his ensemble, dark as it was, showed the glinting diamond pin surrounded by sapphires at his throat that was almost lost in the folds of black silk. He wore a matching wool waistcoat, silver pocket watch chain hanging from its buttons. His black-gloved hands rested on the top of a large thick cane, and it would not surprise Letitia if within was a sword. How passé.

But Letitia could ill afford to offend him.

"Now you've had your turn," he said, with an amused quirk of his lips at her inspection. "Can we discuss business?"

"I do not have more than one session a night," Letitia said, "and not without a prior engagement. You will need to book an appointment."

She turned on her heel, eyes drifting to the veil. He'd already seen her face, so it would draw attention to her fear to don it now. Crossing the room, she picked up the black leather appointment book on a sideboard and returned to the door. He hadn't moved, except for where his gaze followed her movements. She pretended not to notice his examination as she read him.

Letitia stretched her senses. His temperament formed a hot wind, the heat of the desert, pervasive and endless. It made her skin itch, and she fought not to scratch the bead of sweat gathering on her temple.

Physical manifestation of her sensory perceptions was the

sign of an overwhelming persona.

Either that or a dramatic one, she thought, as she scanned her entries for an availability.

"Do you perform your sessions here?" he asked, and she nodded, scanning the book. The book denoted a little over a week of appointments, but something made her keep turning the pages of days he couldn't see. The sensation of his personality on her skin hadn't abated. Whomever he looked for in the beyond might not wish to be found. She always investigated her patrons before performing a session.

Death in wars was terrible, and accidents and sickness were far less traumatic but carried intense grief and regret. The elderly were a rarity and passed in a confused peace.

Murder was the one death she would not accept under any terms.

The longer she stood there, the surer she became that she didn't want to perform any services for him.

"My apologies," Letitia said, hopeful she could put him off with an excuse, "I'll need a preliminary appointment and then a secondary one for the actual session, and I'm unavailable for another three weeks—"

"I can't wait that long," he said, reaching into his suit pocket to pluck out a brown envelope. "If you require a provisional report to better assess the situation, you can come by my office in the morning, where I will have legal paperwork for matters of confidentiality. I believe most of your consultations are in the afternoon, so it should not interfere with your appointment book."

Letitia snapped the ledger shut. "I have other errands I must attend to tomorrow."

"I wasn't asking you, Ms. Hawking."

She had guessed he'd spoken to one of her patrons, which would explain his presence on her doorstep, but now she was certain. Only during private consultations did she give her name, and only to those who treated what she gave them with due dignity. All clients had to meet her conditions, and each made a substantial payment for her service. It varied on the time passed and the trauma of death, but each one carried a price—for them and for her. Letitia always finished her sessions by asking patrons for their discretion and giving out a card with a telephone number and times to call. She was happy for a client to refer her to others, but rather than call he was here in person, making demands. He was not the kind of clientele she sought, especially one connected to a patron who had broken her request for privacy.

"I don't appreciate your tone of voice," she retorted, "or opening my door without invitation like a common thief, never mind you haven't even bothered to introduce yourself."

"I believe I've already apologized for my error," he said, and Letitia would have responded in kind, but he was instructing her again. "And under the circumstances of your profession, I'm being more than reasonable in my request as well as reimbursement for your time."

He attempted to hand her the envelope, and when she didn't accept, he dropped it where she still held the ledger. It brushed her bare fingers, and a shadow grew behind the stranger.

The captivating dark absorbing her being, Letitia fumbled for the mental defenses against a true apparition, stunned as she was by its vivid form.

A cloud of darkness without face or features hovered over the man's shoulder, but deep inside it, she sensed it staring at her. Broad arms that could have grasped her in its embrace lay by its side. Letitia couldn't draw breath to scream at the darkness within the figure, the soul-sucking despair rendering her voiceless at the shadow's presence.

Before she could gather her wits, the stranger left with a swirl of his cloak, and the figure vanished. Letitia stood several seconds more before slamming the door shut, bolting it, and reaching for an ornamental ceramic jar by the door. Hands trembling, she uncapped the lid and sprinkled the crumbling white contents across her threshold. Salt, the purifier and protection against the unwanted. She did the same to the windows, shutting the open one while checking the rear alley behind her second-story rooms. There was nothing there but the kitchen herb and vegetable patch and empty cobblestones. Still, she drew the curtains tight before going straight to the narrow fireplace hidden behind a wrought-iron screen to throw more logs onto the fading embers. Usually, she would have let it die, but not tonight.

Letitia trembled before the oncoming wave. Shaking started deep within her, the growing fear of being helpless rising with every breath. An uncontrollable scream bubbled in her throat and she couldn't allow it to pass.

Pulling a plain handkerchief from her pocket, knotted in a ball, she shoved it in her mouth. The wadded material became saturated with saliva, thick and choking, killing the demonic noise she wanted to utter in complete and endless terror. When her jaw tried to open to release the foreign object, Letitia slapped both her hands over her mouth, tears welling in her eyes and spilling down her cheeks. Falling to her knees, she crouched before the fire, terrified of the dark.

Time passed, but it mattered not, as the emotion of the past threatened to overpower her.

When the tremors faded, Letitia fell onto her stomach in exhaustion, spitting out the mucus-covered cotton onto the carpet.

She lay there for indeterminable minutes, listening to the fire chirping away as the flame swallowed sticky gobs of sap, dancing in delight at the little treasures. It absorbed her gaze, allowing her to drift as she thought on the shadow she'd seen.

No face. No eyes. No personality she could gauge to judge its motivations. It held a malevolence that drove her to absolute dread. She'd reacted in fear. There'd been no logical thought.

Sinking into the scrying bowl and reliving the moments before death differed from seeing a specter with her own eyes.

The past trauma awakened memories of horror and disgust of an event so horrendous her rich chestnut curls were streaked prematurely with gray, the same as her honey brown eyes. People mistook them for hazel until they saw the flecks within were not a golden green but silver gray.

So light for such a dark time.

Refusing to let herself dwell on the past, she got to her feet, scrubbing her face with her sleeve in an unladylike fashion and collecting the spit-covered rag. She was about to walk through the doorway that led to her bedroom when she saw where she'd left the appointment book and envelope on the table. She didn't remember putting them down.

Wary of another vision, she picked up the letter, scanning the room for another shadow, but nothing appeared. Upon examining the envelope left behind by the stranger, Letitia noted a label on one upper corner. It named Driscoll Barristers & Lawyers and an address in downtown Los Angeles, a streetcar ride away.

Letitia flicked it open. Inside were fifty American dollars.

Even with the exchange rate as it was after the Great War, it was near the same amount in British pounds.

An obscene amount of money to meet with a lawyer.

She checked within the envelope, and seeing a note folded there, took it out.

Consider this a gift. All I ask is attendance.

9 a.m., sharp, at my office.

Mr. Driscoll.

Chapter 2

M r. Driscoll noticed Letitia through the glass pane of the door despite her late arrival at his office. An older gentleman and a man with a similar profile sat before him, but whatever business they were discussing was discarded as Mr. Driscoll rose to his feet at the sight of her.

Any plans to leave the envelope with the clerk vanished as Mr. Driscoll came around the desk and opened the office door.

"Ms. Hawking." The nonchalant voice came out with all the civility of her being as important as a client when he only hoped for the opposite—that he would become her patron.

"I came by to return this." She held out the envelope of money. "I have no need or want of it."

He glanced down at the dull paper. "Give me a moment."

The door closed and Letitia wanted to lay the money before the clerk and whirl away before Mr. Driscoll could return. But she didn't want to be accused of theft should Mr. Driscoll think to slander her by stating the funds weren't all there.

After several moments and dark, sidelong glances from the

men within the office, they rose from their chairs. Their pace was notably slow, the elder man hunched over a walking stick and assisted by the young man who could only be his son from his profile.

There were no courteous smiles as they left, and Letitia had none to offer them in return, as she avoided the blatant anger at her presence from the young man. The elder man gave a sniff of distaste as they passed.

It flared her growing resentment of Mr. Driscoll for his high-handed attitude. She was not the one who had banished them from his office.

She strode into Mr. Driscoll's office, not about to dally with the situation.

"Please take it back." She stood facing him when he shut the door. He didn't accept her outstretched hand but instead resumed his seat at his desk.

"Don't you at least wish to inquire why I have asked of your services?" The cool tone denoted his displeasure, at her late arrival or refusal she didn't know, but she'd made up her mind. "Or care to even explain why you ignored my simple request on timeliness?"

The urge to leave pressed upon her. But with no sign of last night's horrifying shadow, Letitia relented and took off her coat before bracing herself for the next few minutes of his arrogance as she sat across from him. If she didn't explain her reasoning with clarity, he may not give up the pursuit. She wanted nothing further to do with him.

Mr. Driscoll's brows rose at her bright day dress, a sunny cream that lightened her spirit.

"I didn't miss the appointment, Mr. Driscoll," Letitia said, "because I never agreed to come."

"Ms. Hawking." He drawled her name, and she heard a brogue that hadn't been there before. "I would like to think you were perfectly aware the compensation for your time would be considerable—"

"I would hate so very much for you to think I only engaged with patrons who thought my services were a matter of price," she said, continuing on when he frowned at her, "when in fact, it is regarding what they need most—comfort. They are grieving for someone who is gone, and what I offer is a chance to move on despite a loss I am intimately familiar with."

"Shouldn't that have been something you asked me if you'd ever planned to book me among your empty appointments?" he said, and Letitia avoided flinching at his knowledge of her schedule. She took care to book her patrons when it best suited them, but some nuances of her growing list were difficult to hide, such as future availability.

Letitia's mind drifted over the last week, and a woman came to mind as she looked at Mr. Driscoll. She'd had a rounder, softer face than his, her hair closer to strawberry blonde than the auburn of the man before her, but Letitia assumed the woman was a relative. Not the same name, from memory, for the patron had been a Mrs. Quinn and come about her departed husband. He'd died in a building accident the previous year. Mr. Quinn missed his wife's smile and the curls of his daughter's hair, but there was no time for much regret. The crossbeam that fell on him at a construction site hadn't allowed for it, so swift was his death.

"Tell me, Mr. Driscoll," Letitia said, "do you take every client who comes to your office for legal assistance?"

"We at least hear them out," he said.

"All of them?"

He hesitated.

"You see," Letitia said, with the patience of her former profession, "there are people beyond your abilities to assist, and you decline the offer to serve them no matter what they will pay. Consider it a virtue of my person I didn't feel comfortable taking any of your compensation when I already knew I couldn't help you. Whatever it is, I wish you well, but I'm afraid this is where we should part ways."

When she held the envelope out to him once more the bemusement gracing his face dripped away, his clenched jaw and darkening eyes revealing an uncompromising hardness beneath.

"Some other means of persuasion, perhaps?" His voice was so soft she nearly didn't hear it. Letitia's dislike grew to twist her blank smile into a grimace. Blackmail had that effect.

"You'll find no change in my disposition," Letitia said, "as you may bully others when someone says no, but not me."

He fidgeted with the paperwork on his desk before casting it aside. It appeared to be the deed to land from the title, but he discarded it as though it caused him a personal offense.

She cared not for his annoyance, grateful no further threats on her person or profession were made, but his sudden quiet was disconcerting.

"What if I told you the nature of what I needed was delicate?" He didn't meet her gaze.

"Many cases are," Letitia said, giving way for a moment. "But my rules are firm and for good reason."

"The person in question is too young to speak for themselves," he said, "and not of legal age. I require the utmost discretion in my business matters, which is why I would like you to sign these before we discuss the specific nature of my inquiry."

He lay a folio before her, but Letitia didn't spare it a glance. Instead, she lay the envelope on the open page.

"No."

"I can make it a lucrative contract—"

"I've already made my position clear." Letitia rose to her feet and collected her coat. "As have you. What I do is difficult, sensitive, and not a cheap theatrical trick or for someone else to manipulate with legalities. I am not sure why you called on me. Moreover, your lack of transparency denotes the matter not to be one of the heart."

For all of his cold composure, her comment was received as a slap in the face.

"I appear to have made a misjudgment about you, Ms. Hawking." He stood, the abrupt gesture knocking back his chair.

"Would you have stated your intent in a clear manner, perhaps it wouldn't have occurred," she said. If his tone was frosty, hers was glacial.

"If I thought some other person of your talent was available, I would look elsewhere," he said, and rather than let her retort to such an insult he went on. "But I've already examined similar services and decided for myself that other *spiritualists* don't hold a candle to your insight. It could be fiscally rewarding, and you would have my gratitude as well."

The glint in his green eyes spoke of money, his every manner unused to refusal, but at the mention of other people using her craft Letitia flinched. She did not want to be near another who thought they could dabble in her dark arts and not become burned.

"Be that as it may," she said. "I cannot and will not involve myself in such proceedings. Good day to you."

Letitia did not stop or wait, opening the office door and whisking out into the street. Whatever plans she'd intended passed in a blur among the crowds, and she stopped for a few essentials before returning to her apartment. A once open veranda remodeled to enclose the stairs led to her apartment. With two apartments available on the second story, Letitia held one and the other accommodated a Ms. Imogen Harland, who worked as a dressmaker. Imogen worked long hours and the pair didn't often cross paths, but she was charming when they did.

At the bottom of the stairs, Letitia heard the phone and raced up to answer it.

Another bad mark on Mr. Driscoll's name—he'd made her late for the hours she should be home for calls.

The phone sat on a little stand at the end of the hall under the window, so she and Imogen could share its use. At this time of day, the call would be for Letitia, and she dropped the packages on the windowsill before picking the receiver up.

"Hello?"

"I...someone gave me this phone number..." the speaker cleared his voice, and Letitia became attentive to his grief.

"There is someone you miss," she guessed, opening her purse and taking out her appointment book.

"Yes," he said, coughing away the tears, "my daughter..."

"And you'd like to know her final moments," Letitia said, tone soft enough to engage him yet not draw from the wellspring of his sorrow.

"No," he said, "I need you to find her."

That was not something she did, or at least not a service she offered. Letitia confined herself to her strongest gift of reaching beyond the veil of death as one who had transgressed before. Though Old Mother Borrows had assured her she was capable of more, Letitia confined herself to this alone to alleviate the power she carried growing out of hand. She had to ensure she never fell victim to the falsity of those beyond the veil who had never experienced life but still sought it out. It didn't change the fact that she could find the man's daughter. Old Mother Borrows' compression of a decade of training into two years ensured Letitia's iron grip on her gift, and that gave no room for error. It had forced Letitia to break—her past, her regrets, and her soul.

"Are you there?" the voice asked, rising an octave when she didn't speak.

"Yes," Letitia said, "I'm here. I'm very sorry, I don't usually do this, but I can meet with you to discuss it. I must tell you I have a fee, which I hate to ask when I don't know if I can help."

"You'll be able to confirm it, though," he said in a rush, a fickle bridge of hope. "You'll be able to see if...if she's dead or not."

"What is your name? A first name will be fine." Letitia could at least tell him if his daughter was dead or alive, and she wouldn't do a further consultation should the former prove true.

"John Barkley," he said, "I don't know if you've seen the case in the papers..."

An eleven-year-old girl, who'd been walking home from school, had disappeared. Letitia had read the story weeks ago. She regularly kept an eye on the papers for such news, since she never knew when it would be related to a prospective patron, the call a case in point.

Letitia thought the girl dead. Tempted to refuse him, she could at least offer closure by confirming what he suspected was true. It was a better fate than leaving the loss open and the life unfulfilled. Letitia's compulsion to give what comfort she could won over rather than let him seek someone else who would do more harm than good.

She refused to let anyone else be marked by the scars of her ignorance.

"Mr. Barkley," Letitia said, "if you'd come by tomorrow afternoon, I'll see you before my other patrons."

"That would be—" his voice cut off, and she heard his breathy sigh through the line, "it would be very kind. I will bring about twenty dollars. Will that be enough?"

"It's far too much, Mr. Barkley," she said, but he talked over her.

"It will be fine," he said. "I just want to see what you think."

"Very well. Could you please bring something personal of hers? A comb, a toy, or even a book."

"Yes, I have something."

"Excellent," Letitia said. "If you'd like to come by tomorrow afternoon at four, I'm in apartment B on the second floor of Six Trellis Lane. It's behind the shops on Spring Street—do you know it?"

"Yes," Mr. Barkley said, "and...thank you."

He hung up, and Letitia put the phone down in relief.

She needed to find a better way of screening patrons if she wanted to continue. Meeting at her home wasn't ideal with the likes of Mr. Driscoll thinking he could stop by whenever he pleased. Perhaps she'd keep it as a place of business but find a new house to let or even buy. Mrs. Finch wouldn't mind, and Letitia was carving herself a small niche in the vibrant, boisterous city. Though there was security in staying in a house full of other women.

Mr. Finch died during the war, but Mrs. Finch hadn't stopped the family business of soap and oil making. Mrs. Finch's products came from a long line of tried and tested recipes and concoctions to delight the skin and senses. Scented soaps, conditioners, and ladies' products. The two daughters convinced their mother to move into cosmetics and were quite successful. They sold their merchandise in a boutique store on the ground floor that opened onto Spring Street, the other half closed off for manufacture of the goods and access to the garden where all their herbs grew and the soaps dried. The family lived below Letitia and Imogen, though there was a front room on the second floor Mrs. Finch had all to herself.

The arrangement was pleasant enough and Letitia didn't want to lose it yet.

The possibility of buying a house was becoming more difficult with the war and growing film industry, but she had funds yet. After her husband's death and the subsequent incident, she could not stand the sight of the house that had once been her home. Letitia sold everything she owned and took only a suitcase when she moved to London. A hazy idea floated in her mind to return one day and buy a cottage on the coast where she'd grown up before Daniel swept her off her feet...

It was a thought for another day. Picking up the packages, she hurried to her rooms. She needed time to prepare the meeting room before this afternoon's guests and tonight's session. Unlocking the door, Letitia was proud of what she'd accomplished with the décor, conscious of its purpose.

People were suggestible, and while she wanted to assure her patrons of her abilities, there were certain expectations. With Mrs. Finch's permission, Letitia coated the walls in a burgundy velvet wallpaper and covered the windows with a thick damask fabric in a plum wine color, darker than the walls. She used wrought-iron candelabras in four corners of the room and a chandelier over the table for atmosphere. The rounded walnut table stood in the center, two chairs opposite the one Letitia sat in. It was a suitable room for what she did and put patrons in the right mind frame to be receptive to her gift. It was a little dark for her tastes, but she'd learned to appeal to the theatrics in people's own heads when it came to her unique talent.

Her clients didn't want to hear the final moments of their loved ones over a white lace tablecloth in a bright green room. The wall's previous color hadn't been suitable for any décor that Letitia could think of, and Mrs. Finch had welcomed Letitia's changes.

The gloomy room still smelled of the salt she'd swept up that morning. She'd need to burn incense to remove the odor. It was hard to assure patrons of her profession if her working room smelled like a kitchen. The next room she used as a bedroom since it had far more space, and it contained another small fireplace that kept the room warm, with an iron arm over the hearth she used to make tea. Far brighter with sun yellow wallpaper and soft cream curtains, Letitia kept it as her refuge from the dark of her profession.

Two large windows let in sunshine, the lace curtains giving privacy from the houses opposite.

A large bed sat in one corner. The room was meant for a couple, but Letitia liked the big bed. It gave her flailing limbs space to thrash during night terrors. The blanket lying over them belonged to her mother, the blue down made of soft angora wool.

She dropped the packages there, shrugging out of her coat, relieved to be in the privacy of her own space.

In another corner sat a desk for letters and correspondence with a small series of files on her patrons. It was slender, but she didn't worry over it. Instead, she turned to the wardrobe and hung her coat among the other simple items. Her black brocade dress was in a cloth bag to one side. The somber tone of the black dress was suitable for her evening affairs, but her simpler day dresses were far different.

English in its modest cut, as were all her day dresses, today's dress was a soft cream and of a good wool, but the style was out of fashion here with its far more conservative hemline. Her hands brushed over it, remembering the way Mr. Driscoll stared, in surprise she thought, but something else glimmered in his eyes.

No, it was nothing more than surprise, and she discarded the notion. The last thing she wanted was attention from an amorous man, but after the war, most ladies could take their pick. The veil she wore at all times was enough to dissuade any gentleman from coming too close, and the frosty manners of a former schoolteacher did the rest.

She hadn't given it much thought when talking to Mr. Driscoll, but the pale white hat with its lace cover that hung over her face would have obscured any chance he would have had at guessing her emotions. She'd take whatever shields were available against such a personality.

Odious man, she thought, unpinning the hat and putting it with the others in the rack above her desk. Every hat was small and discreet, each one with a veil ranging in size and obscurity. She never left the apartment without one.

Smoothing her hair back into place in the mirror beside the wardrobe, she turned to the packages, leaving her gloves on her hands. Her touch attuned itself at odd times, and she didn't need to see the manufacturing process of ladies' stockings. Those went in a drawer in her wardrobe, along with a few other sundry items. American fashions extended themselves to simpler trends than English ones, but it was the opportunity to not have to wear such thick corsets that appealed to Letitia.

Another package perfumed the air when she opened it— dragon's blood incense for the session room. Waxed paper held more of the fat white candles for the candelabras. The last items were a box of bergamot tea and shortbread. She loved the semisweet treat after a session, though it did no favors for her waistline. It was why her corsets were getting snug.

Resolving to walk around the city more but not to stop eating shortbread, Letitia went to the little firebox and put several logs on the fire. The box was low on wood, and with a groan of annoyance she tied a smock over her dress and picked up the battered basket she used to haul wood. She went downstairs.

At the bottom were two doors with a coat rack between them. One led outside to the laneway, the other into the heart of the Finch household—the kitchen.

A long room, the kitchen at varying times of the day smelled of food or soap. A great iron stove dominated one end of the room with enough cooking space for a feast. The table, broad enough to seat twelve, performed the dual duty of dining table and workplace for the making of soaps.

Stacks of the perfumed bars sat dripping onto the cloth underneath, waiting to be taken out into the cool afternoon air.

"Good afternoon, Mrs. Finch," Letitia said as she came in, heading straight for the wood box.

"Hello, dearie," Mrs. Finch said from where she was counting off a list. She finished her row and then turned to Letitia. "The wood box is running low, so I'll have more delivered tomorrow."

"I'll just get enough for this evening then," Letitia said, getting on her knees to pick up the smallest pieces and load them into the basket. She left the fat round ones for the chugging iron stove. The great behemoth of an oven warmed the kitchen but not the rest of the house. On its wide flat top pots of oils were simmering. There was an array of bottles on the table ready to scent the soaps. Letitia recognized the labels.

"You're running low on the lily," she commented. "Would you like me to get more for you?"

Letitia's addition to the house had been rarer scents. Since Letitia needed the incense found in specialty shops in Chinatown, she was more than happy to share with the household. The Finches were broadening their expertise and giving patrons wider range of choices.

"Just hold off on that," Mrs. Finch said, putting the pencil and tally to one side. "I think we've got another batch, and then I will move into getting spring scents. Do you want to have lunch with the girls and me? There's a kidney pie in the oven."

Letitia was glad her face was turned away. She loathed kidney pie.

"No, thank you," she answered instead. "I have files to review before this evening."

"Suit yourself," Mrs. Finch answered, before hoisting the racks of soap outside. "I would have thought you'd need a solid stomach before looking at those horrid things. I know I would."

Letitia didn't respond and took her load up the stairs.

She enjoyed Mrs. Finch's easy acceptance of and lack of questions about Letitia's abilities. Letitia had proved a quiet lodger and a prompt payer, which Mrs. Finch assured was all she wanted. The last woman in the room was tardy with payment.

Setting the basket down, Letitia built the fire up to make tea. Her routine was to spend the early afternoon reviewing the files for the night's session, but it also helped quiet her mind.

This evening the Normans were her patrons. Their youngest son, having taken to drink after the war, had fallen asleep outside and died of the cold and alcohol poisoning. Mr. Norman had banished him to the guesthouse when he'd come home drunk and interrupted a dinner party. They'd assured her of their grief and regret. She believed them.

Inadvertently causing the death of one's own child was a familiar intimacy she'd never forget.

The Normans had given Letitia their son's picture and a watch they had gifted him before he'd gone to war. Such a treasure was precious, and to survive along with its bearer made it resonant of the deceased's experiences in life. It left an impression on the object, enough for Letitia to pick up the thread of who they were. She took it out of the drawer she kept personal items in, having asked the Normans to hold them before the session and promising to return them after.

"Now, Joseph Norman," she said to the silver pocket watch, "who were you?"

Taking care to pull her doeskin gloves off one finger at a time, she studied Joseph's profile. Far more handsome than his father, Joseph was feminine—soft mouth, thick lashes, and a languid pose of self-assurance that was beguiling. It was a face she suspected would have been bullied in school and at home for being too feminine. The youngest son of the gruff old man that was Mr. Norman, who Letitia guessed held high expectations of his sons.

The kettle whistled and Letitia dropped the photograph on her desk.

There was a small sideboard where she kept foodstuffs, and Letitia fetched out a basket with bread wrapped in a cloth and another with cheese. Making a plain cheese sandwich and Earl Grey tea, Letitia also cut an apple to eat while she looked over her research.

Mrs. Finch was a wonderful landlady and cook, but she invited her solitary two residents to only breakfast and dinner in the kitchen. If they planned to be out, Mrs. Finch needed to be advised at the start of the week when she did her shopping. Sometimes Letitia would have a guest stay too late and find Mrs. Finch had placed a plate in the cooling oven.

Letitia kept her own meager stores in her room.

Her funds allowed her the luxury of the apartment while only taking two bookings six days a week, but she lived with as little expenses as possible. Not all her appointment spots were taken, though she offered reasonable rates after a conservative study on the more flamboyant clairvoyants laying claim to similar gifts. While there were a few spiritualists in town, they steeped themselves in phantasmagoric airs. Letitia suspected each was a fraud. She did her best to avoid them, but superstition and the thriving world of Hollywood lent itself to the impossible.

The world was open to her, and Letitia could have found herself anywhere, but America had called to her. Old Mother Borrows warned Letitia there was a fate out there waiting for her.

She would not look for it. The last time she had, she'd lost her only connection to Daniel.

Their unborn baby.

Chapter 3

It was cold when they kicked him out of the pub. Joseph only wanted to buy a bottle to take home. They hadn't sold it to him after he vomited in the gentlemen's. But tonight, of all nights, he needed it.

Just like every other night, really.

The rain drenched him, but he didn't care.

All he wanted was a drink.

He didn't want to see his family, sitting around the table praising his brother John for the promotion at the bank. Declining the dinner invitation, Joseph had made excuses before John's mocking laughter caught him at the door.

"Let him go, mother, he's tight already."

Joseph had proven to himself that his level of sobriety was nigh on angelic then, compared to what he was now. The world swam, and he struggled even to see in the dreary night.

He was lost.

The streets kept turning about, the normal route that should have taken him up Beverly and onto Gardner found him on Vista. Rain turned to sleet as he stumbled through the sleepy streets.

It was lucky, he thought, because if he hadn't been drunk the cold would've bothered him. He'd get home. The rain had momentarily confused him. As the downpour turned to frozen slush on the pavement, the slippery surface caught his unwary feet.

There was a flash, and the sidewalk was level with his eyes.

He blinked away stars, feeling an echo inside his head, and the world went black, streetlamps dying out...only to come back. Joseph studied them, fading in and out, waiting for it to stop.

A part of him assessed the damage, cold and distant. This was bad. He'd fallen and given himself a severe concussion. It wasn't the first time. The last time had been...had been...

Joseph tilted his head to the side so he could retch, agony rushing through him, sharp this time as he spat out the contents of his liquid dinner.

"This no' good," he muttered to himself, staring at the amount of vomit on the pavement.

Joseph got to his knees, and his stomach regurgitated yet more liquid, the stench of alcoholic bile bringing up everything until his body was curled in its own excess.

Pain lanced through his head, an iron spike that squeezed his eyes shut, and he didn't see the men walking toward him.

"Tad ossified, sir?" one asked.

"Might be." Joseph slit an eye open to see two policemen there and breathing a sigh of relief. At least he wasn't about to be robbed. That would have been the highlight of the evening. Or possibly it had turned worse; it was the police after all.

"I'm trying to get to 161 South Gardner," he said, searching for excuses not to be dragged to the drying out tank. His father wouldn't bail him out, and when he threatened like he had tonight, he meant it.

"All good, sir," the policeman said. "We'll get you home."

They picked him up under the arms, the journey foggy until he was standing in the porch's light. The policemen knocked on the door and Joseph couldn't stop them in time.

The maid opened it, her mouth dropping open at Joseph's state and the presence of two officers.

"Oh, I'll get Mr. Norman." She dashed off.

Joseph tried to pull away, to stand on his own two feet, but even with his stomach empty of alcohol he was still drunk. His head hurt, thumping in pulse to the angry pounding of his father's footsteps.

"Thank you, officers," his father said and shook their hands, a glimpse of paper in his palm. The officers' smiles were wide at the thick wad of money—the cause for their kindness, which continued as they tipped their hats and left.

"Walk around back and get in the guesthouse, boy," his father intoned, not letting Joseph in. "I will not disgrace your mother by letting you into this house. I will not let you ruin John's good fortune because you've pissed your own pathetic life away. You were a doctor, and then you drowned in a bottle. I should have told you I was disowning you, but I didn't want you to come home like this, you're a disgrace..."

It went on.

Joseph stopped listening, and he didn't even notice when his father shut the door. How long he'd been standing out on the porch he was uncertain, the world's tears falling on his shoulders. He turned around, walking around the outside of the house and down the side path to the guesthouse.

The door handle didn't want to open.

The deck chairs around the covered pool were inviting, even with the cold, but the bitter chill was getting worse. He had to get into the guesthouse. There was a gas heater inside if he could concentrate long enough to open the door.

Another shove pushed the door open, and it slammed when he fell against it. Stumbling steps took him to the center of the room, but looking about it was as welcome as the rain covered chairs outside. Dust sheets covered the furniture and became the ghosts of his past. Silent and accusatory, he waited to hear their pleas to make the pain stop, though they were naught but memories.

Standing alone in the dusty space, Joseph fell to his knees and cried.

No family.

Friends dead in the war.

Few who understood what being in the medical tents was like, what it did to you, night after night. The endless screams and the visions that haunted him.

During the day now, it was worse, he could see them during the day...he could see them right now...

Letitia wrenched herself away, manifested as physical reeling, and her hand slapped down on the table. The end had been so subtle, it had wrapped about her with the tentative touch of a spider, coming closer to bite her and share the death with Joseph. She gripped the wood, absorbed the warmth in her palm, sweat on her upper lip, and a chill on her skin from the cold of Joseph's death.

"Ms. Hawking, are you all right?" Mrs. Norman asked.

"Please," Letitia said, before quieting her tone. "A moment, please."

The traces faded, fingers of death slipping her by as she recovered her breath and grounded herself in her own body.

Letitia didn't know what she would tell these patrons. They wanted to know it wasn't their fault and to be sure Joseph hadn't passed with regrets. The guesthouse was an eerie reminder of their transgression, but it wasn't because Joseph was there, since he was glad to be gone from the world. It was their own guilt.

"Ms. Hawking," Mr. Norman said, voice gruff, disbelief on his face. Opening his mouth to contest her, she cut him to the quick.

"You were there, at the door, when the policemen brought him home."

She watched the skin of his pale cheeks become reddened, and she pushed on.

"You told him how...unimpressed you were after the police left." Letitia didn't stop, even as Mr. Norman glanced with shame at the now sobbing Mrs. Norman. "You told him to go out the back, not to make a fuss."

Letitia changed the sentence, rephrased it so Mr. Norman wouldn't be any more embarrassed than he already was, and at least now Mrs. Norman knew what had happened. She could guess for herself what exchanged between her husband and son.

"And...at-at the end?" Mrs. Norman asked through a series of tearful hiccups.

Letitia chose her words with care, wanting the Normans to go away at peace but warier of how to treat their other children.

"Joseph was relieved to pass on," Letitia said, watching the father close his eyes in reprieve. "You were right, Mr. Norman, he wasn't fine after the war, and he didn't know how to make it better. This would not be the first time someone has come to me with a son or husband who was stolen by the war long after it ended. But Joseph saved many lives, he did dreadful things for those lives, but there are men who went home because of him. Not whole, but they went home."

She let silence fill the space.

"But he never said," Mr. Norman exclaimed. Letitia didn't expand as he stared at her, fury and shame burning pink brands on his cheeks.

"He isn't here," Letitia said, "and he's far better for it."

Mrs. Norman clung to her husband, who was now wrapping an arm around her.

"I'd like a moment with my wife."

"I cannot leave the room, Mr. Norman," Letitia said, apology in every nuance of her words, "since what I have done today is difficult and leaves behind a residue."

"We should leave, William," Mrs. Norman said, composure returning as she rose with the help of her husband. "Thank you very much for your time, Ms. Hawking."

"I hope I've brought you some level of closure," Letitia said, coming to take Mrs. Norman's outstretched hand and allowing a brief embrace before she pulled back, both arms on Mrs. Norman's shoulders. "Now, go home, and when spring comes clean the guesthouse from top to bottom. There is nothing there than an echo of another victim of the Great War, and he does not reside there."

Sniffling, Mrs. Norman went to the door.

Mr. Norman was behind her, holding out his hand for Letitia's, and like the incident with the policemen, there were folded notes in his hand. At least another twenty dollars.

Letitia stared down at them before lifting her eyes to see the desperate hope of Mr. Norman.

If she took them, he would close the matter, the last page of a book. The certainty was so stark in the lines of his face she didn't need to open herself to see his personality. He was revolting enough as it was, and it left a sour taste in her mouth.

"Mr. Norman," Letitia said, low enough for his ears alone. "You've paid me for my services already. And now you need never bring your family the shame of disowning your son."

"You saw—" he stopped, hands clenching around the money. She met his gaze, and after a long moment, he was the first to break away.

Letitia went to the door where Mrs. Norman had put on her coat, and the pair left, Mrs. Norman the only one to look back for a final goodbye.

There was no sinister figure on the landing, and Letitia closed the door.

But something about the session was wrong.

Nothing too untoward occurred. It was smooth from beginning to end, except for one small anomaly.

Letitia went to the table and sat back in her chair, and instead of looking at the bowl, she tilted her head back to glance at the chandelier over the table. It had candles in some of its holders, placed to cast the right light on the mirror that hung from its center.

Round and twice the size of the scrying bowl, the mirror was suspended from three chains, making it secure and avoiding sway as much as possible. It was tilted at such an angle so that when Letitia looked into it, she saw the scrying bowl.

This was a different type of seeing. The bowl would drag her in and take her to the critical moments before death to experience it herself.

Letitia always found the exact cause before she sought a person's end. Innocent and accidental deaths were easy—she'd take a few gentle moments to relate to loved ones without getting too close to the cause. Others were in sickness or injury, even the battlefield itself. She'd be with them until their death approached. Those who died at the hands of a murderer were not forewarned, or what little they saw came too late to Letitia. It was why she would not take murder cases. There were instances where the victim succumbed to shock before death or were even taken unaware. Delving into their fate when she wasn't sure what was coming risked her dying with them.

Old Mother Borrows hadn't wanted to talk about what happened if Letitia got that far. But then she hadn't needed to tell Letitia. Her own experience had cut her to the bone, tore her soul to shreds, and left her a wreck. Old Mother Borrows was lucky to find enough sense within to repair.

When Letitia used the mirror, there were simply visions, the sensation akin to the images that played in her head as she read works of fiction or watched a silent film at the cinema. But like the bowl that could drag her into the death, so too was the mirror dangerous. She could become lost in a reading...

The chair was her safety. She would fall to one side, or on the table, when she became too tired.

There was no such safeguard against the scrying bowl.

She read the scrying mirror.

It was far easier to slide into its vision, which reflected the remnants left in the scrying bowl of Letitia's last visit. Though it was still distant to her, she knew what she sought.

Joseph's death replayed in her mind, but this time she was only an observer, not lost in his emotion. She was a figure on the street, following him home, watching him fall over, remembering his subsequent pain. The humiliating scene at the front door was a thousand times worse at a distance without the alcohol or splitting pain to distract her from the horrible words of Mr. Norman. For a moment Letitia wished she could have made Mr. Norman squirm all the more, but it was a brief and selfish wish. His tirade abated when Mrs. Norman came looking to see who it was, and Mr. Norman shut the door without a backward glance.

Letitia studied the scene from across the street, but now she came closer to Joseph, not watching him but the shadows.

Nothing alerted her senses or was wrong about the situation, but she followed, fading into the guesthouse. Joseph stood in the center of the room, crying before falling to the floor and curling up into a ball against the cold and all the nightmares the world had given him.

Letitia knelt beside him, aware of what was coming and unable to stop it, but still she touched Joseph's forehead with a cool hand.

A figure leaned over her.

She shrieked, slamming onto the floor as she came off her chair. Broken out of the vision, she stared around her ordinary session room. The shadow had disappeared, but there was no mistaking its presence.

The figure, while terrifying her, had a discernable difference from the one she'd seen behind Mr. Driscoll. In the world of visions, she could evade its form, even if the sense of dread was triggered by her own underlying fear. Unlike the being who'd glared over Mr. Driscoll's shoulder, this figure had emanated no such ill intent within the vision of Joseph's death.

But if a being of shadow haunted her sessions, then being anywhere near Mr. Driscoll could risk the very damage that left her body scarred and her mind on the edge of insanity.

No amount of money would bring Letitia willingly back there, not when she'd already experienced what lay beyond the veil.

Chapter 4

Letitia sat in bed, eating the breakfast she'd retrieved earlier from downstairs, when the phone rang.

Mrs. Finch didn't frown on her lodgers dining in their rooms, provided they brought the plates straight back and cleaned them. It meant Letitia could snatch warm toast from the kitchen and take it to her room so she could read a book or the paper in bed. Letitia justified her indulgence after last night's dreams of dark hallways and a figure behind every door.

Getting lost in the fripperies of the Bennet family was the balm she needed. She'd read *Pride and Prejudice* since she was a child. A far more welcome alternative to her lonesome upbringing, it allowed Letitia to pretend she was one of the sisters when she'd been young. Years later, it was the book she picked up and read after the worst of the nightmares. Comforting as a childhood teddy, the amusement of the familiar words chased away the dark.

Someone knocked on her door.

She'd forgotten the phone was ringing.

Leaving her book open, she put aside the plate of half-eaten toast and slipped on her gown.

"Tisha, it's for you," Imogen called through the door. Only her mother and Imogen called her Tisha. Her mother could no longer, and Imogen was a wounded soul Letitia had spent time with when she first moved here. Imogen lost her husband to the war, and Letitia helped her find him and see he had gone on without regret. It had given Imogen the strength to keep going on with her life. She'd been much closer to ending it all than anyone realized from her bright and happy personality.

"Who is it?" Letitia called as she opened the door.

"Woman to book an appointment." Imogen had her hand over the receiver. They both knew it was odd for one of Letitia's patrons to call this early. The cards said to telephone between the hour of eleven and twelve. Letitia took the phone.

"Hello?"

"Ms. Hawking," a breathy female voice said, "I'm not sure you remember me. I came a few weeks ago about my husband killed at a construction site."

"Mrs. Quinn," Letitia said. It could only be Mr. Driscoll that wanted her. There was no reason for Mrs. Quinn to call her again. She gave her patrons as much closure as she could, and Mrs. Quinn had gone away satisfied. One of her earliest patrons, Mrs. Quinn gave Letitia a few referrals after their productive session. Or so Letitia had assumed.

"I was wondering if you'd like to meet for lunch?" Mrs. Quinn said. "I have a proposal I'd like to discuss with you."

More likely a luncheon attended by none other than Mr. Driscoll.

Letitia contained her annoyance. "If you'd like to book another session, I'm afraid I can't—"

"No, no," Mrs. Quinn said, "it's not for me, but I understand you won't accept my brother's invitation and I hoped that I could explain. It's about my daughter, Finola."

The haunting words of Mr. Driscoll came back, a delicate

matter he'd mentioned but no detail without the signed forms. Letitia hardened her resolve. No amount of empathy would sway her to involve herself if Mr. Driscoll sought to put legal restrictions on her.

"You must forgive me, Mrs. Quinn," Letitia said, "but unless she's passed away, I am not sure I can help."

"Please, I need to explain, you can't understand how critical it be you who helps us." Mrs. Quinn sounded fit to cry, but it was not her Letitia began to soften toward. Who was the daughter, and why did she need Letitia's help if she weren't dead?

"Could you meet me at twelve?" Mrs. Quinn asked at Letitia's silence. "Or even for coffee this morning?"

Letitia gripped the phone, holding her buttoned gown against her throat. Imogen touched her arm, and Letitia smiled at the tall blonde, shaking her head.

"I would prefer a tea," Letitia said, "and I'm not sure how useful I can be, but I will be there. Shall we say ten o'clock?"

"Yes, that would be so kind of you," Mrs. Quinn said. "There's a little French place a few blocks from where you live, Monsieur Pierre. Do you know it?"

"Yes, I know it," Letitia said. "I'll see you at ten. Goodbye."

"Goodbye, Ms. Hawking, and thank you."

Letitia put the receiver back.

"Are you all right?" Imogen's hand hovered near Letitia's arm.

"Fine. Just a taxing patron," Letitia said, brushing away the apprehension tightening her shoulders.

"I know all about those." Imogen rolled her eyes. "I grabbed the phone because I thought it was for me for work. A little early for you to get a caller."

Dressed in a trendy olive suit cut to the knees, Imogen had been about to leave for the day. She'd stayed behind when she'd seen Letitia's subtle unhappiness at the call. They did not share much, but these small moments connected Letitia to the world. Imogen's presence was like bright sunshine on Letitia's face after she'd helped chase the clouds of Imogen's past away.

"Thank you," Letitia said, "but it's fine. Off to work?"

"Yes," Imogen said with a grin, "going to be a long today."

Her beaming face said far more than words could about Imogen's enjoyment in her career. Letitia was happy for her. Not that she disliked comforting grieving people, but there was an element to it that drained her of joy in her own life.

It must have shown on Letitia's face from Imogen's next words.

"Say," Imogen said, having gone into her apartment to collect a hat and using pins to hold it in place but leaving the door open, "we should go out for dinner sometime. There's a place I like to go to unwind, not too rowdy but good jazz music. Fancy a night out this Friday?"

Letitia warmed to the idea of time with Imogen after all the darkness of the last few days.

"Truth be told, it sounds delightful," Letitia said with a smile.

Imogen's grin grew wider. "Great! But you can't wear those old English frocks. It's a fancy place, so borrow something of mine."

Letitia eyed the tall frame, narrow hips, and small chest of Imogen with a laugh. "What on earth do you have that will fit me? And I like my dreary frocks."

"Oh, I'll pick something up today," Imogen said distractedly, looking Letitia up and down. If Letitia guessed, she'd think Imogen was taking measurements with her eyes. Given Imogen's profession, Letitia suspected any dress Imogen gave her would fit as though tailor-made.

"As long as it's not too..." Letitia waved her hands at Imogen's ensemble, and Imogen chuckled at the gesture.

"No, my dear, I'll find something appropriate. Good luck with that woman." Imogen picked up her coat and bag, closed the door, and raced to the stairs. Letitia retreated to her room.

Imogen hadn't meant to hurt with the comment, but it still stung.

Standing in front of her wardrobe, Letitia looked over her dresses. The cream she wore when she went to the market was an English fashion tone. They were not new or bright like what Imogen wore, but their softer tones reminded her of home, even when walking through this strange city. There was a sense of discovery every time she ventured out, the world of Los Angeles still new enough to her senses and different from home.

Letitia stared at her closet, forgetting flamboyant clothing or soft day dresses for something appropriate for her afternoon consultation. She selected a severe woolen dress in drab gray. Even as she touched the folds of cloth, the scents of lavender wafted over her, filtering into her memory, a reminder of a different time. She'd worn the dress during graduation and other ceremonies at the school where she taught. Her mother had bought it years ago when she'd first interviewed for the position of a teacher during the war.

Her hand fisted on the material, as nostalgia for chalk dust, cheeky faces, and the sound of children overwhelmed her.

Yanking the dress off its hanger, she got dressed, planning to do some research before her meeting. Regardless of whether Mr. Driscoll was there, Letitia needed to know more about the family before she met Mrs. Quinn.

She did her hair up. The gray was striking against her youth, streaming from her temples, not a single stripe but the subtle threads of a spider's web. She'd thought about coloring them, but the reminder helped her stay focused. Every time she was surprised at their presence, it changed to chagrin at forgetting, even for a moment, that she caused them to be there.

Letitia pinned on a black hat with a veil that covered only half her face. The netting was so thin, just strands of thread, but she wouldn't have to take it off to have tea. Black leather gloves and an umbrella for the rain, Letitia's last collection was the slim case used to protect her research on patrons.

Forewarned was forearmed. As the words hummed in her ear, she could almost hear them in her husband's voice as she left the building. *Always know your enemy, always know more than they think you know.*

Daniel didn't often speak of what he did for the navy, but Letitia remembered the advice.

Letitia locked her door before heading out, making her way through the dreary streets to the Los Angeles Public Library. Intent on finding out about Mr. Barkley's little girl, she knew it wouldn't hurt to familiarize herself with what the papers were saying about the disappearance.

Walking through the doors of the library, Letitia left her umbrella in the entry hall with a host of others and nodded to the woman behind the desk. Letitia didn't know her name but recognized her from previous visits. Letitia borrowed many books, but that was not her errand today. She headed straight for where the newspapers were stored and began her search in the reading room.

Mr. Barkley was easy. There were only a few articles, and all that was said was that his eleven-year-old daughter, Maisie, had been walking the five blocks from school to the Barkley house and never arrived.

What Mr. Barkley hadn't expanded on was that this was the third girl to go missing under such circumstances in twelve months. The paper was known for being wildly speculative, but the police dismissed any connection owing to the nature of each one. Different times, different ages, and a flagrant quote from a detective regarding young women trying to make it onto the silver screen.

Not appropriate for their ages, but there were no other articles on the subject.

Letitia looked at Maisie's photograph. Taken two years earlier, the family portrait was simple as they came. A fidgeting child made to hold still and smile. Maisie had a cherubic face, blonde curls tied into pigtails, and a mischievous glint in her eyes.

Letitia knew she was dead.

Photographs didn't speak well to her, but there was an emptiness in the girl's eyes when Letitia looked at the picture.

She didn't want to embroil herself in a police investigation should she be able to see more in a vision. Even pointing Mr. Barkley toward Maisie's body would make the police want to know the source of information.

Witchcraft was still considered a crime in England, and most assumed the current occultism was a con. There were enough grieving widows and family left after the war that such people were easy marks. It had been difficult in London to prove her talent was not trickery and shadow play. The delicate balance between what she did and what others offered tipped over. Letitia received invitations to attend parties and to display her ability as though she were a circus act. She had refused.

Thinking it wouldn't affect her, Letitia continued to offer her services, and her reputation had grown.

The proverbial straw had been when a detective came by asking about her sessions.

It was time to move on from London's streets too full of fakes and on to new horizons.

Given the sensationalism abounding over séances and the like, Letitia wanted to flee to less satirized cities. She was not a charlatan, and the respect she paid her craft was not false or something to show off.

She helped people past their grief. She helped them regain their lives.

Returning the articles on Mr. Barkley and the missing girls, Letitia moved on in search of the Driscoll family heritage. She had already read the article detailing the death of Mr. Quinn when Mrs. Quinn had first approached her. It had noted the attachment to the Irish American Driscoll family, but it hadn't interested her at the time.

Now she read about it the papers, intent on noting anything she could learn about the family. There were articles about the court cases for the business, many to do with real estate, including an article about a property further to the north that was once a retreat and had fallen into disrepair. She was reminded of the deed on Mr. Driscoll's desk, the transaction he hadn't wanted there with the papers he cast aside. But there was no address listed for her to check and she hadn't paid it any mind in his office.

Unsatisfied with the level of information, Letitia packed up her things and went to the catalog for the books.

"What are you looking for?" the desk clerk asked when Letitia sighed, finding nothing under the Driscoll name.

"I'm looking for a local family history," she said, careful not to give a reason for her search. "There is a firm for lawyers here under the name of Driscoll."

Recognition lit up the librarian's features. "A small family, but there is a book that may help."

She went to another section for history, handing Letitia a card for Irish American families. Letitia thanked the clerk and looked through the shelves of books until she found the hefty volume. The tome weighty in her hands, she took it to a nearby table and sat to search for the Driscoll name.

The family had come out to America in the early 1700s, before the initial wave of Irishmen. Like most, they started out in New York, but then they moved west for the gold and cattle and became successful enough after a few generations that a branch of the family could afford to move out to Los Angeles in the 1850s. The eldest son used part of his income to attend university in Boston before coming back to Los Angeles and setting up the law firm. It had been a family-owned business since then.

There was nothing specific about Mr. Driscoll.

Closing the tome, Letitia thought back to his grim face, ignoring the tremor of fear crawling up her spine at the memory of the shadow behind him. The man was...angry. The spirit possibly more so.

It hadn't translated well, but the visit the following day

had only worsened her disposition to Mr. Driscoll. Despite his desperation, he appeared used to getting his way, and Letitia took a dim view of people who thought they controlled the world in such a way.

Letitia had only accepted Mrs. Quinn's invitation to tea because Letitia feared if she did not, Mr. Driscoll would find a way to interrupt her life again.

She didn't want to know what other means he would use to ensure that she did as he asked, and the concept of upsetting a lawyer hadn't sat well.

Letitia didn't even know what he wanted, and Mrs. Quinn would at least give her all the information to decide for herself rather than just assuming Letitia would do it for money.

That was not why Letitia helped people.

Her motivation was penance for her guilt.

When her husband had died in the war, she'd had dreams of him drowning at sea, and she was unable to save him. When she'd sought help from the church, the promise of prayer did little to still the dreams that left her exhausted and weary to her soul. Her growing stomach carried her grief—the babe of her lost husband.

She'd sought out help, for someone who could reach beyond, to tell Daniel a part of him still existed. What was supposed to be a moment of love and consolation became a nightmare, and tangled in its web, she'd struggled for years to be free from it.

Letitia offered the same help she'd never found.

The book tumbled out of her hands, banging on the floor of the quiet library. A few heads turned to her, and she retrieved the book, apologizing to those nearby. Face aflame and heartbeat fast as a rabbit fleeing a trap, she gathered her things in haste, shoving them into her case before placing the book on the returns shelf and leaving.

Outside the cool air swept the heat from her cheeks and chased away the dark corridor of her past. Letitia let the drizzling rain fall on her for a moment before opening her umbrella.

She'd walked all the way to the library but would need to catch a streetcar if she wanted to meet Mrs. Quinn on time. She also wanted to be early and to have the matter over and done with.

She would leave their family to its own troubles. Mr. Driscoll had arisen an uncharitable nature in her that did not often come to the surface.

It made Letitia uncomfortable, for she knew that she should be kinder, but self-preservation was a stronger force, fear of the past bending her to its will.

Upon the streetcar's arrival, Letitia climbed aboard and paid her fee, not bothering to sit on the crowded service. The sway of the vehicle reminded her of the voyage across the ocean, and she'd tried in vain not to imagine Daniel there or how the ocean had swallowed him. What he'd endured before the end.

Her grip on the railing tightened.

It haunted her thoughts ever since she saw that shadow over Mr. Driscoll's shoulder.

Letitia wanted to stay as far as she could, but she'd seen a figure in Joseph's final moments, something that shouldn't have been there.

Yet for all its disturbing presence in her vision, it didn't exude the same vindictiveness she'd first witnessed looming over Mr. Driscoll's shoulder.

Death wasn't a phantom that haunted victims.

Letitia had come to America to escape her past, to hide in a burgeoning city of odd souls, and to make a small corner to hide in...alone.

She didn't need the Driscolls' ghosts. She had enough of her own.

Getting off at her stop and reaffirming to herself that she would hear Mrs. Quinn out but still say no, Letitia didn't like the hollow feeling in her stomach. When she saw Mrs. Quinn had already arrived at Monsieur Pierre's, the sensation grew.

The little café was an embodiment of Paris, offering French pastries, coffee, and Swedish chocolates kept in a glass display, with little boxes allowing people to take them home. Letitia didn't like chocolate much, but she saw above the display case jars of biscuits, including butterscotch. An indulgence during her meeting would be acceptable, given she would not get time for lunch.

Round metal tables were full of people finishing a midmorning repast, people talked in French and English, the tone pleasant on the ear. The warm lights overhead contrasted with the dim day outside, casting shadows across the room and leaving an intimate setting despite the full café.

Mrs. Quinn had taken a table near the back and was being seated by a waiter when she spied Letitia in the doorway and raised her hand in greeting.

Letitia threaded between the tables, stopping before Mrs. Quinn, who rose with a smile.

"Ms. Hawking," she said, "I'm so glad you could make it."

"Mrs. Quinn," Letitia answered, holding out her hand, which Mrs. Quinn shook. The similarity to Mr. Driscoll was elusive, but there in the faint bone structure was a determined jawline that did not bode for a dissimilar personality. Mr. Driscoll was tall with loose curls of graying auburn, while Mrs. Quinn was a strawberry blonde, far younger than him, and a little plump. She was a far cry from the broad-shouldered mountain that was Mr. Driscoll.

"What do you fancy?" Mrs. Quinn said, gesturing to the chair opposite as she sat.

"Earl Grey tea," Letitia told the still hovering waiter, "and the butterscotch biscuit in the jar on the counter."

"Madam does not wish to see the menu?" he clarified, holding it out for her to inspect.

"No, thank you."

When he'd gone, Mrs. Quinn took a deep breath, smiling at Letitia, who braced herself.

"I'm so sorry about my brother," Mrs. Quinn began in a rush. Letitia held her tongue but returned the smile with a smaller one of her own, prepared to let Mrs. Quinn ramble until she said something useful.

"You see," Mrs. Quinn went on, "Alasdair and my husband were close, and there was trouble just before his death. My brother feels terrible about it, but our concern is not, in fact, Mr. Quinn."

"You said on the phone that this was regarding your daughter?" Letitia prompted, hoping Mrs. Quinn would get to the point. The evasion on the subject from Mr. Driscoll bespoke a serious matter, but not why it should concern Letitia. It was annoying.

"Yes, my Finola," Mrs. Quinn said, lowering her voice. "She's sick."

"Have you summoned a doctor?" Letitia said, holding onto her patience.

"We have...and it's not a physical condition," Mrs. Quinn said. "She had an awful turn a while back, when she was with Alasdair—I mean, Mr. Driscoll."

Letitia stared at her, the overeager woman cagey, her gaze darting about the crowded restaurant rather than resting on Letitia's face.

"Please forgive me, Mrs. Quinn," Letitia said, "but this affects me how?"

Mrs. Quinn was silent for a moment, clasping her hands and wedging them between her body and the table, almost as though she were praying. Letitia had a foreboding Mrs. Quinn would not call to an unresponsive god but plead to Letitia instead.

"You are a very gifted woman, Ms. Hawking," Mrs. Quinn said, her voice hushed and wary of nearby tables listening in, "but I wonder, have you ever met anyone else like yourself? Able to...contact the dead, I mean? And the other things—I can only assume that's why you wear the gloves and veil, so you can hide."

Letitia flushed at the slight, aware now the woman was far more like her brother than she'd realized. The schooling of her features slipped and she eyed Mrs. Quinn with distaste. Mrs.

Quinn waved her hands before her, mouth open as she gasped for words.

"I'm sorry," she said, "it didn't occur to me that would be such a rude thing to say."

Biting words wanted to snap along Letitia's tongue, but the order arrived and she remained silent. The waiter placed tea and two small biscuits before her, asking if there was anything else before leaving.

Mrs. Quinn had a black coffee and that was all. Letitia was a little surprised at her choice. It was enough to make her pause when Mrs. Quinn dumped three spoons of sugar in her cup.

Letitia studied her.

Mrs. Quinn's lips were bright and tinted red, her face powdered, hair in neat curls.

At first, Letitia hadn't noticed the makeup that covered the swelling of sleepless nights under Mrs. Quinn's eyes or the fine tremble in her hands she'd hidden with gestures. Her lips weren't just crimson from an application of tint—she'd been biting them. Little tears in the flesh peppered her skin.

"Mrs. Quinn," Letitia intoned as Mrs. Quinn stirred her sugar in, "what is it about your daughter you think I can help with?"

The gentle tone Letitia used caused Mrs. Quinn to whisper as though it were a last confession.

"She's being haunted by a phantom that attacks her in her sleep," Mrs. Quinn said with despair, "and if you don't help her, she must go to an asylum."

Chapter 5

Letitia's throat constricted. A python of terror wreathed around her neck, squeezing the breath out of her. Her thoughts narrowed on the desperate plea of Mrs. Quinn as she struggled to regain her composure. Her fingers twisted, clutching the first thing they touched, the teaspoon for her tea, and she bent the metal with her fingers, willing back the memories.

Gurneys and straps, white jackets and buckles, and always the screaming.

The spoon snapped.

Mrs. Quinn gasped, and Letitia shut her eyes to block her out.

Wresting control from her fears took labored breaths, but she heard Old Mother Borrows in her mind.

"You control just one thing; your breath. Breathe through it."

Several heartbeats later, Letitia could open her eyes, and she swallowed. Her throat was dry and scratchy. Helping herself to the brewed tea as though nothing had happened, she dropped in a wedge of lemon and left it black, sipping it to soothe herself. When her self-possession had returned, she glanced at Mrs. Quinn. The other woman sat motionless except for darting eyes flicking between the rest of the café and Letitia, and then down at her own lap.

Her averted eyes bespoke her shame and fear, but Letitia didn't care.

She could not—no, *would not*—allow herself to be embroiled in whatever was happening with Mrs. Quinn's daughter.

Even now, on the edge of hearing, she caught the echoes of doctors' voices. They'd prescribed bizarre and unnecessary treatment for Letitia's hysterical condition. Ice baths and isolation, cold food and confinement, drugs and dismissal.

With no family to care about her, Letitia survived because of an empathetic nurse.

The nurse had whisked Letitia to a solitary sanctuary far from the darkened halls of the asylum. They'd arrived in Scotland where Old Mother Borrows had welcomed Letitia, and together they began a journey through the difficult pathways of Letitia's uncontrollable gift.

Because her nightmare had not ended. She'd trapped herself in her own dark power.

An edge of guilt prompted Letitia to ask at least a few questions. That wouldn't hurt, and she might help guide Mrs. Quinn into a kinder action than those of Letitia's experience.

"Why haven't you taken her to a physician?" Letitia murmured, focusing on the girl.

"We did." Mrs. Quinn took her cup but set it aside in an instant. "We even thought to take her to the seaside after she... after the incident. But travel more than a day away is hard when she has such night terrors. You wouldn't believe the noise she makes."

Letitia would. The echoes were still there when she woke.

"A prescription of sedatives perhaps." Letitia was loath to suggest drugs, but it was an easy way to distance herself.

"It doesn't help." Mrs. Quinn shook her head, curls in a disarray. "I shouldn't even be speaking to you on this as Alasdair wants it to remain in the family. He doesn't want anyone to think—"

Letitia rose a brow at the hesitation. "What? That his niece is insane?"

"He is reaching out to anyone he thinks can help," Mrs. Quinn said. "We've even seen a priest who suggested an exorcism. Alasdair would not allow him into the house."

For a brief moment, Letitia thought better of the arrogant lawyer.

"A nurse gives her laudanum every night." Mrs. Quinn bit out the words. "And yet she can wake up in spite of it. The doctors say she's just a growing girl with hysteria, but I know something is wrong with her soul. She's very...special. If you would just come and meet her."

A part of Letitia longed to find this girl and discover what was wrong. But Letitia was not Old Mother Borrows, and she could not fix a broken soul. She couldn't even guess why both Mr. Driscoll and Mrs. Quinn were convinced only she could help.

But most of all, she didn't have it within her to fight the darkness that had cost her so much.

"What you are asking is not something I can provide," Letitia said, being careful in her words, "but I can write to a friend of mine in Scotland where you may take your daughter—"

"No," Mrs. Quinn shook her head, the emphatic gesture undoing a pin in her hair, letting a curl fall. "Finola can't travel. Forgetting the fact she can't sleep, it wouldn't be safe."

"For whom?"

Mrs. Quinn fell silent.

"I'm very sorry, but I cannot take this case," Letitia said, surer with every passing moment that whatever plagued Mrs. Quinn's daughter, Letitia couldn't help her. Not at the risk of her own sanity. She'd clawed it back, one shred at a time, built walls, and protected herself after traversing through her own private hell.

She could distance herself in the readings and use her gift without it spiraling out of control as it had before, endangering others. If Finola required the same help as Letitia needed at the time, then there was no way Letitia could risk her own mind to save the girl.

Letitia made to rise when Mrs. Quinn's arm snapped across the table. Rather than the tight clutching grasp Letitia expected, Mrs. Quinn's fingers lightly touched the exposed skin between Letitia's glove and dress.

Letitia jerked her hand back, but it was too late.

Over Mrs. Quinn's shoulder was the figure, as it had been all along, watching Letitia with the quiet intensity she'd seen in her vision with Joseph. Too close, too much, too dark.

The malice in its eyeless stare was so intense it seemed to strike at her as she stared wide-eyed, unable to look away.

Not something from another realm, but something that had once been human.

Letitia got to her feet and stumbled away.

She ran into another table, spilling their cups and apologizing in her haste to get out the door. She dared not look behind her as she sought the sunlight. The cleansing rain. Overcast as it was outside when she burst into the street, the soft gray light was better than the gloom of the café.

The drizzle from earlier had turned to a freezing downpour. Her forgotten umbrella lay inside. Letitia left it, taking quick steps at first and then near to running down the slick pavement, catching glances as she fled from the café. Dodging pedestrians, Letitia ignored a shout behind her, flinging an apology over her shoulder.

The rain was what she focused on, drops on her face, streaking down her dress, the mud on her shoes as she ran back to her apartment. She gave no mind to the dirt as she rushed up the stairs, grateful her purse was still on her arm as she unlocked the door and slammed it shut behind her. She had forgotten everything else.

Her umbrella, her case files.

She would go back and retrieve them later.

For now, as she leaned against the door, the terror that had goaded her on vanished like burning paper, filtering away to nothing as she collapsed to the floor. Dread threatened to overcome her and she could not let it, and with her hand on her heart, she tried to regain control of her breathing.

"Push out whatever seeks to control you with your breath," Old Mother Borrows' voice came to her, *"as though each exhale is the taint, anger, and fear. Regain composure with deep, even breaths."*

Letitia lost time fighting the demons of memory, exhaustion eating at her consciousness, and she fell into a trance focused on her breath, but still, she was dragged into dreams of dark corridors and screaming. The endless screaming.

Letitia awoke. Staring around her, she was confused as to why she lay on the floor of her session room. Memory filtered back, bringing on a fine trembling from the chill of the room, the wet cloth of her dress clinging to her skin. Her handbag lay on the floor, its contents spilled out where she'd dropped it. She plucked out the ladies' pocket watch, cursing when she saw the time. Sweeping up the contents of her purse, she ducked into her room to slide the curtains shut and lit the fire, shivering in the cold, skin clammy from the damp dress.

Turning about, she saw the mud she'd tracked across her own room, meaning it would still be in the session room and in the hall. Annoyed at her stupidity, Letitia swept up the drying mud, even going out onto the landing. It was still there, so Mrs. Finch hadn't seen the mess she'd made, or at least she hadn't removed it herself.

After everything in the hall and session room was clean,

Letitia went to her own room, still feeling the numbing sense of cold, exhaustion dragging her movements, escaping time pushing her on.

Mr. Barkley would be here in another thirty minutes and she wasn't ready.

She stoked the fire in her bedroom and put the kettle on.

Letitia didn't like not having time to study the file before a potential patron turned up, but she had no other choice.

Ignoring her rumbling stomach, Letitia had a kitten wash in warm water from the kettle before putting on her things. The gray dress would need proper cleaning if she hadn't ruined the wool, but she hung it close enough to the fire to glean its heat to dry but not shrink.

Refreshed in dry clothes, Letitia forwent food for a quick cup of tea to steady her nerves before the punctual knock of Mr. Barkley.

Letitia crossed to the session room and placed the veil over her face with practiced ease, pulling on black leather gloves before she opened the door.

A gentleman stood there, by himself, with a bag in one hand. His blue eyes lit up when he saw her.

"Ms. Hawking?"

"Yes, Mr. Barkley," she said, stepping back, "please come in and have a seat."

He did as bid, already holding out the things she'd asked for—a photograph and an item belonging to the girl.

It was a worn book, pages musty brown and cover ragged, but the title struck a chord in Letitia's heart. *Pride and Prejudice.*

Her pulse pounded in her ears, a headache developing behind her eyes.

Mr. Barkley turned about where she was still standing by the closed door.

"Tea?" she asked, escaping through to the other room when he nodded.

When she was alone, she reached for the wall to steady

herself.

Her head swam, apprehension drawing her shoulders tight.

Reaching for the kettle, she followed the routine of serving tea. A jug of milk, the pot of English tea, sugar in a little ceramic jar. Placing it all on a tray, Letitia picked it up to carry it to the next room.

She had cups there that she used for guests, so she didn't have to use them day in and out herself. Made of paper-thin china, the cups gave clients the impression that she held high standards.

Letitia poured tea, avoiding looking at the book or photo. She held out a cup and saucer for Mr. Barkley, who took it without a word.

Having a moment to absorb his face, she saw he was a plain fellow, with mousy brown hair thin and fine under the hat he'd since placed on the table. She waited until he'd taken a sip of his tea, but his hands fidgeted with the cup, eyes darting about the room.

"Now," Letitia said, bringing his focus back to her, "I want you to understand how this will progress. I will examine the picture and the item to see if I can help you. If I cannot, that will be all, but if I can, I will need you to move onto the next step."

Mr. Barkley pulled his wallet out, and it was the twenty-dollar note.

Letitia was ready, giving him ten back as she took the note.

"Please." He slid it back, but she placed a gloved hand over his, putting gentle pressure on him so he stilled.

"I have rules, Mr. Barkley," Letitia said, her voice quiet but firm. "I will not do you the disservice of over charging you when I'm not sure if she's alive. If she has passed on, and it wasn't with trauma, then I can try to reach her for you. There will be a fee based on what is involved. In some cases, this can be hundreds of dollars."

She let that sink in, drawing back her hand. After a moment he took the change and slipped it into his wallet.

"I'd like to apologize, Ms. Hawking," he said. "I am desperate to find out what happened to my Maisie."

"I will study the picture and book," Letitia said, not about to let him fall into his grief and worry. "I'd like to ask that you don't speak during this time. One of the things I'll be able to offer if I see her is something only you would know about her. That you come by reference is flattering, but I find everyone has a measure of doubt. This session is to affirm in your mind I can do as I promise."

"What would that be?" Mr. Barkley asked.

"That should Maisie have passed, and it wasn't violent, I can share her final moments with you." Letitia pitched her voice low and soft to lessen the distress her words may cause. Mr. Barkley grimaced and closed his eyes as she continued. "I will not tell you if someone murdered her, Mr. Barkley. I cannot do that. Often the victim is taken by surprise, and this can drag me into death with them. I will at least be able to give you some measure of closure, simply by reading what I can of Maisie's things."

His eyes cracked open though the grim features didn't change. "Thank you."

She took off her gloves and picked up the picture. It was the same one she'd seen in the newspapers. A girl of eleven, hair in pigtails, grinning at the camera.

Letitia focused on her eyes. The liveliness there was a dim and distant echo compared to actual life. She let her gaze soften, imagining what the girl would be like, letting her ability paint a picture of Maisie. This would be one of many photographs. She had laughed too much in the others. Letitia put it down and picked up the book.

It didn't belong to Maisie.

The knowledge was as instinctual as breathing. Letitia embraced it, bending it to her will.

"This isn't her book," Letitia said, setting it down and looking to Mr. Barkley. "It belonged to someone else, a much older woman...her mother?"

"Died six years ago of tuberculosis," he said, "and almost took Maisie, too."

Letitia nodded, turning the pages, feeling the love in the paper under her fingers, and opening to a white satin ribbon inside. As soon as Letitia touched it, darkness overwhelmed her.

There was a fall, and she was tumbling down a long shaft, no light, only the reek of brine and rot.

Letitia yanked her hand back as though stung by a bee. She shook it, the prickle on her fingers stinging into her hand. Rubbing away the pain, she looked to Mr. Barkley.

"That belonged to Maisie," she said. "It was her christening ribbon."

"Yes," Mr. Barkley said, eyes now wide and eager. "You saw her?"

"Not quite," Letitia said, "but let me try again."

He fell silent and Letitia used the book to slide the ribbon onto the table in front of her without touching it. It was grubby in some places, fraying at one end, and it was these teased tassels Letitia reached for, this time ready for the images she received.

Maisie was curled next to her mother on a big bed, playing with the ribbon as her mother read, content to lie next to her in the firelit room. Her father came over, picked her up, and took her to bed, but she took the ribbon with her.

Years later, she still had it, held it tight in her hand, wrapped between her fingers, while she stood by her father's side at the funeral of her mother. Her friend Tommy waved at her across the church, but Maisie didn't wave back. Today was not a day to be happy.

Maisie threaded the ribbon through her mother's book and kept it by her bedside. Though she never read the pages, she sat up and flipped them like her mother had, eyes lost to memory, her fingers plucking at the thread of the ribbon.

Letitia stretched her mind for what was beyond, but while she was sure the girl was dead, there was no sense of her beyond death. It didn't take much to imagine why the little girl was taken and what might have happened to her. Letitia drew back before the lingering soul would become aware she sought it out.

As much as Letitia wanted to tell him more, there was nothing else to see without scrying. Short of going into a trance, she wouldn't be able to see anything but Maisie's final hours, which wouldn't help Maisie, her father, or Letitia.

And Letitia had a grave fear the girl had not passed the veil. Maisie was on the wrong side of death.

Her spirit was out there, somewhere, lingering on this plane. Whatever tragedy had befallen her was keeping her here. Meaning if Letitia went looking for her, Maisie might find Letitia.

Under no circumstances was Letitia foolish enough to open herself to a restless soul. She'd seen firsthand what regret, anger, and frustration could do.

"I'm so sorry," Letitia said, and she didn't get to finish as Mr. Barkley wept. His hands came over his face, and he bowed over the table, wracking sobs shaking him.

Letitia waited, aware she could give no further comfort.

"She's gone?" he asked, after several minutes, wiping at his face with a handkerchief.

"I'm afraid so," Letitia said, putting her gloves back on, and sliding back the possessions. She made no move to stand, knowing Mr. Barkley would still have questions.

"Did you see...?" his voice trailed off.

"Please understand, Mr. Barkley," Letitia said, "I talk to grieving clients to help them move on. I accepted seeing you to help bring you closure should the worst have happened. But I cannot tell you more than that. I know that Maisie carried that ribbon with her everywhere, including the funeral of her mother. Tommy waved to her, but she didn't wave back. Instead, she went home and pretended her mother was there reading the pages of the book, and Maisie was curled up next to her, playing with the ribbon. I imagine you often found her like that, asleep with the book."

Mr. Barkley's face paled, but he uttered not a word.

"I did not want to tell you this," Letitia said, hearing the emotion in her voice, and she cleared her throat. "My patrons know that their loved ones are gone. As unpleasant as this is, I'm hoping at least the part of your concern whether she is alive will pass."

"How did you know about the ribbon?" he asked, ignoring her speech.

"I saw it," Letitia answered, "the same way you see pictures in your head when you read a book or listen to a story. The only difference is I'm reading from the veil between life and death."

"But that's witch—" he broke off, horrified at his own words as his hand came to his mouth, wiping it before glancing at her.

"Forgive me," he said, a blush creeping up his cheeks, giving them some color back. "I was told what it was you did and that your gifts were precise, and you've proved it beyond a shadow of doubt. I just...it's one thing to see and another to know. And I've tried everything to find my little girl." The tears came again, and Letitia's heart wanted to weep with him, but she could not allow herself to fall into his sorrows or to be convinced of seeing more of Maisie's death. It was a fast path to retribution of which she would take no part.

"Does it matter how such a thing was done, as long as you know she's no longer in any torment?" Letitia asked.

Reminded of his grief, Mr. Barkley shook his head.

"I won't ask that you book another session, Mr. Barkley," Letitia said, "as I will not reach further into her death." Letitia didn't elaborate that this was because the spirit was still here, somewhere in the mortal realm.

For souls that passed beyond the veil, there were traces of them on its fabric, a weave to its cloth that with the right items Letitia could find and read in her own way. She was able to slip herself into those final moments before their death.

When a soul didn't move on, there was nothing on the veil.

Maisie was not there, but she was most certainly dead.

Chapter 6

Smoke curled through Stephen's lungs as he inhaled it from the cigarette. The winter's chill caused him to cough against the phlegm building in his throat.

"If I get bloody sick again, the boss won't be pleased," he muttered to himself, scanning the waiting luggage. Fancy trunks sat on a wide trolley. He'd wheel it up to the ship at the stroke of midnight. Passengers had until then to submit their luggage to the liner leaving at dawn.

The transport of the luggage left him shivering in the cold. He'd told the other porters to go home. It was already after eleven, and he could close the gates on his own.

Instead of waiting outside, he went to the little house by the gangway. It kept out the worst of the wind. The room was small at six by six but room enough to have a potbellied stove and desk. There was also an old armchair with springs sticking out of the folds of cloth. Putting his lamp on the desk, he sat down to warm his hands, loading more coal into the belly of the little black stove. The kettle had long since been washed out by one of the younger lads before he left.

"What's his name?" Stephen thought aloud, mumbling around the cigarette. "Mark? Matthew?"

He shrugged, since it wouldn't matter he'd forgotten. The boy had been there a week, and many of them didn't last that long. The work was too hard. Being a stevedore wasn't a career choice—at least not for lads just finding their feet. But Stephen was the assistant dock master and had his eyes on that last step. But one thing stood in his way.

Making sure there was no one about, Stephen pulled a book from under the desk, which lay hidden away in a little cubby hole.

He mumbled through another chapter of Alice in Wonderland. The words became harder, and with frustration and a furtive glance to be sure he was alone, he tried saying them out loud.

"They were indeed a...queer-looking party that ass-assembled on the b-bank—the bird with drag-draggle... damnit!" He put the book down with a thump on the armchair, and it tumbled to the floor. Glaring at the book as though it had offended him, he clutched the arms of the chair, shame hot on his ears.

It didn't matter, for he could read the paperwork that came across his desk—numbers, passengers, and ship names—and as far as he knew that's what the dock master needed. Unbidden, Stephen remembered the scene from last week when he'd been invited to Mr. Carrick's office to talk about Stephen's recent ill health. Mr. Carrick had been having lunch and reading a book by Sir Arthur Conan Doyle.

Stephen already believed he was stupid when talking to Mr. Carrick.

He ignored his boss worrying about Stephen's health. Mr. Carrick moved him to the day schedule as of next week to help with Stephen's chest complaints.

The dryer weather of Los Angeles should have made him better, but nothing did these days. Not even the bottles of medication that the doctors prescribed.

No, Stephen hadn't focused on Mr. Carrick's words.

He'd been too busy staring at the bloody book.

Just as he did now.

This book belonged to Bethany, and she'd left it out on the table for him.

She said nothing. She never did. Silly girl was quiet as a mouse, but she had a voice filled with birdsong, tiny thing that she was. No, she wasn't a girl anymore. Bethany dreaded turning fifty, though he was closer than her. There should be no reason to regret their ages. They had a grown son who'd survived the war and worked on navy ship engines. A daughter who married a grocer, and at her suggestion they were adding flowers. They were doing well.

But he wanted to read.

He wanted to talk like Mr. Carrick. Use all those fine English words.

The old fellow sat in his tower, told people what to do, and the dock was above reproach.

Stephen did his part, but he didn't think he deserved Mr. Carrick's praise. Neither of them had been young enough to go to the war, but they'd seen their fair share of ships pass through here.

They'd even shared a nightcap or two, and though Mr. Carrick invited Stephen to call him by his first name, Stephen refused. He wasn't like that. Mr. Carrick was his boss, and he'd do as he was told, first and foremost. It was about respect.

Looking at the book still on the floor, he leaned down to pick it up.

"Excuse me?" A voice startled him into dropping the book yet again.

"What the—" Stephen looked up into the face of a young man who was dressed in a suit and coat against the cold.

"Sorry, old boy," the stranger said, "got a few things for you. It's before the curfew, isn't it? Only we got caught up at the theater and my wife's maid hadn't packed all our things."

English.

"Sorry, sir," Stephen said, "you gave me a start. I'll come right out."

Stephen waited until he left before picking the book up. That had been quite a fright.

But a grown man sitting reading children's stories didn't bear thinking about. Dusting off the book and seeing one corner had dented, he resolved to buy Bethany a new copy, or another book, if she liked. He'd tell her about it all. Maybe they could read together.

Smiling at the thought and putting the book back in its hidey-hole, Stephen went out to get the luggage.

Only...his legs wouldn't move...and he couldn't breathe...

Shadows danced in his vision, and he was falling...

Letitia saw his death come, and she avoided it when Stephen became confused. She had what she needed. Studying the small woman across from her, Letitia found it no wonder that Stephen still thought of Bethany as a young girl. Dark hair showed few threads of silver, and her wide brown eyes and youthful skin made her appear far younger than her nearly fifty years.

Bethany was quiet and reserved, any signs of grief hidden by the same respectable nature Stephen displayed. But her eyes were red, and thin bony hands clutched her handbag. If she was slim before he died, she was a whisper of her former self now.

"He wanted to buy you another book," Letitia said, deciding to start on the sweetest note. "He read *Alice in Wonderland* in secret at work. He wanted to be like Mr. Carrick."

Bethany said nothing, turning her head to blow her nose before she gestured for Letitia to continue.

"If you go to the dock house on the pier," Letitia said, "there is a desk in that office. Behind the drawers on the left-hand side, there is a space under the desk. You'll find the book there."

"He took it..." Bethany's tremulous voice emulated her

birdlike persona, the cadences of her voice beautiful to hear.

"There's a corner bent where he dropped it," Letitia added, "and he was going to tell you so you could help him learn to read. He wanted to know all those...fine English words."

Bethany sat there for long moments, staring at the table, and Letitia stayed silent, letting her absorb Letitia's words.

"Did he...at the end..." her voice drifted off.

"He had an easy passing," Letitia assured her and ventured to say more. "He didn't even know. We could all hope for such a painless death."

Bethany cried then, fat drops that rolled down her cheek that she brushed away.

She got to her feet, so quick her chair tilted, and she snatched it before it fell, with a smile of apology at the near-miss.

"I think I should get home now, and you look peaky my dear," Bethany said, collecting her coat from the rack by the door.

"I'm fine," Letitia said, even as fatigue nipped at her heels, "as long as you've received the answers you were seeking."

Bethany's hand was on the doorknob, but she looked over her shoulder, and Letitia knew for a moment why Stephen had cared for her. The beaming smile, so full of love, told Letitia how Bethany missed him but would carry on. The presence was a spring breeze on Letitia's face, warm and soft, speaking of the hope Letitia never allowed herself.

"Yes, Ms. Hawking," Bethany said, opening the door, "you told me what I needed to hear."

She closed the door behind her, and Letitia was bereft. The sudden loss of a gracious woman chiming the bell of her soul, echoing through her lonely heart, filled her with profound grief for her husband. If not for himself, then for the companionship his presence had meant to her.

Nagging tiredness washed over her, forcing her to withdraw inside herself again.

Letitia's head felt full of cotton wool, her feet heavy as she stood to cleanse the room. She should have been starving but food had no appeal. She collected her night things and dressing gown and went down the hall to use the bathroom she shared with Imogen.

The windowless room had only enough space for the commode, a sink, and a great clawfoot tub Letitia had yet to work out how they'd gotten into the room. Deep, it would cover her to her neck, and Letitia's aching body longed for the warmth to sink into her bones. She turned the taps on, checking the temperature before sliding off her shoes. The tiles were cold on her stockinged feet. Grasping the gas knob of the heater, she turned it high before laying her dressing gown across the bars. By the time she finished her bath, it would be toasty.

Testing the water with a hand and turning up the hot tap, she took a vial of oil, the extract of juniper, and laced the water with drops. The sweet scent tickled her nose and comforted her.

Letitia took off her black dress, and when she held it up, she resolved to go to the launderers tomorrow, adding it to her sodden gray dress. She shed her underthings, making a mental list of items to collect in the morning before dipping into the water.

It scorched her skin and she gritted her teeth against the burn.

The water would never be too hot as long as she remembered the asylum baths.

Her skin turned red while she soaked in the water, but it made the white scars show like whiplashes on her skin.

Across her belly, the hasty surgeon's knife left a harsh reminder of her past, the puncture of the stitches she'd torn in her anguish-driven madness akin to bullet holes. Ugly as they were, the thin lines on the inside of her arms from wrist to halfway up her elbow were delicate by comparison.

Letitia's finger traced one of the lines, the memory of making the incision as hazy as the darkness of the days following the fated event. The police had taken her to hospital, covered in more blood than her own, keening without words, full of a broken soul.

They'd drugged her, if only to stop the sound, and when she'd awoken the anguish came back. More violent than before, no amount of time or consolation eased the growing pit inside her where life had once been. Her dead husband's lawyer paid for the submission into the asylum the doctors had insisted on. Letitia hadn't been coherent enough to protest.

Fog surrounded every memory of the institution, full of insane remnants of once-human minds reduced to ramblings of childlike pleading, animal noises, and demonic howls.

All the while a shadow stalked her. The specter of the past hadn't vanished. She'd cursed God and begged for his mercy, told Satan to send his messenger away, and yet pleaded for him to take her until she'd paid for what she'd done.

Asked at night's darkest if it was Daniel and if he came to punish her for losing their son.

The doctors increased her medication and treatments.

She'd lost time, lost herself.

There were only the drugs, given to her when she woke up screaming, the bindings when she would try to hurt herself, the confinement when they couldn't silence her...

A nurse had been helping her into a real bath, warm and comforting, to help clean her hair, and she'd leaned forward to take Letitia's hand.

"I see him, too," she'd said, and Letitia didn't believe her. Remaining mute, she didn't answer, afraid they would do something worse. She'd be put in isolation again. The nurse was one more tormentor who'd rather her ramblings were on another ward.

Letitia curled in a ball, hiding herself and touching as little as possible. If she did, she was bombarded with images that didn't belong to her. She avoided eye contact because of the overwhelming nature of others' personalities and seeing their judgment, rousing her hatred and disgust at herself. Worst of all were mirrors or reflective surfaces since they contained dark nightmares of what had once been within.

She could not even laugh at her own condition—her mind was too busy running from everything making her afraid. But the nurse was there, she wasn't judging, and she could see the figure that haunted Letitia.

"He's just a shadow of his former self," the nurse insisted, "and you needn't be afraid. He will not hurt you."

Letitia pursed her lips, looking away.

"He never touches you," the nurse went on. "He only watches, but it's scary when he isn't where you are expecting him to be, and when you have such terrible memories of what happened."

Water poured over Letitia, warm and gentle as the nurse's words. She kept talking as she ran her fingers through Letitia's hair, combing it with lotion, rubbing it into the matted knots, untangling them with gentle tugs.

"How do you know?" Letitia said. It was the first time she'd spoken in weeks. The first time someone had been civil in far longer than she could remember.

She'd come to believe the doctors were right, and it was her mind manifesting its guilt for her sins. Madness had driven her to attempt to take her life…and to take someone else's.

The nurse smiled, pouring another jug of water down Letitia's back to wash the soap suds out of her hair.

"How long have you seen it?" the nurse asked.

"Since…since the séance…"

The nurse would have seen her file.

The patient is suffering post-traumatic stress from a miscarriage during attendance at a séance. Patient present to contact husband who died in the war. The host of the séance attacked the patient, who defended herself and killed the host. Patient has been incomprehensible, prone to violent outbursts, and sees false visions. Motivated by guilt over the loss of her child from her deceased husband.

Letitia had seen the file, too, when it was left on a doctor's desk during a session, and she'd read it. The paper didn't note what had happened, citing the cause as female hysteria. A group of widows meeting to commune with the dead and hoping to say a final farewell to their husbands.

It was an easy excuse to the truth Letitia had tried to explain.

She didn't blame them for thinking she was insane.

The nurse took a furtive look around the empty bathroom. The other occupant was an old woman who stared at the walls. With a quick smile at Letitia, the nurse's hand darted into the pocket of her smock. Letitia drew back, afraid of another needle or a scrubbing brush. She'd not always been amenable to baths, unable to stand the sight of the shameful scars across her abdomen.

The nurse only held aloft a small brown glass vial, and she opened it and held it under Letitia's nose. Juniper flowers filled Letitia with lightness, the scent stirring deep within and awakening a sensation that wasn't pain, anger, or sadness.

It was the tentative touch of peace.

Not forgiveness, never that, but a reprieve.

When she didn't protest, the nurse put several drops in the bath, and Letitia felt something other than the weight of her past. She did not want to die in this cage, and though at one point that had not been true, it was now.

It took another three months of therapy and convincing the doctors she was fine before they released her into the nurse's custody. With postwar soldiers scarred by what they'd seen, the hospital needed beds and discharged her.

Letitia let the nurse take her to the far reaches of the Scottish Highlands.

Her name was Moira Borrows, and her grandmother saved Letitia's soul.

y

Chapter 7

Letitia rolled away from the morning sun's rays. The light was a bane to her eyes, her nose stuffy, and a headache pressed on her temples. She felt altogether wretched. The rain yesterday and an extended bath had left her with a chill. To top it off, a large glass of brandy on an empty stomach after her bath hadn't helped. Lured by the fire, she sipped her drink and watched the flames, and she'd been content until shivers from the dying fire had prompted her to crawl into bed.

Sitting up, she reached for her purse and pulled out the ledger.

She had a consultation in the afternoon, but her evening was free, and there was no session booked for Friday. She had dinner planned with Imogen then, but she should feel better on the morrow. Checking the time, Letitia discovered it was only a little after eight, and the ache in her stiff body forbade her from more than thinking about moving.

Deciding to be virtuous later, Letitia burrowed herself back under the covers after twitching the curtain so no sunlight would pierce her sleep.

She'd only just drifted off again when there was a knock on the door. Not Imogen's tentative hand, but a far heavier one.

Staring at the adjoining door, Letitia closed her eyes and laid her head back.

She heard another insistent thud on the door.

Sighing, Letitia sat upright and swung her legs to the bed's edge. They dangled there a moment, and she wondered if whoever it was would leave before she got up. Seconds passed and yet the call came again. Three hard knocks.

Shoving her feet into her slippers and struggling into her gown, Letitia rubbed her eyes on the heels of her palms as she walked to the door.

Whoever it was should have in all politeness given up. Perhaps it was Mrs. Finch.

Letitia's session room was dark, and she left it like that, not wishing to alert the knocker she was awake. She bent down, observing the twin shadows she could see from the crack under the door. She would have put a draft snake there but had forgotten in her cold-induced stupor.

Someone was still waiting outside. They knocked again.

"Who is it?" she called.

"Mr. Driscoll."

Letitia's hand hovered over the knob.

"It's rather early," she said, hearing the quiver in her tone.

"I thought it wouldn't be appropriate to call while you had one of your appointments," he said, baritone rumbling through the thick wooden door, "and it is after nine now."

"I've already told your sister I can't help her," Letitia said, raising her voice, but her throat scratched, aching at the louder tone. "But I'm more than happy to give you the name and telephone number of a woman in Scotland who can."

"My apologies," he said. "I only wanted to return the items you left at the café, Ms. Hawking."

Her case files and umbrella.

"Please leave them on the telephone stand," she said.

"I'd like to give them to you in person."

She heard the brogue in his voice, but there was an undercurrent of desperation. Letitia leaned her head against the door frame, thumping it, and was unable to hold back the wince of pain.

"Ms. Hawking?"

"Just a moment," Letitia said, sure this was a silly idea, but she needed those files. A simple enough request from a woman whose son died in the war. It was a familiar but easy appointment and would not require any additional effort but to look at a picture. Still, the photograph was in her case, and Mr. Driscoll may well leave with it when Letitia needed to give it back to its owner.

Ensuring she was decent, Letitia unlocked the door and opened it only enough to let the hall light filter through. He had taken a step back but didn't hand her the leather case in his arms when she held out her hand for it.

"I also wanted to...are you quite well?" he asked. Whatever he'd been about to say was wiped from his tongue as he took in her appearance.

"As it happens, I am not," Letitia snapped, her resolve to stay on her feet weakening.

"Then I won't take too much of your time," he said. "I have something I wanted to give you."

Letitia drew back from the door, retreating to the table to hold herself upright on one of the chair backs. She was being unspeakably inhospitable and didn't care as he came into the gloomy room.

"Please just give me the file," Letitia said, her voice rasping. With every second that passed a weariness threatened to overwhelm her.

"Here." Mr. Driscoll placed it on the table, and then took out of his pocket a box and lay it on top of the file. "Mrs. Quinn felt dreadful about what happened yesterday, and she wasn't sure why you ran—"

"It doesn't matter," Letitia said over the top of him, "but I must ask that you leave now."

She brought her hand to her temple, catching the beads of sweat. As her hand drew back, she saw the moisture, her vision swam, and her grip tightened on the chair until the wood groaned.

"Would you like me to call a doctor?"

"Go away, Mr. Driscoll," she muttered, her legs shaking.

"You look ill." His feet appeared in her downturned vision. Realizing he was too close, she looked up at him, afraid. In the streaking light from the door, his features were stark but not unkind. When she didn't respond his brows furrowed.

"You left without your umbrella yesterday, and it was raining..." he said. Letitia scowled.

"It's no concern of yours." She gestured to the door, but even as her arm swung her trembling legs gave out. He caught her outstretched hand, letting her crumple against his shoulder as he wrapped an arm about her.

"Running through the rain because of bloody Abby," he said in a furious curse. Her head was spinning too much to respond, vision swimming in and out as her consciousness faded. The world tilted as he brought his other arm under her legs. Her head fell against his shoulder and she couldn't utter another protest. The thuds of his steps reverberated through her like heartbeats as he walked across to the door to her room.

There was a disgusted sigh, no doubt at her meager lodgings. Standing her up by the bed, he flung the covers back with one arm and then sat her on its edge. She looked up at him with fear of the shadow that followed him, but there was nothing there. Instead, a shaft of light was striking his head, surrounding it in a crown of rose gold and silver. The nimbus effect robbed her of any timid response at indecency, and the once-stern lines of his face were of concern.

He studied her in equal measure, fingertips brushing sweat-slicked strands from her face, touch tentative and warm. Letitia fought against leaning into his hand, taking meager comfort in the gesture of tenderness.

She willed herself to sit upright, grasping at what little strength she had remaining to undo her dressing gown, but her fingers fumbled with the buttons.

He pushed her hands away, undoing the buttons as her fingers would not.

"I can't...insist enough...how inappropriate..." Her voice trailed off as he helped her out of the dressing gown. She still had her nightgown, but the thin cotton was all that covered her. For all of his help, his gaze was minimal on her person in assisting her to bed.

"Another time, Ms. Hawking," he murmured. "Right now, you need rest and a doctor."

"It's just a cold," she said. "Please, I'm fine, just shut the door on your way out."

"Or it could be the damn Spanish flu," he said, holding her with care despite the angry words. "How long have you been in the country?"

He took care to lift her, pulling away the dressing gown and cradling her against his chest as he assisted her.

"About six months," Letitia said, the truth tumbling out. He tucked the sheets into the bed, the motion gentle even though he glared at her all the while.

"Damnit." He placed a hand against her forehead, the soft gesture a cool balm though his calloused palm was rough against the hot skin. "You would have landed in New York about the time a carrier ship from England brought the flu with it. Never mind all the traveling you must have done or all the clients you meet. Hold on."

He disappeared, returning moments later with a cloth and the bowl she kept her fruit in. Now empty of fruit, it slopped with water. Dragging a chair to her bedside, he wet the cloth and lay it on her forehead. It was bliss. The coolness was almost painful in its relief, bringing clarity to her thoughts but with it sleep and a growing fever.

"Mr. Driscoll," she whispered, licking her dry lips, "you can't stay here."

"Propriety be damned, Ms. Hawking," he said, putting on the kettle and taking off his coat. "I'll get a cup of tea, ring for a doctor, and at least wait until he's here to assess you aren't in any immediate danger."

"That's not what I meant..." Letitia felt herself fading, but she couldn't have him here while she knew something dark followed him. Not while she was sick and weak, unable to stand, let alone face a malevolent spirit.

Mr. Driscoll ignored her, making tea and taking stock of the things in her cupboard. Selecting the tea box, he made a cup and put it by the bed. "You need to keep your fluids up. I'm going to make a call or two and be right back."

Letitia couldn't even answer. She lay in bed staring at him, aches stretching throughout her body, heat building in her limbs, and sweat beading under the cool cloth.

"I'm...I'm sorry," he said, touching her hand where it lay on the cover. She wasn't wearing her gloves.

Warmth flooded her, hotter than the fever, but burning it back and leaving her hand light. The cleansing wind across the desert left her breathless, but it eased the tension under her skin. She grasped his hand, wanting the sensation to fill her, body trembling with the sweet relief of his persona.

He gasped but kept holding her hand, staring down at where she gripped him. Fire within him ran along her nerves, stemming the fever's advance and flooding through her. The accidental touch brought back her clarity, and with horror, she snatched her hand back and drew it under the covers, but it was too late.

She'd drawn on a sliver of him.

It should mean nothing, it wasn't too much, and she hoped she didn't dream of him when she fell asleep.

"Please go," she said, weeping as she rolled over and away from him. There was silence behind her, and then the rustle of cloth and footsteps. Prone, Letitia was unable to open her eyes, the dry desert heat fading under the rush of the fever as it overwhelmed her.

Letitia lay in a bed of a stonewalled room, desperate for water and her skin on fire. A part of her knew it was in the past, nothing but a memory, but she could no more have stopped it than she could change history's events. At least it was her own dream and not Mr. Driscoll's, but it was her last thought as the vision swept her away.

Fever rocked through her, trying to claim her body. She was ready to give in.

She could not scratch—they had bound her hands. She could not move—they'd tied her feet.

"*Please*," she begged the figure by the fireside.

"*They spent a year filling you with poison*," the old woman said. "*Did you think it would all go away?*"

No, she didn't, but Letitia had never guessed it would be like this, the sweat pouring from her body and saturating the sheets. A stranger changed them, paying no mind to the bindings, but Letitia never lost sight of the woman in the rocking chair whose words stole any inclination to cry for help. Gimlet eyes pierced her soul and when Letitia wanted to scream, she found the compulsion absent.

The woman studied her, smoking her pipe, piling more wood on the fire, and making the room hotter and hotter. Not a bead of sweat was on her, though covered head to toe in wool as she was. She was there while Letitia burned, with watchful eyes that never blinked. They became Letitia's anchor, drawing her back to life and sanity.

On the third day, Letitia awoke, calm and still. The old woman got up and unbound her legs and hands without Letitia asking. Letitia couldn't even lower her arms by her sides or curl her legs up, so the woman did it for her. A buxom frame with the arms of an ox moved Letitia about as though she were nothing but skin and bone. It's what Letitia had become.

"*Who...who are you?*" Letitia asked between cracked lips.

The woman smiled for the first time in days, and not the toothless grin of a hag but the wide smile of a Cheshire cat, with perfect teeth and all the secrets.

"*You can call me Ol' Mother Borrows,*" she said. "*Everyone does.*"

"*What do you borrow?*" Letitia said, weak and light-headed.

"*Lost souls. Like you, my girl.*" She picked up a cloth and wiped away the last of the sweat from Letitia's forehead. "*I'll borrow you for a time and make you whole again.*"

"*After what I did?*" Letitia said, able to think of her pain and loss without falling into the void of grief.

"*There's another fate waiting out there for you, tangled up in your past,*" Old Mother Borrows said, "*and you've got to go find it to get through it, even if it means revisiting your worst fears.*"

Letitia opened her eyes.

A hazy memory lingered. Sunlight streamed into the room, but it was from the afternoon sun. Had she slept all day?

Stretching against her tired limbs, she felt feeble as a kitten as she lifted her head. Scanning her bedroom, Letitia caught sight of her bedside covered with bottles of medicine. Upon the bureau across from her sat a leather bag, open at the top. Other things that weren't hers were strewn about.

Mr. Driscoll sat in a chair across the room.

Ankles crossed, he slumped in the chair, a book in his hands. The top of his shirt was unbuttoned and the sleeves rolled up, and he'd hung his coat and waistcoat on the stand she kept in her session room. He was reading her battered copy of *Pride and Prejudice.*

The trickling light etched the lines on his face about his eyes, haggard but at ease, as he turned another page.

There were footsteps across the session room, and Mrs. Finch came in, carrying a tray.

"Here you are then, Mr. Driscoll," she said.

"You are a godsend, Mrs. Finch." He put the book to one side and placed the food on his lap. Letitia puzzled over their easy companionship before Mrs. Finch noticed Letitia was awake.

"Oh my," Mrs. Finch cried, bustling over to Letitia, "you're back with us, dear!" She came over to the end of the bed and patted Letitia's foot under the covers.

"How long was I ill?" Letitia asked, her throat raw. Mr. Driscoll set aside the tray, getting a glass of water before Mrs. Finch could move.

"Three days, no less," Mrs. Finch said, a fond look at Mr. Driscoll, "and your intended hasn't left your side."

Letitia raised a brow as Mr. Driscoll blocked Mrs. Finch's view, saying nothing as he held out the glass. She lifted her hand, the glass almost slipping through her trembling fingers before his hand tightened around hers. He sat on the bed beside her, his free hand coming around to cradle her head and lift her up so she could sip the water.

She gulped it down, and he took it away before she was ready.

"Not too much. You haven't eaten in a few days," he said, easing her head down and getting up before she uttered a word.

The water eased the dryness in her throat, revitalizing her. When Letitia tried to sit up, he was there again, one hand under her back and the other keeping her decency as he held the covers to her chest. She wasn't in the same nightgown.

When she widened her eyes, there was an amused glint in his eye, but he said nothing. Letitia wanted to know what he thought he was about but was silent as Mrs. Finch put a pillow behind her head.

"Thank you," she said, puzzled and uncomfortable at the turn of events.

"You're welcome, Ms. Hawking," Mr. Driscoll murmured.

"I'll get more broth," Mrs. Finch said, beaming at Letitia. "You're so lucky to have such a good fiancé, Ms. Hawking."

Letitia couldn't stop the color burning up her cheeks, and from Mrs. Finch's sly twist of her lips, she was aware Mr. Driscoll was not her partner. "That man hasn't left your bedside for three days, Ms. Hawking, for it's Sunday afternoon, I'll have you know."

With that, she picked up her skirt and swept out.

"Three days?" Letitia croaked, searching for her purse and appointment book. All those clients she'd have to call and apologize to. She struggled to find an excuse.

"Looking for this?" Mr. Driscoll was holding the little black book, picked up from where it rested on the desk. Letitia held out a hand for it, but his stern expression gave her pause.

"Don't worry," he said. "I called them all and explained you were ill. They'll wait until you call them again."

At his cool expression, Letitia became aware he'd seen she didn't have as many appointments as she'd claimed. Not that he hadn't guessed already, but now he'd be sure. She drew back her hand, her scattered brain finding no excuse to give him as they stared at one another, the seconds ticking on.

She cast her gaze to the floor.

There was nothing she could say to a man as determined as he was, and instead, she turned to other embarrassing subjects.

"Thank you for taking such excellent care of me." She tugged the ends of her hair fallen loose from their plait.

"It was the least I could do," he said. "Whatever was said and done, it was never meant to hurt you. You were in this predicament after the duress placed on you by me and my sister."

Letitia opened her mouth to deny that it had been anything Mrs. Quinn said, almost mentioning the figure before she fell silent. To confess would only make Mr. Driscoll wonder what had made Letitia run. He did not need to know of her fears.

"Besides," he went on when she didn't speak, "if you had Spanish flu, there was a good chance I did as well when the doctor arrived, and I didn't want to bring sickness to my own home. By the time the doctor could have organized a nurse there was no point."

Letitia's brows puckered, wondering if Imogen or Mrs. Finch and her daughters could not have assisted, and he must have read it in her face.

"I didn't want to impose on the people of this house," he whispered, "or make them ill, too. They have livelihoods of their own."

Suitably chagrined, Letitia instead dwelled on having Mr. Driscoll stuck here for three days, trapped in this tiny room with a sick woman he didn't know. A sneaking suspicion of his motivations burned in her cheeks, replacing the fever. Would he demand her help now?

"You've been very kind, and I am much better now," she began, and his mouth quirked as he blinked at her.

"Are you about to ask me to leave?" he said, soft as the hearth fire, and far hotter. Letitia wanted nothing more than to have her apartment back. To untangle herself from his insistent advances. She longed for a slender thread of his tenderness to be for her and her alone—and not her abilities.

"I cannot thank you enough," Letitia said, but not denying she wanted him to leave. "But doing so does not indebt me to your niece's cause."

Mr. Driscoll froze, staring at her. "It might surprise you to know, Ms. Hawking," he drawled her name, anger burning in every word, "that I did it because it was the right thing to do."

Then without another word, he stood up and walked out the door.

Letitia would have breathed a sigh of relief had it not been for all of his things strewn about the room. A reminder of all he'd done, and a promise he'd be back.

Chapter 8

L etitia wasn't surprised when she opened the door and Mr. Driscoll stood there.

He hadn't returned for several days, and by then she was better.

The scope of his aid came to Letitia long after he'd left. Imogen, returning from work, came to check on Letitia. Imogen had nothing but kind words for Mr. Driscoll, who'd called for a private physician and rang all of Letitia's clients to apologize and rebook or promised a return call on Wednesday when Letitia should be better. He took her calls as well, making notes of times and numbers so Letitia could get in touch with ease. He left the book with all the numbers on the dresser for when she was ready.

And he'd not done it for her help. His words echoed back to her every moment she uncovered another facet of the days he'd spent there. A pile of papers in a briefcase indicating he'd worked away from his office. A delivery came with her laundered dresses. Her cupboard was full of food she'd never bought, even the tin of shortbread full.

She hadn't asked him to do any of it, didn't remember the days as it was, but she still carried a conviction he meant to win her gratitude for what he wanted.

Yet the thoughtfulness needed to be acknowledged.

Letitia met his eyes, a thousand questions on her lips but most of all a beseeching why, which his return gaze did not answer.

And something twisted within, an admission she never wanted to make. She couldn't ignore him any longer.

Stepping aside, she opened her door to him, and there was the briefest flicker of relief as he passed her.

He carried a box under one arm. She hadn't even noticed it until he placed it on the table.

"I brought you a gift."

It was she who should be thanking him, but he came with a present not knowing his reception.

Another time...

His words still echoed in her ears. The whisper he'd uttered when he'd helped her to bed—in her anxious state in the days after he left, she'd wondered if she'd heard them. She did not expect him to have had such thoughts about her.

The vivid memory of him standing over her, with her in nothing but a nightgown, caused raucous butterflies to skip over her skin and slip under it to writhe in her chest at the sight of him in her rooms once more.

Now they came again, a thousand times louder, not with dread but the foreign touch of anticipation.

Letitia's gaze flickered between him and the box, the prickling sensation of wariness warring with the tightness in her throat. Though she'd invited him in, she wasn't sure she wanted him to stay. Some measure of fear, or of betrayal to her once love, nibbled at her thoughts during Mr. Driscoll's absence.

Despite it, she'd collected all Mr. Driscoll's belongings, had laundered his clothes in kind, and even mended a loose button on his waistcoat. It had seemed a trifling, silly thing to have done for someone she was both drawn to and feared, yet she had bought the right color thread and made the stitching as small as possible to fit in with the fine cloth of the garment.

It was his respect for her position that rattled her most.

Her appointment book was full.

There had been quite a few names on the list he'd left for her, along with the people she needed to book. Calling them all had been a tedious but rewarding affair.

But whatever hope she had of balancing the scales between them was hollow in her chest. For all her prejudice, he was a kind man.

"I have your suitcase packed," Letitia said, ignoring the gift. She went to his bag and rather than giving it to him put it beside the door. "Would you like tea?"

If her offer surprised him, it didn't show as he nodded. Letitia collected the tray from the other room and brought it into her session room. Though he had made himself comfortable in her private room, she wasn't about to entertain him there. When she returned, he hadn't sat but stood staring at the garden below her window.

He still didn't turn about as she poured, helping herself to a cup.

Whatever was weighing on his mind, Letitia thought it would take time to divulge. Perhaps she should have listened to him before. But she would do so now.

"You have recoiled yourself in fear from both me and my sister," he said, "and I would like to know why."

Letitia's fingers pressed hard to the porcelain cup's side, willing the heat to sink into the coldest reaches of her troubled mind. She'd allowed them the time to converse on what he wanted most, but that he chose to start with such a question had her scrabbling for an answer.

Letitia sought a way to escape confessing her dread from her cup, but it didn't help. Nor did his assessing eyes as he came to join her at the table, drinking the tea but waiting with all the patience of a mountain.

And he was like a mountain, even without the heavy coat on his shoulders. She'd seen it when he'd worn only his shirt. Long arms and broad chest. He was strong, even if he did work as a lawyer, so there must be something else he did to keep such physical fitness. She'd told herself to discard any idle inclination to let her eyes rove over him and wonder.

There was no fear of a shadow that followed him, giving her a measure of calm and an ability to speak of why she would not help him, though her resistance weakened.

"You and your sister have had something dark happen to you," she said, choosing her words with care, "and it follows you, this shadow and its purpose. It is not beyond the veil, or it could be something....not of this earth."

"I am not sure I understand what you mean," he said, though he sat forward when she spoke, clear in his comments but not with condescension.

Letitia struggled to find the words to answer him with an honesty he might understand.

"We all have souls," she said. "Those souls cross over when we die, but to where isn't for us to know here and now. These souls go through what I like to think of as a veil between life and death." Letitia didn't miss the way his eyes darted to the one she wore now. At the wry twist of his lips and subsequent irritation, she took it off.

His expression changed from slight mockery to one of satisfaction. At what, she wasn't sure, but she put the veil to one side so as not to distract from the conversation.

"When someone passes through the veil, they leave a... stain of their passing." It didn't sound nice, even as Letitia said it, but it was the only way to phrase it. "I read that remaining mark through a scrying bowl, see the world from that person's eyes before they die, for a time. I cannot stay when they die, because it can drag me into their death if I'm not very careful.

Dying is one of the most profound things we experience. When it's happening, it can be easy for it to overwhelm me, for me to become lost in the death itself."

"It's why you don't take murder victims." He pursed his lips, brows furrowed in confusion. "But you help war widows and other people who died in accidents. Like my brother-in-law. They are sudden deaths. They are dangerous, too."

"Yes," Letitia said, "and I always find out the circumstances so that when I see their final moment coming, I extricate myself from the vision. I don't let the vision extend into active combat—just the moments leading up to it. That way, even if the death is unexpected, I won't fall into it. Emotions can run high and be confusing. To the untrained, you can believe you are *becoming* the person, and so when they die, you don't know who you are and you can die."

Mr. Driscoll pushed away his cup, folding his hands on the table in front of him.

"But that isn't why you won't help us with Finola," he said. "And you're afraid of us because of this...shadow that follows us."

He wasn't dismissive of her fears, there was no contempt in his voice, but all the same, his eyes were cold as they regarded her. Letitia guessed he might think her a coward without accepting what the risks were.

"I've had a similar spirit follow me," she said, being clear in her warning while remaining cautious not to give too much detail, "and it stole my life and my sanity. And it is my burden to bear. I still do not wish the same burden on you. There is something different, and far more treacherous, that slumbers in your shadow."

"What kind of danger does it pose?"

"The kind that taints the soul forever." Letitia's voice lowered to a whisper. "The kind that never fades, that stays with you in nightmares."

Mr. Driscoll swallowed, his Adam's apple bobbing. "Finola

has such terrors. Do you?"

Letitia rolled her lips and considered denying it but after a moment gave a clipped nod.

"That's how you convinced both my sister and me you weren't there for our money," he said. "I thought...I thought if I gave it to you, I could dissuade Mrs. Quinn from trying with anyone else. You were right about my brother-in-law. For a moment you made her believe." The sentence sounded unfinished, as though he would have added himself, but the words never came.

"There are many people out there who would fool you for your money, Mr. Driscoll." Letitia sipped her tea. "I am not one of them."

Something about her empathic tone drew him to study her.

"I've gathered as much," he said. "It doesn't serve you to cause a scene like what happened at the café without due course. You are aware in ways I am not of this...darkness that follows those of my home."

She could hear the fear in his voice and that he took her words with due consideration, but so too was doubt there.

"You didn't come because you wanted to know Mr. Quinn was thinking about his job or his family before he died," Letitia countered. "You came because something happened to your niece, something unexplainable to anyone with an ounce of reason. There is something you aren't telling me about the situation, but here's what I can tell you. A dark spirit has attached itself to your family and will hurt them in unspeakable ways."

His knuckles turned white as he stared at her, but whatever he opened his mouth to say, he appeared to think better of it, as his lips became a firm line and his hands relaxed.

"I can't send her to Scotland to recover," he said. Letitia knew he had spoken to Mrs. Quinn, but then Letitia hadn't given him all the information he may need.

"And if you send her to the asylum, she will die."

It was a cruel thing for her to say. She saw the shock on his face and shook her head at it, and his stubbornness.

"Did you think I didn't know?" Letitia said, wanting to hammer home the gravity of her fears. "I was a widow, alone and friendless. Your niece is not. They locked me up, and only the kindness of a stranger brought me back to sanity."

Gone was the surprise but his gaze drifted to her abdomen.

"Is it why you have those scars?"

Letitia went numb, head light and reeling.

"The doctor told me," he said, allying any concern he had seen them himself. He had the grace to avoid her furious gaze as he explained. "He mentioned the scarring when commenting on your constitution. I merely listened. It was Mrs. Finch and Ms. Harland who changed your gown."

Letitia's face burned with intense embarrassment, shame, and dread that a relative stranger should know something so intimate about her. More than one, in fact—the house she resided in full of women who would empathize with such scars now would consider her with sympathy, if not pity. She stood, and he braced himself, but she turned away and paced the room. She withdrew her hand from her stomach to her hip, her gesture self-conscious under his assessing gaze.

"You had no right," she said, wanting him to leave. "I never asked for your attentions. My past failings are now common knowledge, and you have displaced me within my own home."

"My apologies," he said after several moments of watching her. "I didn't mean to offend you."

"Yes, you damn well did," Letitia bit out as she tried to compose herself. What would Mrs. Finch's kindness turn to knowing the wounds on her body? Would the sunshine that came from Imogen change now that she had seen Letitia's weaknesses? It was several minutes before she could resume her place at the table.

"Yes," she said, "those scars were how I ended up in the asylum. Can you imagine the experiences that went with them? Don't send your niece to the asylum if you love her."

It was his turn to be furious.

"I do love her," he said, biting out the words one at a time, "and it's why I am here. It isn't why I stayed, but if I could but tell you, you might be the one person who can understand why I may not have a choice—"

He broke off, clenching his jaw to hold back the words, the muscle tensing and releasing. Whatever he would have said next Letitia waylaid it.

"You must understand," Letitia said, "if I fail—if something were to happen, I may not be able to remove myself from it. I may make it worse."

There was a bark of laughter, sudden and sharp, so surprising Letitia started. There was no humor in Mr. Driscoll's face, nothing but a hard sneer that held no nuance of amusement.

"Finola can't sleep," he said. "She's kept awake by nightmares of someone coming to take her, to do…the most awful things to her. At night she makes the kind of plea no family would ever want to hear, as though some being is torturing her as she sleeps. There is no rest, only waking hours of fear and the assault that comes at night. She is living in a waking nightmare. We've had to start a dosage of morphine and have a nurse on hand to help manage her. Aside from having her committed, Abby and I are at a loss as to what to do."

As though it was the last stone pillar in the wall of her defenses, he knocked it down. Letitia's quest in America, and her purpose in London, was always to avoid the fate she herself had experienced. Denying assistance now only disproved her own philosophies and how far or how much of herself she would be willing to sacrifice.

But those morals she clung to, which she held dear when patrons demanded more, would make her out to be a liar if she didn't help Mr. Driscoll now and go to Finola as someone had once come to her. But this time Letitia would arrive long before the darkness consumed this girl.

Even if she did not yet know the cost.

For all Old Mother Borrows' teachings, she never meant for Letitia herself to become a tutor but only to contain the darkness within, the power Letitia wielded with such ease because she was so strong. So much stronger than she had any earthly right to be. And it was because she was tainted with something not of this realm.

"I'll meet her." Letitia was proud her voice didn't tremble, wiping sweat-slicked hands on her dress. The fear there, sitting behind her eyes, made her feel like prey looking for any chance to escape its predicament. But her spine straightened with her experience. She would not let another girl such as herself into the hands of doctors who didn't know what they were doing.

Mr. Driscoll's eyes drifted closed and the lines of his face eased. He wasn't old—a handsome profile had been rendered fearful by his perpetual scowl.

"Thank you." He got to his feet and went to the door.

"You can't mean for me to see her now?" Letitia asked, shocked.

"I do, Ms. Hawking," Mr. Driscoll said, "as I am afraid you will say no later, and I will not let this matter lie a moment longer. Someone needs to help my niece in a way I cannot."

Letitia hesitated, her decision's sudden ramification causing her to catch her breath.

"If-if I cannot help her," Letitia said, "I mean, if I do try and cannot, will you consider taking her to Scotland, despite the risk?"

Mr. Driscoll froze.

"You may have to drug her the whole way," Letitia pressed on. "But I promise you, there is a woman in Scotland far better able to handle this than I. I would ask you to send for her, but she will not leave her homeland."

Old Mother Borrows hadn't come herself to collect Letitia— she'd sent her granddaughter. Letitia never found out why the old woman would never leave her home, but she was in no position to ask.

"I will," Mr. Driscoll said. "But please, only if you come now."

Letitia bit her lip, the last vestiges of fight slipping away.

"Will you take me home when I ask, without question?" she clarified, and he nodded.

Letitia collected her veil, coat, and purse, and as an afterthought grabbed a small vile of juniper oil before she joined him at the door. Waiting until she locked it, he led her down to his car where the driver opened the door. Mr. Driscoll let her slide across the leather seat and placed a rug about her knees as he got in beside her.

"Are we going far?" Letitia felt a clenching worry she had allowed Mr. Driscoll to commandeer her.

"My house is on the far side of town," he said, "and I do not wish for your cold to return."

She turned to the window as the driver pulled the car out into the late afternoon traffic. People were thronging from businesses to return home, and at some moments they crawled along. Mr. Driscoll fidgeted beside her. He took out his pocket watch, glancing at the time, and put it back with a sigh.

"Are we in a rush?" Letitia asked as the driver got around a slow horse and carriage to pull out onto a stretch of road leading away from the city.

"I have been fighting for weeks to have some hope, so you must excuse me if I cannot wait to see if you hold the answers Mrs. Quinn hopes for." Mr. Driscoll added nothing further, and Letitia wondered again if he was speaking for himself and not Mrs. Quinn. "If you can see her at night, when things are at their worst, perhaps you may understand why I think our time grows short."

"What in her behavior has changed?" Letitia asked, suspicion sharpening her words.

"The visions are stronger, and she lashes out at people around her more often. She can see thoughts of the unwary," he said, rubbing his brow with one hand, "and though it affects my sister and the staff, it doesn't seem to reach me, and I assumed someone such as yourself would be immune against it."

The girl was gifted. Whatever had happened to Finola was not unlike Letitia's passage through the flame—emerging from the other side gifted, forever altered but not the same. There would be little Letitia could compare to her own suffering.

"You could have warned me." Such a power of mind reading was intimidating. Letitia would not allow a young, traumatized girl to see her innermost darkness.

"I just did," Mr. Driscoll replied, staring down at her. In the back of the car, he was close, and it reminded Letitia of the woody scent she'd gleaned from him when he'd helped her to bed. The way his fingers trailed over her skin, and with such tenderness as he pushed her hair from her eyes. The heat of his body when he held her, so unlike the fire of her fever. Fiercer, brighter, purifying.

And she would never tell him the effect it had on her.

"You must understand that my presence could make things far worse," Letitia said, disbelief he'd kept such a thing from her. "If Finola can see my past, then this could be disastrous."

"It isn't the same strength that I have come to understand of your gift," he said. "I assumed it was guessing, but my sister says it is not so. There is enough in Finola's words that lead me to believe she is...gifted. But so, too, does it come with a taint. Finola knows things that she should not. That nobody should ever know, least of all her."

The latter was spat out with such bitterness it stunned Letitia to silence.

"What matters is that she is just a girl," he went on. "She turned fourteen three months ago, and she shouldn't be robbed of her innocence like she is with these abhorrent nightmares. The things she describes when she is asleep are the last words you want to hear, let alone from your own flesh and blood."

"What happens in them?" Letitia asked, determined to know the details before she faced whatever had driven Mr. Driscoll to such measures.

He clenched his hands on his knees, trembling with rage as he uttered words that should never be spoken. Of a violence and perversion, and the darker nature of men...

She comprehended his meaning with stomach-churning revulsion, bile coating her tongue. It was every woman's worst fear to have a man take them by force.

Finola was just a girl...

"When did this first start?" Letitia began, forcing herself to ask. "Was she alone?"

"No," Mr. Driscoll shouted, startling the driver who swerved before straightening the wheel. "The doctors checked all of that for me. She wasn't out of my sight for more than a few moments, perhaps ten minutes."

"What do you mean she was out of your sight?" Letitia's gentle tone simmered the anger roiling off Mr. Driscoll.

"I recently bought an old hotel north of Los Angeles," he said. "It promised to be quite the retreat, but the building needed much work. I took Finola with me one day when she was driving Abby to distraction. Finola went exploring and I left her to it. She wasn't to go far but I found her crying in the cellar. I was looking at the piping to see what repairs we needed when I saw her. She was alone. There was no one else there. I made damn sure of that."

"No workers or tradespeople?" Letitia said.

"None." Mr. Driscoll's arm slashed through the air. "I would never allow any harm to happen to her. The men who were working on the repairs have worked for me for years. They knew her. I did not see it in one of them to have caused it."

"What about before then?" Letitia said. "Could whatever have happened to her have occurred at another time?"

"There was nothing before then, and I've told the doctors that," he snapped, and Letitia drew back at his vehemence. "She was laughing, spinning around the ballroom and pretending to dance when I wouldn't play with her."

Letitia bit her lip but pressed on. "What did she describe

happening?"

"She said a figure in the dark threw her to the floor," he said, his once-bright eyes darkening to terrible vengeance. "It ripped her dress...but there were no marks, no sign of violence, but she was screaming as though it had all happened in a matter of minutes. She'd gone down to the cellar to explore, even though it was empty. A crew had already cleared it of garbage because I wanted to use the space. Anything of value I had taken to my house cellars. I was inspecting the plumbing in the kitchen when I heard screaming. There was no one in the cellar but her, and only one way in or out. She was alone."

"What about the house, this old hotel." Letitia scrambled to find a source and to arm herself against an unknown foe.

"It's not been in use in years." Mr. Driscoll rubbed his eyes. "Mr. Calbright apparently inherited it from his father and did nothing with it. His son wants to sell the family's useless assets so he can focus on his shipping company. The hotel is in a bad way but given the price they sold it for, I thought it a bargain. It's well built and a good investment if you're willing to do the work yourself. Or, in my case, Mr. Quinn, before he died. He was trying to finish another job so he could begin work on the hotel."

Mr. Driscoll's voice faded, and his gaze focused out the window.

He had more than one reason for his guilt. It wasn't just Finola he felt responsible for, Letitia guessed, it was the father Finola knew—his sister's husband.

Letitia drew her arms around her, tucking the blanket in tight to her waist, wondering what could have happened. The miles passed, the lights of the city fewer and farther between, until the car climbed up the hill toward a house that overlooked the city.

Built as a castle with a modern flair, the house was made of stone with plaster white walls, the roofing all black tiles. Towers dotted the edges, sharp jagged teeth, and within the wolf's mouth were lights, warm and inviting.

Letitia reached her senses out, but the house held no true fear, and she bit down on her ability. In preparation, she imagined herself surrounded in a pleasant light from which nothing but what she chose could penetrate.

It wasn't an ability she actively used, but it was always there in the background, humming away, filtering enough out so that she wasn't surprised but still knew of people's attitudes around her. Her innate ability to do this had saved her life and the life of several other women once. It was only instinctual until Old Mother Borrows had shown her otherwise. It was a shield against things not of this world.

By the time they pulled up at the doors of the mansion, Letitia was in control.

If there was a malevolent force in the house, it could not reach her without her permission.

Mr. Driscoll offered his hand, helping her out of the car.

His palm was warm against her leather-clad one, his disposition kind in his relief to have her at the house. The sun was an orange sliver on the skyline and fast fading to nothing, even in the few seconds she took to admire the view down over the gardens, bare as they were with the winter breeze. Still, she hesitated, staring at the perfect landscaping that was so like the old houses of England.

Mr. Driscoll strode to the door, a footman already opening it as his master approached. She knew now not to wonder at how he'd thought he could buy her off. He was accustomed to wealth and the American manner of assuming everything was simply a matter of price. For all of his appearance of kindness, his earlier behavior was clearer to Letitia—money solved most problems.

She only wished it were true.

Walking up the stone steps, she entered the hall through the wide wooden double doors.

Inside, the castle motif was apparent only in the white walls and exposed wooden beams of the ceiling, which were better suited to a European castle than the modern-day city of Los Angeles. Modern electricity powered the low lights in alcoves that highlighted the beams.

"Glad to have you back, sir," an elderly butler said, who was using a walking stick. "Mrs. Quinn is in the study, and the nurse is sitting with Miss Finola."

"Thank you, Hargraves," Mr. Driscoll said, taking his coat and hanging it himself before accepting Letitia's. "This is the Ms. Hawking I spoke of before. She's come to help Finola."

Letitia wasn't sure she could but said nothing as she smiled at Hargraves. "Pleased to meet you."

"Oh, ma'am," he said, tears filling his eyes, "I'm so glad you could come. You've got to help our poor little girl. She suffers so much all in the house hear her."

There was a desperation that clung to the butler as he dropped his professional manner in sorrow. She let a sliver of him in and was touched with a chill from autumn wind passing through bare trees. It was a stronger reaction than Letitia expected. She feared the situation may be worse than Mr. Driscoll told her but wasn't sure how possible under the awful circumstances. That he was gritting his teeth and avoiding her glance did not ease her.

"Ms. Hawking?" Mrs. Quinn was standing in the corridor, staring in amazement before scurrying toward them. "Alasdair, you got her to come."

She rushed to embrace Letitia, who shrank away until she found herself against Mr. Driscoll. A steady hand on her shoulder eased her anxiety and he was quick to let go. Mrs. Quinn hesitated, a blush growing on her cheeks, and she stopped a few feet shy of Letitia.

Letitia tried to slow her elevated pulse. Mr. Driscoll held one hand not far behind her back, as though he were a safe haven for her retreat. When their gaze met there was only concern until Letitia dipped her head once and his arm fell away.

"Ms. Hawking has agreed to look at Finola," Mr. Driscoll

clarified to the room. "She isn't sure what she can do to help, but we may have to take Finola to Scotland."

Mrs. Quinn opened her mouth, shaking her head, but Mr. Driscoll was already holding up his hand.

"Please," he said, "let's at least give this a try. We have to do what's best for Finola, and maybe Letitia is right, as she has been about many other things."

He directed the last words to Mrs. Quinn, who bit her lip before nodding.

"Well," she said after a moment, clearing her throat, "if you'd please come this way."

Letitia followed them, allowing the house itself through her shields.

A prickle on her skin made her glance over her shoulder, and though nothing was there, she shivered. There were no shadows on her hosts, but she was cautious all the same.

While no malevolent presence existed, something in the air kept Letitia on guard, eyes darting to shadows and gloved hands on the banister longing to seek out what unsettled her so.

There was something in the house that didn't belong there.

She braced herself and followed Mrs. Quinn up the stairs.

Chapter 9

Finola lay in a room better suited to a princess.
A four-poster bed draped in gauze shrouded the figure within.
A pale pink duvet covered the slight frame, illuminated by a rose
glass lampshade held aloft by a fairy cast in bronze.

Pretty as it was, Letitia focused on the girl in the bed.

Finola's breathing was labored, her eyes twitching beneath
her lids and forehead clammy, with threads of auburn hair
sticking to her skin.

Letitia studied her for several moments.

There was no darkness attached to the girl, though the
room's low light gave too many shadows for Letitia's liking.
Ever wary of self-protection, she took hesitant footsteps closer.

When she stood at the foot of the bed and was sure there
were no dark specters here, she took Finola's measure.

Finola was drugged, but from the girl's eyes flickering in
uneasy sleep, it wasn't working. Even with the morphine, Letitia
could tell what the others could not—Finola would still have the
nightmares.

A nurse sat beside the bed, and Letitia looked to her, letting a sliver of the nurse's personality in.

A warm breeze regarded her, refreshing though it was weak. The nurse stared at Letitia but made no comment at Letitia's scrutiny.

"What's your name?" Letitia asked, coming around the bed to offer her hand.

"Nurse Hopkins." Hopkins had curling brown hair and hard dark eyes. A firm hand gripped Letitia's gloved one, and she maintained eye contact. There was a hardness within the nurse, and Letitia guessed she'd served in the war. Not on the front lines, but she was toughened by her experience.

"What can you tell me about Finola's condition?" Letitia asked. Mr. Driscoll came up beside her, and Letitia held up a hand to silence him. He glared but nodded permission for Hopkins to speak when the nurse hesitated.

"She has terrible night episodes," the nurse said, "like those of the soldiers coming back. When she's awake she cries a lot, she...bathes often but won't eat much." The nurse's glance dipped between Finola and Mrs. Quinn as though she would say more, but she pressed her lips together.

"What else?" Letitia's gentle tone, and the retreat of Mr. Driscoll's looming form, let loose the nurse's tongue.

"I walk with her in the gardens," she said. "She...doesn't like people to touch her. Appears distracted and nervous, takes to fright, doesn't like strange men—the gardeners and delivery men and such."

It was succinct but what Letitia needed to hear. "Thank you, could you give me a moment?"

The nurse needed another nod from Mr. Driscoll before she took her leave.

"Well?" Mrs. Quinn asked, standing on the far side of the bed, touching her daughter's forehead. The girl flinched, and Mrs. Quinn drew back her hand with a disappointed frown.

"Please don't," Letitia asked, and Mrs. Quinn's glower

turned to acute displeasure.

"She's my daughter and she's sick." Mrs. Quinn's voice held a razor's edge that hadn't been there before.

"She also can't distinguish who is touching her when she's dreaming," Letitia said, and Mrs. Quinn covered her widening mouth, gaze darting between Letitia and Finola. She must come do this often, and what should have been the comforting gesture of a mother made the nightmares worse.

"I need quiet," Letitia said, turning to Mr. Driscoll. "She shouldn't wake up. All I'm going to do is slip in and see if I can ascertain what she's dreaming about. Perhaps get to the source of the problem. But...if it becomes too much, and I ask you to take me straight home, will you?"

She couldn't run like she had last time or wait until she was alone to let her fear get the better of her. In hindsight, she should have asked that they bring Finola to her, but it was too late now. Letitia could at least be sure before she started that Mr. Driscoll would do the right thing by her.

"What do you want us to do?" He said, and Letitia took it as an acceptance he would do as she asked.

"Please just stand by the door," Letitia said, gazing at Finola, "and don't distract me. I cannot insist on how important that is, and do not speak."

She waited until they both agreed. She received another curt nod from Mr. Driscoll, while Mrs. Quinn murmured something that sounded like acquiescence. She sat in a chair on the far side of the room and Mr. Driscoll stood defensive by the door with his arms crossed.

Letitia cast their presence from her mind, tugging her gloves off one finger at a time as she studied Finola.

A part of it was a delay as she waited for the last possible moment to extricate herself, but with every second that passed a fierce anger rose within her—at her own treatment, the doctors with the best of intentions doing more harm than good. In the asylum, Letitia was an adult at least, had some mettle of sense within, or Moira Borrows would never have gotten her out.

As a young girl, Finola would have no such constitution.

Letitia had no way to judge while Finola slept, but as she looked at the forlorn figure an old fear crawled along her throat and she swallowed against it. An asylum's good intentions would break a girl like Finola.

Taking a deep breath, she followed Old Mother Borrows' mannerisms even though a fine tremble skittered over her skin. Her hands clenched, and she willed the sensation away, gritting her jaw as she prepared herself for whatever haunted the Driscoll home.

Holding her naked palm over Finola's forehead, Letitia didn't touch the girl but opened her senses to whatever was emanating from Finola.

There was the sparkle of a stream, fish slipping beneath the surface. Letitia almost jerked back in shock; Finola held latent abilities. Animals in any impression often denoted psychic intelligence. Old Mother Borrows found within Letitia a dark wood settling with snow and deer walking between the trees, eyes wide and watchful.

But while Letitia marveled at seeing it in someone else, so too did her mind's eye behold the fresh stream pouring into a fetid pool held in place by a rock dam. Fish choked in the sludge, their rotting corpses buoying to the surface. And on the walls of the dam stood a figure. The malice within its eyeless gaze reached into her soul and left her awash in the slimy sensation of the dead fish as though she'd plunged into the dam waters herself.

Letitia drew back, eyes wide as she looked about, but there was no shadowy specter in Finola's room. But its presence lingered in Finola's mind.

Wherever the spirit rested, whatever its attachment, the trails of its foul presence staining the girl's soul was the cause of Finola's distress. Mr. Driscoll was right—no doctors would find anything because it would leave no physical marks—only the ones on her psyche. Drugging her wouldn't keep the vile creature at bay.

But it was not there now. For the present, Finola's subtle twitches were wholly bad dreams.

Relief almost crashed into Letitia. Her hand lifted to her chest to still her beating heart, rising to protect her throat and stop the sudden desire to scream. Letitia wouldn't allow her fear of the past to distract her. She could not have an attack now. She retreated to the nurse's chair by the bed, breathing through her fluttering pulse, her legs shaky as she sat.

"Ms. Hawking?" Mr. Driscoll was at the end of the bed.

"Please," she said, desperation making her voice soft, "come no closer."

When she looked up at him, she was drawn to the concern in his deep green eyes and the hand held out as though to help. The perpetual desert warmth rolled off him in waves that swept away the chill of the nightmare.

He wasn't touching her, but he wasn't far enough away. She needed distance to think but also to explain what was wrong.

"We should not discuss this in front of her," Letitia said, fumbling for composure as she dropped her gaze.

"Yes," Mr. Driscoll said, "and you look as though you could use a brandy."

"I'll stay until Hopkins comes back," Mrs. Quinn said, coming to take Letitia's seat. Letitia got to her feet and left the room. At the door, she gave a single glance back at the bed. The familiarity of the girl's mind was tugging at Letitia to the point where she wanted to stay and do as Mrs. Quinn had and stroke the girl's forehead.

Instead, she let Mr. Driscoll escort her downstairs to a library.

Books on law lined the shelves, thick green carpet covered the wooden floor, two leather armchairs sat before a roaring fireplace, and a desk littered with paper dominated one end of the room. Letitia could have slept on the desk, it was so large.

The stacks of paperwork denoted that Mr. Driscoll was a busy man, or perhaps he had been working from home. Someone had brought the briefcase he'd left behind at Letitia's apartment from the car, but he ignored it all.

"Please make yourself comfortable," he said, going to a sideboard to pour her a drink.

"I'm fine, thank you," she said, holding her hands out to the fire to try to replace the warmth she'd gleaned from Mr. Driscoll's personality.

His presence was beside her, too close, his hand on her elbow and sliding down to her wrist where he lifted her hand and placed the drink there.

"If it rids you of your pale appearance, I'd be grateful," he said, hand not leaving hers until her fingers wrapped around the crystal cut glass. He held on a few moments longer, searching her eyes, but let go to pour his own generous glass. Glancing down, she saw he'd only given her a nip, and when his back was turned, she placed it on the mantle without another thought.

She didn't want a drink. She wanted out of this beastly mess.

"What is your verdict?" He sat behind the desk, and she saw his eyes drift to the glass though he said nothing.

It was as though they were back in his office, and she hoped he didn't try to make her sign anything again.

"This isn't a piece of paper or business transaction," Letitia said, snapping at his cavalier attitude.

"I'm aware of that, Ms. Hawking." Mr. Driscoll gentled his tone, beseeching her. "Help me understand what I can do for Finola. Anything you ask."

When she met his gaze there was a seriousness there, determination an easy mantle for him, but to her, it was a shaky bridge at best. She took one deep breath, and then another, collecting her thoughts.

She hadn't eaten yet and was still fatigued from the fever. She also didn't know what to do about Finola. The girl needed the help Letitia thought Old Mother Borrows could provide, but they were running out of time.

Her thoughts returned to the dark stain filling the waters of the dam, the creeping tendrils staining Finola's mind surely as weeds growing through a stream, choking it off.

Even if they took her to the old woman, Letitia felt Finola wouldn't make the journey. It would be several weeks, a month's travel at most, and Letitia knew Finola could be insane or dead by then.

Whatever the presence was, she would have to find it and face it. Her hands wrapped about her middle, swallowing against the rising terror that she may have to face down a spirit. Or something worse.

But her choices were slim—it was either that or leave Finola to the darkness.

Dread pressed her to leave but she wouldn't abandon a young girl to face such a creature alone, in spite of Letitia's growing concern.

"There is a monster hunting and hurting her within her dreams," Letitia began, and Mr. Driscoll raised his eyebrows.

"We know she's having nightmares—"

"No, it's more than that." Letitia tried to articulate what she had seen. "You know how when you are having a nightmare you almost know? Or you at least wake up?"

He nodded, and she came to stand in front of his desk, hands clasped in front of her, willing him to understand what she was about to say.

"It isn't like that for Finola," Letitia said, "she is being made a prisoner of her dreams. Everything that happens she feels, the pain as genuine as if it were happening to her body. The presence for Finola is real, so even when she wakes up, she sees it, even if no one else does."

"Did you see it?" he said, alarmed. "Is it there now?"

Letitia was caught off guard by his sudden question.

"Yes. I mean, no." She hesitated over her next words. "It's left its impression on her, and she's having nightmares about it.

But it wasn't there in the room, not now."

Her gaze had fallen to the floor, the seconds ticking onward.

"That's what you meant about a darkness that followed us. You've seen it before. That day I first came to your house and why you ran from Abby."

"Yes." Letitia didn't dare lift her head. She was ashamed she'd behaved in the manner she did, but it was worse now Mr. Driscoll knew more about her past and subsequent fears.

"Does that mean that this monster should be in our nightmares?"

"I'm not sure." Letitia returned to the fire. So much was uncertain, yet Mr. Driscoll and Mrs. Quinn were trusting her with Finola. A trust she wasn't sure was misplaced. Letitia may be familiar with what had happened, but too much was out of her scope, and she did not have Old Mother Borrows' gifts.

"What is it?" he said, and for the longest time, she wouldn't answer. When she heard his chair creak and footsteps cross the carpet, she faced him before he could reach her.

"It could be anything," she said. "The soul of a person who hasn't passed the veil, or something far, far worse." She closed her eyes on the last part, trying not to remember the séance. The longer she thought about what she'd seen standing on the weir of the dam, the more the trepidation grew within her.

"What aren't you telling me?" he asked, voice icy.

Her gaze shot to his, ignoring the fury there because underneath it she saw the same fear. "That there are far worse things than being tormented by the souls of the dead."

"My daughter believes she is being ravaged by someone in her sleep," his voice was rising with every word, "and you think there is something *worse?*"

He stopped, and Letitia had been about to remind him of her scars when she realized what he'd said.

"Your daughter?" she asked, shock in her voice.

"Yes," he bit out, "my daughter." He reached for her, and she cringed until his hand passed her to take the brandy she'd left on the mantel, which he gulped down himself.

Letitia took several steps away, moving to the door.

No wonder he had been so determined. It wasn't his niece that this was happening to, it was his daughter, and he'd been there when it started and hadn't been able to stop it.

This was far more complicated and personal than Letitia wanted to know, but it didn't seem to stop Mr. Driscoll as he refilled the glass and returned to the fireplace. He leaned on it, taking comfort from the glass as he spoke.

"The woman in question was supposed to marry someone else," he said, "but we were in love, and it didn't stop our foolishness or our indiscretion. Her family hid her away, tried to stop me from seeing her, but she kept the babe a secret long enough to bear Finola. My intended's father was the kind of bastard who would have paid a doctor to be rid of it had he known. She told her parents they'd have to see her married or shamed. They relented. It would have all worked out had she not died in childbirth. At the time, Abby and Seamus—Mr. Quinn— had discovered they couldn't have children, and so I gave Finola to them to raise as their own. Finola needed a mother, and I could still be her uncle. It worked for everyone in the end."

"Everyone but you." The words were out before Letitia could stop them. He didn't turn from the fireplace, but his eyes drifted to hers before they slid closed.

"I suppose," he said, finishing the drink.

He fell silent and Letitia was at a loss for words. No solution on what to do was coming to her, and she'd laid all these problems at his feet. Mr. Driscoll barely believed, let alone possessed the tools to banish such a creature. She wasn't surprised at the resentful silence.

But when he wasn't demanding, she found Mr. Driscoll's presence an easy balm.

Enough so to open herself to his presence and to sense that summer heat.

But even as she basked in that fire Mr. Driscoll unwittingly exuded, her stomach being to roil, and despite having had her walls up there was an unsettling wariness creeping about her.

Like people, houses too emanated their past. But houses weren't as direct, the subtle nuances often lost in other overt senses.

The house wasn't saturated with the memories of English castles, but enough people had lived within it that there should have been a sense of the past lives. She'd blocked the impression when she first came in, protecting herself should there be anything untoward, but she sought out the house's atmosphere now. As it slipped through her shields, she saw something else.

There was a darkness beneath her feet, extending through the wood and stone of the floor and down into the cellar. She could see the basement cluttered with furniture covered in dust sheets and boxes of dusty and worn goods as if the floor she stood upon were glass.

Down in the depths of the house was the specter.

She stood frozen, afraid it would stretch incorporeal hands through the floorboards and carpet to wrap around her ankle and drag her into darkness. Letitia couldn't believe how long it had been there, waiting and watching like a sulking viper in a pit. It had lain dormant until she'd sought the source that haunted the people of this house.

At Letitia's attention to the phantom, waves of hatred crashed over her, violent and destructive.

Her instincts screamed for her to flee before it overwhelmed her, but the longer Letitia stood staring at it she realized it wasn't staring at her, though from the twisted resentment it acknowledged her presence.

It focused its attention past her to the ceiling. Letitia lifted her head, wondering what it sought.

The world slowed to a pause as the sounds of Mr. Driscoll breathing, the fire crackling, and the floorboards creaking faded away into velvet silence.

Finola screamed.

Letitia whirled about, flinging open the study to dash for the stairs. Slipping past the butler and avoiding a maid in the hall, she hurtled through the door and to Finola's bed.

"Get back!" she commanded the nurse and Mrs. Quinn, as she strode into the room.

Finola lay as though pinned, hands bound by invisible ropes, mouth wide, her high keening filled the room. Under the duvet her legs thrashed, but she seemed to grow weaker by the moment as she lost the fight against her demon captor.

"Finola," Mrs. Quinn pleaded, "it's a dream. Please, my darling, wake up!"

Letitia pushed her aside, swatting the nurse with the needle away.

"Don't touch her," she snarled at the well-meaning Hopkins. The nurse drew back in horror.

Letitia hadn't put her gloves back on. She couldn't sit by and do nothing regardless of her terror. She would not leave Finola to face such a demon, not when Letitia had conquered her own and come out the other side. Scarred and broken, and defeated in every possible way, but alive.

There was no telling what it would do to a mind so young, and one more attack may be the last one.

Letitia didn't hesitate, touching Finola's temples as she reached for the veil.

Chapter 10

There was darkness. There was always darkness. More inside than out, which made this the perfect place. Stairs descending into the earth, each one filling him with elation at the freedom to be himself. No more gesturing and posing, a smile on his face and courtesy in every word.

He'd help them with their dinners, make sure the beds were made, and smile for the senile old woman whose son only visited to pay the bills. There were always fresh flowers in the rooms and throughout the hotel. The lawn out onto the headland was always manicured. Everyone who stayed thought well of the place, and he orchestrated it all.

And it was a face he wore, a mask. Everyone had masks.

They'd wrinkle their noses at the smell under talcum powder and oil of lavender.

Avoid his gaze when their loved ones shat themselves.

They'd leave, and he'd clean it up.

All the while a greater reward awaited. For the kindness and patience he afforded everyone who stayed at his home, *there was a counterpart to the compassion he showed them.*

Cruelty akin to hell lay below as the domain above was heaven, and he was master of both.

This was his space, his time, everything he was or would ever be.

He didn't mind the poor patients above who needed him so, the elderly and feeble. But it left a corner of him unsated, lonely, and full of relentless anger. It had taken many years to find out how to express his displeasure, and by happenstance had found the perfect place.

Afterward, he'd found the perfect person and brought them here to defile that perfection.

Here, where he was free.

Humming a lullaby for his loves, he came to the heart of his darkness.

The smell of rot was a tang on his tongue. He licked his lips, anticipating the taste of salt, sweat, and tears. Another scent assaulted him—urine, excrement, blood. That wasn't as pleasant. That would have to be removed.

Chains rattled in the dark. He heard a whimper, and his fists clenched.

Holding himself back, he stayed on the last stair absorbing it all, no point in even closing his eyes it was so dark. He could reach by feel he knew the way so well. And it wouldn't matter the sounds they made, for no one could hear them.

The snivels grew to sobs, each one drawing heat to his loins, but he held out, wanting to savor every second that ticked by. To feel the shadows caressing him, urging him on, sending shivers up his spine.

Satin skin, soft bodies, and endless tears.

He couldn't wait for the shrieking to start.

Letitia screamed.

Hands were on her shoulders, helping lift her from where

she fell onto the floor. She scrambled back from the bed, the low light blindingly bright. People were shouting, there were calls for a doctor. Letitia covered her eyes, curling up as much as she could, trying to remove herself from the vision she'd just witnessed.

The threads of their pain sunk into her skin along with the satisfaction of the killer, staining her with his joy and arousal. Disgusted at the impression, she rolled over onto her stomach trying to retch, but nothing would come out. She brought her hands over her face, sobbing to release whatever she could of the vile emotion that held her captive.

Hands again pulled her from the floor, brought her close, and enfolded her in warmth. She was safe, she wasn't in the cellar, she wasn't the killer, but the abhorrent thoughts were trapped in her throat, and she had to say them.

"He's a vile beast." She uttered the words between panting gasps of despair and revulsion. "He kept them chained in the dark, and nobody knew. Nobody knew!"

Tears flooded down her face, and she trembled all over, unable to open her eyes.

"Ms. Hawking." A voice called her name and hands gripped her tight, but she couldn't look. Someone gave her a light shake, but it was her name that brought her to her senses.

"Letitia!"

Her eyes snapped open and met the emerald gaze of Mr. Driscoll. She was sitting in his lap, cradled against his chest. His face was pale, but his expression softened as she focused.

"Ms. Hawking," Mr. Driscoll said, relief in his voice, "look at the bed."

Letitia's head whipped around.

Finola lay over the edge, stretching her hand out for Letitia. Eyes the color of a cerulean sea sought her out with desperation. The nurse and Mrs. Quinn were trying to hold her on the bed to make her lie back.

Letitia didn't hesitate, remembering the rotting bodies of

the fish, the dam the man stood over. She scrambled over the floor, pushing past the others to wrap Finola in her arms and use her own body as a shield to stop *him* from coming back.

She poured what little energy she had left into imagining them both surrounded by light, safe from the creeping shadows. Letitia sensed the specter's anger, and that it would attack Finola again.

The lamp was growing dimmer, and the shadows slinked closer to the bed. And on the edge of hearing was the rattling of chains.

"You hear them," Finola whispered, burying her face in the crook of Letitia's neck. "You can hear him."

Letitia had forgotten that she needed not only to guard her thoughts but to keep certain dark parts of herself from Finola's view. The sudden apprehension that *he* would find his way to Finola again through the scars of Letitia's soul made her gasp into Finola's hair.

"Turn on the lights, all of them," she pleaded. "Now!"

Hurried footsteps crossed to the switch and with a flick, the lights banished the dark.

Letitia was weeping—in relief and fear, at the trembling bundle in her arms, at the promise of safety, and most of all at not being in that cellar.

They rocked for several minutes, the room silent, and Letitia brought her breathing back under her control, wondering what they should do now. The immediate threat was gone, but it hovered on the edge of the light, waiting for its chance to reclaim its prey. It was not this house—Letitia was sure of that much—it was somewhere else, but the sinister shadow had attached itself to something in the cellar. That was how it found Finola. It used something within the cellar to attack Finola and finish what it started when she'd first encountered it.

Letitia needed to break the connection and remove the spirit from the house. Once that was done, then Finola could focus on healing. All Letitia had to do was throw out the item the spirit had anchored itself to, but she was not foolish enough to face it tonight.

"Make coffee," she told Mrs. Quinn, "lots of coffee, for we cannot go back to sleep."

Letitia had said *we*, but she looked at Mr. Driscoll when she said it, hoping he took her meaning to refer to Finola.

Mrs. Quinn hesitated, hand reaching out for Finola's arm where it was wrapped against Letitia's waist.

"Please," Letitia begged, "you brought me here, and I broke the cycle, but he will be back."

"Don't scare her!" Mrs. Quinn snapped, seeking to take Finola once more.

"Do as I say or something far worse will happen," Letitia promised, and Finola whimpered.

"Abby," Mr. Driscoll said, "do as she says. Lay out food, coffee—cake as well. I'm sure Finola wouldn't mind a slice if she's to join us. I also don't think our hospitality to Ms. Hawking has been enough. Perhaps some dinner, too?"

Mrs. Quinn's delicate hand curled into a fist, and she left the room, glaring at anyone who dared to meet her eyes.

Finola's breathing fluttered like an expiring flame, and Letitia slid off the bed, changing her grasp on Finola to hold her hands as she sunk to her knees. Finola panicked at first, grasping her, but Letitia spoke like she would have to one of her students.

"I'm here," Letitia said. "I'm not going anywhere."

"Please," Finola said, "don't let him come back." The latter was a despairing sob.

"Listen, hear my voice." Letitia squeezed her hands, the words of Old Mother Borrows pouring out of her mouth. "You can't control this, it's beyond you, but you can control you—how hard your hand squeezes mine right now, your eyes focused on mine. You can control how you breathe, and I need you to breathe with me." Letitia counted, drawing in deep breaths, getting Finola's breath in time with her own, and then slowing it down until Finola's tears stopped.

The realization that Letitia was a stranger grew like dawn on Finola's face, and eyes wide, her lips curled into what might become a smile. Letitia kept her gaze focused on the girl's eyes, which dilated in curiosity. For a moment Letitia felt something she had only experienced with Old Mother Borrows—a sense of being watched from within. Letitia saw then that Finola was aware of using her abilities. She wasn't naïve to them as Letitia had been. It would make explaining to her all the easier, but for the moment Letitia swept a veil between them to stop Finola from learning anything much about Letitia except that she was a friend.

"Who...who are you?" Finola shook her head, looking surprised at the action. "You're Letitia. Uncle thinks of you often."

Mr. Driscoll cleared his throat, a chastising gesture though he said nothing.

A creeping blush tinged Letitia's cheeks, but she didn't look away from Finola's earnest eyes.

"My name is Ms. Hawking," Letitia said, with a little sternness to remind Finola of propriety before softening her words, "but when it's just you and I, you can call me Tisha, if I may call you Finola?"

"My dad used to call me Nola," Finola said. "You can, too, if you'd like."

"I'd like that very much," Letitia said with a grin. There was a pause as Finola still didn't let go of Letitia's hands.

"You'll stay up with me?"

"I promise," Letitia said. "And it shouldn't happen again if we stay awake."

Finola's face threatened to crumple, but after Letitia glanced at her with mock sternness, Finola flushed and took a few deep breaths.

"I think Ms. Hawking will need fortitude if she's staying up all night with you," Mr. Driscoll said. Finola's face burned and she turned away. Letitia wondered if the girl knew that it was not her uncle, but her father, speaking to her now.

"You should get dressed," Letitia said, distracting her. "I'll help you, and we'll see if your mother has any dessert."

Finola's eyes widened before glancing at Mr. Driscoll.

"Can I, Uncle?"

"I did just tell your mother to lay out cake," he said, frown fading with a warm smile. "If I thought midnight dessert would keep away nightmares, I would have fed you French cakes weeks ago, poppet. Your mother be damned." He muttered the latter, shaking his head, as Finola giggled at his swearing.

"You'll be downstairs in a moment?" He hesitated, waiting for Letitia to nod.

With one last look at the bed, he left the pair, shutting the door behind him.

Letitia pulled Finola off the bed and helped her to stand.

"Come on, we shouldn't be alone," she said when Finola hesitated. Finola was quick to retrieve her slippers and dressing gown, donning them before taking Letitia's outstretched hand. Rather than the main staircase, Finola headed down the hall to a much closer set of stairs for servants. She paused at the sight. It was darker than the hallway, the only light was dim at the apex of the switchback. Finola's hand tightened on Letitia's, who also shared the apprehension that if the one light in the staircase went out, they'd return to the nightmare.

"I'm not sure where you are going, Nola," Letitia said with brightness, though her words were edged in caution, "but the stairs are this way. I remember that and I don't live here."

She tugged Finola away from the dark descent and to the main staircase, and when they were in the hall Finola headed down a central passage, sure of where she was going. Finola went to a set of doors, flinging them wide.

Smells wafted through the air, a roast duck from the rich aroma, though when Letitia scanned the large and bustling kitchen it was a cake topped with cream that dominated the table. Finola had stopped in front, mouth, and eyes wide.

"Come here and have cake," Mrs. Quinn said to Finola from where she was cutting a piece, wider than her hand as Finola picked it up. Her mother scowled. "Use a fork."

"Coffee, Ms. Hawking?"

Mr. Driscoll was by the stove, jacket off and sleeves rolled up.

"Please," she said, coming to stand beside him, enjoying the domestic scene but unsure of herself. Mrs. Quinn babbled to Finola, talking about reading and games and how they would stay up all night together. Letitia didn't want to interrupt since she'd already done so several times this evening. Mrs. Quinn was acting like a cat over her kitten and was inclined to spit if Letitia put so much as a toe out again.

Instead, she followed Mr. Driscoll when he ushered her to a nearby room, where a servant was building up the hearth. The lights were on, filling the room with a warm glow reflected off the dappled yellow wall paneling. A long table of dark wood held over a dozen chairs and would have overlooked French doors, but the curtains were drawn against the night.

Mr. Driscoll set the tray down at the far end of the room where a sideboard sat in one corner and took out cups and saucers. Beside the sideboard were several overstuffed chairs, the latest newspapers left on a side table.

She came up behind him, discreetly admiring his broad back as he moved. It was not the same figure as Daniel; Mr. Driscoll was much broader, but for once guilt didn't assail her at the notion of having Mr. Driscoll wrap his arms around her again, if only to transfer some of his endless warmth into her chilled soul.

Looking after Finola had taken all of Letitia's strength, but the thought of not doing so was now abhorrent since she'd seen what haunted the girl. Letitia had witnessed nothing like it, her own situation vastly different. But still, no one else would have understood enough to banish the specter better than Letitia.

More tired than she cared to think about, she didn't notice Mr. Driscoll staring at her. They stood for a moment, eyes locked, and Letitia saw the gratitude there, but there was something else in his gaze that made her palms sweat.

"You can see dawn rise from this room," he said. "It overlooks the garden, which isn't so bright at the moment, but it promises spring is on the way."

"That's very thoughtful of you." Letitia sunk into one of the armchairs by the fireside. It was domestic to see Mr. Driscoll pour her a coffee.

"Cream or sugar?"

"No," Letitia said, "if I have to drink the abomination, then I'll do so with no help."

He grinned. "You don't partake?"

"For you, I made an exception." Letitia watched him over the rim of the cup he handed her before he turned away. She wasn't speaking of the coffee but of her presence here. His head tilted and a small smile formed on his lips; he guessed her other meaning. She had come though he hadn't known what it was he asked of her, but now he might understand a sliver of what risk she'd taken.

"I am...sorry." It was so tentative she almost missed it.

"Thank you," she said, acknowledging the apology, but there was more to do. "But this isn't over. We will stay awake until dawn, Mr. Driscoll, and then you and I are going to the cellar beneath your study."

"What?" he said, spinning about to face her.

"There's something you took from the old hotel. I assume on the same day this entity latched itself onto Finola."

"It was just some furniture and odds and ends." He rubbed his jaw. "The old hotel was full of junk, some of it salvageable but not suitable for what we're doing. I put the saleable pieces down in the cellar thinking of having them cleaned and assessed later."

"You brought back something," Letitia said, "and between

whatever happened in the cellar at the hotel and the specter's ability to find her here, it's been able to continue the assault."

He looked about the room, as though the offending item were there, and when he took long strides to the door, she called to him.

"Not tonight," her voice cautioned. "Not in the dark."

It was enough of a warning that he came back and sat opposite her. "What do we do then? Wait?"

Letitia raised a brow. "I know patience is not your strongest virtue, or perhaps even one you possess at all, Mr. Driscoll, but try, on my part."

His lips curled almost in a smile, and he gave a one-shouldered shrug at the insult before leaning forward to help himself to coffee. With a surreptitious glance at the door, he went to the sideboard and opened a cabinet to take brandy out and add it to his coffee.

"Would you—"

"No, thank you."

"I wouldn't under normal conditions," he said, putting a tipple in his coffee, "but this has been quite a damnable affair."

"And it's almost over," Letitia promised, making herself take another draught of the bitter brew. It tasted like mud on her tongue, and she shivered as she swallowed the unpleasant substance, eyes pinched shut.

Mr. Driscoll chuckled at her, and her eyes flew open to his amused expression.

"Is my coffee that awful?" he said, a dry, self-deprecating grin on his face as he sat in front of her.

"I think it's more the material you are working with," she said, "not so much the maker."

"If the offense isn't with the maker, then please let me know what you need." It was an innocent statement, but Letitia heard something else in the brogue of his voice. She swallowed, the grit of the coffee sticking to her tongue as her mouth became dry.

"Water would be good," she said, getting to her feet, "but I'll get it myself. I want to check on Finola."

She swept out of the room, haste making her footsteps loud on the wooden floor. When she'd closed the door behind her, she took a moment in the hall to catch her breath. Her skin was hot when she raised a cool hand to her cheek.

"Like a stupid schoolgirl," she said, chastising herself under her breath, saying it aloud and bringing censure as she drew herself together and returned to the kitchen. Any attraction sparking within her wouldn't last. She wasn't of his world, and no amount of wanting would transform the shattered remains of her life enough to make her a suitable wife.

Shaking off the notion, she went to the kitchen doorway.

Mrs. Quinn and Finola had gathered several trays of cakes and sweets. The cook was laying out dinner things, several maids hovering nearby for when the cook gave direction. It was a close and comfortable setting, and not at all like the houses in England that Letitia had seen. At the aroma in the room, her stomach became a hard, painful knot in her middle. Whether it was the lack of food, the events of the evening, or Mr. Driscoll's presence, she couldn't say.

"What can I help with?" Letitia asked when they all turned to her as she came in.

"You should eat dinner," Finola said, "or have some of this cake. I thought I felt awful."

Finola's admittance of her perception regarding Letitia's state of mind was met with a sharp chastisement.

"Finola," Mrs. Quinn admonished, "don't do that, you know it's rude."

A mischievous glint in Finola's eyes suggested she knew full well what she was about, but she still waited on Letitia.

"Dinner sounds wonderful," Letitia said. "Can I take that tray to the table?"

A maid picked up the tureen of roast vegetables before Letitia could touch it.

"You're fine, Ms. Hawking," Mrs. Quinn said with a tentative smile, "but if I could speak to you for a moment, if you please. Finola, help with those tea cakes."

Finola's pointed gaze fell on the indifferent Mrs. Quinn's back before Letitia was ushered into the empty hall and the kitchen door closed.

"I have to tell you," Mrs. Quinn said. "I-I cannot thank you enough."

Letitia stared at the bright disposition as it wilted, remembering the wane woman in the café who covered every weakness. Mrs. Quinn wouldn't meet Letitia's eyes and instead focused on her hands held in front of her.

"Whatever has happened to my girl, you've done the impossible," she whispered, low and full of desperate gratitude. "I cannot think to repay such a debt."

"No," Letitia said, damning all the family with their need for recompense. "I could not leave her like that, since she had no ability to fight such a thing, but I can tell you I will not leave until I find its source and remove it."

At that Mrs. Quinn's head jerked up, eyes brimming, and appearing to forget herself she embraced Letitia. Walled in as she was, Letitia allowed the contact for a moment, sensing a tropical sultriness from Mrs. Quinn that she hadn't noticed before. It was subtle, almost weak, but no less warm.

"Thank you," Mrs. Quinn whispered. "And please, call me Abby, will you?"

Letitia nodded, able now to extricate herself from Abby's embrace. Abby beamed at Letitia, and with a quick brush of fingertips over her face, removed the signs of her sudden outburst and returned to the kitchen.

Letitia stared after her, still shrouded in warmth, but she shivered and gave the kitchen a sidelong glance as she returned to the dining room. What goaded her to make such a promise to Abby she could not have said, except that it was true. Letitia would not try to bind or banish it herself, but if the attachment to the house was removed, then she was confident it would leave Finola alone to heal.

With a deep breath, she returned to the sitting room, where another challenge of sorts waited for her. It would be fainthearted not to return, so with spine ramrod straight she made her way back.

"Forgot the water?" Mr. Driscoll drawled from where he still sat.

She'd overlooked it after Abby's thanks.

"I didn't want to get in the way. They're about to come in with the dinner things," Letitia said, hoping the threat of the others' presence would stop the innocuous comments.

Letitia wanted to believe that his interest was motivated by her helping to save his daughter, but as she met his gaze, there was no mistaking the speculative interest within. If she had thought he was a desert wind before, he was now the cooling sultry night air against her sudden bashfulness.

"Anyone would think my niece wasn't the only one to read minds," he murmured.

"Not minds," Letitia answered, licking her lips. "Intent."

She remained near the door, hands clasping her skirt, legs unable to cross the room and resume her seat. He didn't move, but his stare went on, and she swallowed against the rising embarrassment at his perusal.

"I'd ask what it is you see," he said, "but feel I'll only receive another of your cryptic answers."

"When have I ever not been clear with you, Mr. Driscoll?" Letitia said before she saw he was laughing at her.

"I think you make your intentions well known," he said, getting to his feet to stand before her, "but please don't go reading into mine. I don't believe you know just quite what it is I...want."

The last word was a whisper as he scanned her face, trying to read her in return.

Letitia remembered his hand on her cheek, and how despite

all of his airs and position as a lawyer he'd worked hard in his life. She wanted that calloused palm on her forehead again, the human contact something she'd not given herself leave to desire again.

He was almost within reach, but stopped just shy, looking down at her. Letitia had never been so aware of their difference in stature, or the warm tone of his skin at the collar of his shirt where he'd loosened his tie, or the hands held at his side that she wanted to hold her.

To keep her safe.

The briefest moment of yearning came away with a knife-thin sliver of guilt.

She stepped away. "As you like, Mr. Driscoll."

He opened his mouth, frowning at her sudden change, but there must have been a warning in her face for he remained silent. He was aware of her past, but much of it was still a mystery and Letitia intended for it to stay that way. He was not her Daniel, and she was not the same woman Daniel had loved.

Letitia didn't know if she could ever love again and saying no to Mr. Driscoll had proven hard when he was only asking for her help.

She didn't know what she'd do if he asked for her heart.

Chapter 11

Letitia stood at the top of the stairs to the cellar. Fear would have kept her there, trembling on the threshold, but the dawn's light grew on her back and Mr. Driscoll, ready to face any dragon with the courage of the naïve, was at her side.

Down the stairs it was dark, but sunlight streamed into the shadows, fed from the open front door. The cellar's door was tucked under the main staircase, the entrance gloomy and uninviting.

"There are lights," Mr. Driscoll said behind her. "I'll get them."

"No." Letitia's upraised hand stopped him, and she softened her tone when she realized how loud her voice sounded, sucked away into the cellar. "No. I'll do it in a moment. Where is Finola?"

"She's out the back, walking the gardens with Abby," he said.

Throughout the long night, Finola had done much to keep spirits high, gorging herself on cake and making sure no one fell asleep. Letitia suspected she'd done it in fear but answered Finola's endless questions about England. Abby opened the adjoining room where a piano sat in a corner, taking Finola through all her lessons. Finola invited her uncle to cards and trounced him, though Letitia, seeing his hand, knew he let her win. It was a cozy family setting.

But more than once Letitia had found Mr. Driscoll watching her, and when they were alone, he turned his attention on getting to know Letitia better—not her past, just herself. Little questions on her love of Jane Austen and what else she liked to read. The traditional fashions of England she preferred over the more brazen American trends. Not even Daniel had asked her favorite composer or the way she preferred her tea.

In the heart of the night, despite weariness weighing her down, his quiet words and gentle interest kept her afloat in a sea of wariness and apprehension.

When the gentle fingers of dawn had crept over the horizon the family was relieved, and despite any exhaustion, Letitia wished she could keep the mellow and insistent flirtation of Mr. Driscoll forever.

But it was she who reminded them of their grim task, yet unfinished.

When she spoke, Abby took Finola away, and Mr. Driscoll drank the last of his coffee and led her to the stairs.

At the door's maw, guarded by Letitia's vision of light, she let no fear escape the tight bonds within her mind before proceeding.

Tugging her gloves on, Letitia descended the shallow stone stairs into the depths of the cellar with caution. They were a sickening reminder of her encounter last night. What was a joyous submersion into the dark for the specter was an exercise in controlling dread for Letitia. She focused on the distant button that would give unnatural light, hand tight on the railing until she hurried the last few steps in darkness to push it on.

The gloom of the cellar fled under the warm glow of electric lights, shapeless ghosts turning to furniture covered in dust sheets. Stone arches gave way to bays leading deeper under the house. Sunlight trickled in from arching windows high in the walls but at ground level outside and covered in vines and plants. They wouldn't illuminate the murky room if the lights went out.

Letitia gritted her teeth.

No, this was not her responsibility, she acknowledged to herself, but she would not leave until she knew the connection this house had to the old hotel was gone.

She crossed the floor, having mapped out the rooms above, and walked to the section underneath Mr. Driscoll's study. She heard Mr. Driscoll follow her, close enough that his presence was reassuring.

There were several boxes, cutlery and plates, some folded linen, and a few glass vases.

Letitia didn't know where to start. Without the shadow of night oppressing her it was much harder to find the source.

"This is where you keep the things from the old hotel," Letitia confirmed, examining the dusty objects and wondering how she would find which one had caused so much trouble.

"Yes, and I'll have them all removed today," Mr. Driscoll said. "In fact, there will be people arriving within the hour to clean it all out."

"No children or women?" Letitia said.

"Contractors hired to move furniture through the firm. They're all able-bodied men."

"I—" Letitia hesitated, "I'm sorry, I don't want to take any risks."

"Neither do I," he said. "I find your protective attitude admirable under the circumstances."

Letitia saw a twinkle in his eye that might have been amusement and a softness to his mouth that bespoke endearment. His words were one of many compliments on her prowess he'd plied her with during the long hours of the night, and Mr. Driscoll was charming when he wanted to be. Letitia still didn't know how to react to such turns of phrase. The veiled innuendo became innocent with company, but it wasn't lost on Letitia that there was another meaning to Mr. Driscoll's attention.

Her breath caught in her throat when he leaned forward. She couldn't move out of his way with the furniture cluttered around them.

With a whirl of cloth, he'd tugged a dust cloth from a piece of furniture.

"Is it this one?" He asked, not breaking his gaze from hers.

Letitia turned about and knew it wasn't right. "No."

Another dust cloth ripped through the air. "What about here?"

"No."

The dirt-streaked covers piled up in a corner, Mr. Driscoll discarding them as they kept checking under each of the filth-covered sheets. Letitia would check the item itself, and if it had cupboards, she'd open them and check the contents. She didn't know what she was looking for but would when she found it.

Mr. Driscoll's face became streaked with dirt, hair dusted an unbecoming brown. The grime caked her own clothes and gloves.

"How long were they stored here?" Letitia asked, wiping motes from her nose.

"Not long," he said, "but I had them all moved as they were. I didn't clean them beforehand."

"Why did you bother moving them?"

"They're all quite valuable antiques," Mr. Driscoll said. "The original Mr. Calbright spent some time and money making it a fine retreat for those with enough money. People from the gold rush would put their elderly relatives there, assured their hard-earned money paid for the best of attentions from the staff."

He kept working, and she asked no more questions.

They were at the back of the section, in a far corner, with only a dim light from the basement windows to guide them. Letitia looked upward, knowing the study and Finola's room were above their heads. Mr. Driscoll's form and his strong arms had distracted her following any verbal cue she gave but when he touched another sheet, she felt a skitter over her skin and called out.

"Stop!"

He paused and looked at her over his shoulder.

"Move away," she advised, and when he stepped aside, she saw it. Her gaze drifted up across the cobweb-strewn beams to the ceiling. Letitia was standing in the exact spot from last night, one floor down.

A fine trembling took over her hands as she reached out for the dirty cotton, her mind envisioning the ludicrous horror that the figure would be behind that sheet and leap out and clutch her in its dark embrace.

She swallowed against the restriction in her throat, unable to move, sweat breaking out on her skin.

There was a hand at the small of her back, grounding her with its warmth, the life within soaking into her stillness.

"Do you want me to do it?" Mr. Driscoll asked, his breath fanning over her ear, whispering as though her fear had infected him. A hush fell around them while he waited for her to answer, every second stretching on while her heart raced.

Her leather-clad hands were within inches of the sheet.

The cloth rippled.

Whether a breeze caught the folds in the drafty cellar or the cause was her heavy breath so close to the thin material, she didn't know.

An insidious apprehension crept along her senses, exacerbating her own fear, and in the nearby window appeared Finola's wide, terrified face. The girl had knelt before the glass panes to the basement, hands held to her chest, rocking back and forth, eyes unblinking as she stared at the sheet so close to Letitia's hands.

Someone pulled her away, but Letitia could still hear her cries.

"Damn you," Letitia cursed the specter, snatching the sheet and yanking it aside.

A typewriter.

It sat innocuously on a wooden desk, free from the other crowded detritus they'd uncovered, placed almost with purpose.

Tiny. Delicate. There was even a floral brass motif across its sides.

But underneath the oily sheen of its black lacquer, the surface seemed to wriggle like a handful of worms. The keys stuck up like the teeth of a creature that would bite. It might have been small but for all intents it was a snake, curled up, afraid of the light and ready to strike.

"Is that it?" Mr. Driscoll was behind her, and Letitia nodded. She heard boxes shifting behind her, a clatter, and he was back, hammer in hand. He grasped her elbow, drew her aside, and then raised his hand.

"No!" Letitia called out, stepping between him and the typewriter. "Don't do it."

"Why on earth not?" he said. "Then this will all be over."

"Every screw, every key, every scrap makes a difference." Letitia held her hand out to ward him off. "If you smash it here, all it will do is spread, fall down cracks, and stay in your house until it has a hold. Give the hammer to me."

He frowned down at her, and she saw the protest forming on his lips before his gaze shifted to over her shoulder.

Dread rendered his face pale. His mouth widened, pupils dilating and growing. Outside, Finola screamed, but Mr. Driscoll stayed frozen, unable to move. Then she felt the finest brush of fingers across the back of her neck. A cold touch sent a pulse to the base of her spine, and she shuddered in horror. She couldn't breathe, seeing the same fear on Mr. Driscoll's face.

"Alasdair," she whispered the name, just a breath of air. He stood transfixed, and she couldn't turn to face it. Trying to fight the urge to push him aside and run, Letitia took control of the only thing she had. Taking a deep breath, she shouted his name.

"Alasdair Driscoll!"

He enfolded her in his arms, spinning her about to put her out of harm's way, hammer raised to hurt a being made of shadow.

There was nothing there.

Finola was calling for her uncle, and footsteps crunched in the gravel as people bent to see what Finola had been crying about. Letitia pressed herself to Mr. Driscoll's back, hand sliding under his upraised arm and over his heaving chest.

"It's gone," she said. "It isn't there anymore. It was only trying to frighten you."

Letitia said it over and over before his arm lowered, and though his hand tightened on the weapon, he laid it to one side. His hands came up to cover over hers, pressing hard before he cradled her hand. He didn't face her. She kept her chest pressed to his back, the pair watching the corner for any sign, but nothing further emerged.

"Is that...is that what you see?" There was a rawness in his voice.

"Yes." Letitia wept.

"I'm sorry, Letitia," he said, voice breaking. "I am so sorry. It was in my head, and I saw—"

He stopped, jaw clenching as he bit back the words. Letitia waited a moment and then let go of his comforting warmth. "We aren't done yet, Mr. Driscoll." Regaining some composure, she spoke the words with all the formality she could muster.

Her voice snapped him with rigidity, shoulders tense and movements jerky. Picking up a wooden box, he tipped its contents to the floor, letting them smash to pieces. Letitia gave a startled cry at the sudden destruction, but when he faced her, she fell silent.

"I take it you know what to do with this thing, Ms. Hawking?" His voice, his eyes, his face were closed off. Thin lips, dubious eyes, tension throughout his frame. Locked away until such a time as he could deal with what had happened. She recognized the expression. She'd seen a similar one in the mirror.

Letitia did not want to speak to this Mr. Driscoll.

"The typewriter, Ms. Hawking?" he snapped.

"Don't touch it," Letitia said, not sure herself what to do with it. She made to step around him and when he wouldn't move, she glared up at him. "Do you think it wants you? What did you see when it looked at you? What did you feel?"

He dropped the box and stepped away as though she'd slapped him.

Before it was more than a thought, Letitia picked up the typewriter in her gloved hands and plonked it in the box. As an afterthought, she covered it with a discarded sheet. Grasping its edges and taking care not to touch the sheet that covered the typewriter, she hefted it in her arms before holding it out for Mr. Driscoll.

"Dispose of this in the ocean," she said. "Far from the coast."

When he wouldn't take it, Letitia took a deep breath, and walked toward the stairs. She didn't want to stay down here a moment longer.

"Are you coming, Mr. Driscoll?"

There was a muttered cursing in the dark, and she heard the brogue of his voice.

"My apologies," he said, voice tight. "I was not prepared for such a...manifestation."

"Why do you sometimes sound like an Irishman if your family has lived in America for years?" Letitia asked, trying to distract him.

"Because I grew up there," he said, "and when the woman I loved died, I went back."

She didn't ask more when she heard his footsteps on the cellar floor echoing behind her, relieved he followed. The poisonous thing in her arms didn't stir, and when she was in the full sunlight of the entry hall, she breathed a sigh of relief. Letitia turned and tried to give the box to Mr. Driscoll, but he made no move to take it, leaning against the door jamb of the cellar and bathing in the morning light.

"I do not wish to—" he broke off, a grimace stark on his face. "It has an unpleasant effect on me. I do not have the necessary skills you do to defend my thoughts."

Letitia didn't dare leave it lying around. She took it to his study, placing it on the corner of his desk. As she walked out, she ran into Finola, who peered over her shoulder.

"A typewriter?" she asked. Finola couldn't have seen it since it had been under a sheet before she ran, and Letitia had covered it. She'd read Letitia's mind.

Finola's were flushed, hands clenched, a resentment that a mundane machine had been the source of such terrible nightmares. The wave of hatred that crossed Finola's face as she stepped forward made Letitia stand in front of the door to block her.

"Move aside," Finola used the same tone Letitia had used on Mr. Driscoll in the basement. Letitia stood her ground.

"What do you think will happen if you touch it?" she said instead, moving so that Finola had to look into her eyes.

"You don't—" Finola bit the words out before falling silent. "I have to know, to see for myself."

"No." Letitia whirled about and had a moment to be grateful there was a key in the door. She turned the lock and took the key.

When she faced Finola, she thought for a moment the girl would launch herself at Letitia.

"You should at least let me see it," Finola whispered, tears coming so it took only a blink before they were cascading down her cheeks.

How many nightmares had Finola endured? How many touches from that vile thing had invaded her mind and her dreams? Precious moments gone, innocence stolen, and a lifelong fear of the dark.

"Do you want it to come back?" Letitia asked, hating her own soft voice in the face of Finola's wrath. "Because if you touch it, that's what will happen."

Finola recoiled, and Letitia saw the betrayal there before the girl fled.

Letitia stood against the door, catching her breath and shaking away the pressure of Finola pushing on her mind. Her power was great and dangerous, and it was no wonder such a small thing should have such an effect on a girl so young. Finola's untried power had awakened the sliver of a dark soul who'd imprinted on the typewriter, and it gave him a window into her.

Letitia's own experience taught her well that what Finola needed most was time.

She walked into the entry hall where Mr. Driscoll still stood, catching his gaze and something behind his eyes that spoke of defiance. The resemblance between him and his daughter was stark in the morning light.

Though relief should have been his companion, she found a similar resentment, but the petulance in Finola differed from the glower on Mr. Driscoll's face. Letitia sensed the stinging sands of his personality almost strike her with its wrath.

Now the fear was done, the episode over, there was the hollowness of victory without vengeance, a rising anger after the ugliest episode the family might ever encounter. There was little to do with wrathful thoughts but give them time to fade, as Letitia knew for herself.

"The typewriter is on your desk," Letitia said. "I think the best thing to do would be to take it out on a boat. Don't throw it too close to shore or it may end up back on the beach."

"And what of Finola?" Mr. Driscoll said.

"She should recover," Letitia said with a wane smile. "But you were right about her gift, and I am sorry, but I am ill-equipped to train her."

"Hasn't the danger passed?" he asked her, brows furrowed.

"Yes, it has," she said. "And I have done all I can. The rest is up to Finola...and you."

Something in Mr. Driscoll's eyes died. "That's it?"

Letitia bit her lip, wondering what else there was to his question—if she had read too deep into the night's motivations to his attentions or not deep enough. With a sigh she gave way, stepping back from the warmth she found such solace, to retreat into her self-imposed winter.

"I'm rather tired, and I'd like to go home now, Mr. Driscoll." Letitia walked out the front door, collecting her coat and purse on the way out.

She couldn't stay.

To do so wouldn't only continue to jeopardize her safeguards, but Finola needed the kind of strict teaching Letitia didn't have the strength to give.

The sun warmed her skin. There was a soft breeze of winter, a welcome chill from the swirling sandstorm behind her. When she was in her own home Letitia would be relieved, but for now, she enjoyed surveying the castle grounds in the growing sunshine. Spindly, leafless trees and bushes pushed toward a blue sky, and it filled her with warmth, hope, and the promise of spring.

Hearing a car engine, she stood closer to the house so she could get straight into the approaching car and leave.

A bath, she told herself, and some of those biscuits, or maybe go down to the kitchen and make her mother's soup. She's been absent and not told Mrs. Finch, and that would upset the landlady.

Letitia cluttered her mind with thoughts other than the one that wanted to be asked. Would Mr. Driscoll see her off and was this the last she was to see of him?

She didn't know if it was hope or fear that pinched in her chest, but when he arrived it twisted ever more.

He held an envelope in his hands, and without a word, he thrust it at her.

Letitia took it, though she didn't know what it contained. Her curiosity died in disappointment as she saw the thick wad of notes inside, and the cream paper of a check.

She didn't want to calculate it because it wouldn't be worth it.

"Did you think you owed me?" she whispered, staring at his guileless green eyes.

"Honestly, Ms. Hawking, I don't know what to think." He ran a hand through his dust-streaked hair. "You did what you came here and promised to do, and I wanted to be sure you didn't leave empty-handed."

Letitia stared at him, her disenchantment growing at his callous nature. After all, she had done, the risk to herself, and what it would add to her nightmares, here he was with his bundle of paper to ensure that whatever slate between them was clean.

Shocked, she didn't notice the car behind her until he reached for the door to open it.

At the dismissal, her fury knew no confinement.

"Your impertinence, sir," she said, as coolly as she could muster, "is superseded only by your complete inability to understand my motivations or need for self-preservation, despite what you may have seen or what I have done."

"What you mean is that I never should have asked you," he snapped. "No matter that you saved a young girl's life who is irreplaceable to me. You have rendered us a great gift given the lengths I went to in order to facilitate your aid. I only thought if that were the case you be duly compensated."

Letitia's choking rage fell out of her throat to spike her tongue in bitter words.

"From the start, you only ever thought about what money could buy you," she accused, "and from that same start, I said no. I came here to help you, and you thought *this* was worth what I could have lost?"

She held up the envelope to him, and he narrowed his gaze.

"That was all I had to hand." Bitten out between clenched teeth, Letitia gave up.

"I didn't help you for this," she said, dropping the envelope near him, not stopping to watch if he caught it. She stepped into the open door of the car and gave the driver her address. The driver didn't wait, pulling out at once, and Letitia was glad she didn't need Mr. Driscoll's permission to leave.

She refused to look back, but she still wondered if he turned away, done with the matter. And with her. Would he come to regret his actions? They were about to swing around the drive when she dared peak over her shoulder.

He had not stayed.

The budding attraction she'd had for him burned to ashes that coated her tongue the whole way home.

Chapter 12

She clutched her son, hoping they'd be ignored and that the letter from the lawyer's office would go unnoticed in her handbag.

Fear hammered at her heart, and she squeezed her son's arm, but he looked so full of rage she thought he might pull away and do something stupid.

"What's in your purses?" the man in a mask shouted. "You came to deposit—give it!"

He stank of alcohol and nervous sweat. The copper stains on his clothes weren't his blood.

There was a guard lying on the floor. She could see where he was going bald from where his cap had fallen off and rolled to one side. It couldn't stay on his head, for he had to have more skull for a hat. The rest of it was splattered on the surrounding floor, shotgun pellets still smoldering.

She hiccupped into her gloved hand and clutched her son closer.

"Line up you useless f—!" The man was screaming again,

and she didn't know what to do. She had no money, and they would ask why she was there.

The lawyer's check was to give her access to an account worth a thousand dollars. It was her son's entire future. It was everything she had left to give him.

There had been a mistake, a dreadful, horrible accounting error that had left them destitute after the war. For three years she'd scraped by selling what few goods were left from the house she couldn't keep. Her mother's silver hairbrush. Her grandmother's sewing machine. Her engagement ring.

"Mom," her son said, "lemme go, I gotta do this."

"Don't be stupid, Elijah," she whispered, but she'd drawn the robber's attention.

"Are you talkin' back?" The spitter was in front of her, looking her over, but it was the gleam in his eye when he glanced at her son. "Looks like we got ourselves a hero!"

"I got a hellovalot more honor than you, cur," Elijah said, rising to his feet despite how she pulled at him to come back down by her side.

But he was near eighteen now, not a boy, no matter how she tried to protect him. He could have gone to war like his daddy, could have fought, been brave, done his country proud if he'd been old enough. Instead, the work at the sawmill had changed him into a broad, strong young man.

Elijah squeezed his fists, and the knuckles cracked.

When he stood to his full height, he wasn't taller than the robber, but he didn't have to be. Not when he could swing like his fists were made of battering rams. He swung.

The robber tumbled down, like strings cut on a puppet. It was so sudden, the other robbers turned only when they noticed the absence of his cussing.

"You all best leave," Elijah said, "police gonna come, women in here fair set to screaming until the angels descended themselves. So, go on now, you got the lion's share, you stole what us folk couldn't afford."

Dead silence descended over the bank.

None of the robbers moved.

"What's your name, boy?" A fellow asked, coming out of the opened vault. He was tall, hat low over his eyes, bushy beard covering his face, but gimlet eyes burned above a smoking cigar.

"Elijah Farnsworth."

The strange robber glanced down at her. "That your mom?"

"Yessir," Elijah said, standing in front of where she still knelt. "Been taking care of me since my daddy died in the Great War."

The stranger paused, taking a long pull of the smoke. "Son, everyone died in that war."

He raised his pistol to shoot Elijah.

She was rising, unstoppable as the light of dawn and as bright as the flash of the muzzle as she stood in the bullet's path. When she caught it, it pushed her back, hit her like the big goats when she'd been a girl on her uncle's farm. She felt Elijah's body behind her, catching her weight, but she was already crashing to the floor.

"Mom...?" The quivering voice of her son came from so far away.

She glanced around. People were screaming and running for the doors despite the shots. Men were overpowering the robbers. None of it meant anything as she stared up at Elijah, he was so tall above her. A tower of strength, not short at all. She saw that now.

"Mom?" He called again, and she felt the pain then and knew it was only a matter of time. She held up her handbag, and it stirred him to action. Dropping to his knees beside her, he cradled her in his arms.

"Take the lawyer's letter, Elijah," she gasped, "and you go get an education, or go buy land and farm it. You go make everything of yourself I couldn't give you."

He took the bag but stared at it in confusion.

"But you can't go..." he cried.

"Oh, my love," she said, "I'll be with your daddy, and I'll always watch over you."

Elijah was crying, but a robber came up to him with a gun, and before he could get within arm's reach Elijah lunged for him. Watching the fight, she couldn't call him back. Some kind woman came up and put pressure on the wound to her sternum.

She was numb now as the shadows danced, but she wasn't alone. She thought she saw someone watching them fight.

No, watching her...

Letitia sensed it. It reached up through her stomach, fastened its hand about her throat, and squeezed. There was no breath to scream, no way to fight, and for a moment she thought it would hold her in the vision and force her to endure the final moment as she passed the veil and into death.

She choked, the breath lodging in her throat like a piece of food, the blood rushing to her face. Letitia coughed, forcing the fear aside and dislodging the breath to take dry heaving gasps that brought her little relief.

"Ms. Hawking?"

A voice called across the table, and her nails slid across its surface until she found its edge. Gripping hard, she dragged her body away from the scrying bowl to focus on the twisting wooden surface of the table. Dark, light, the smooth transition between the two. Always warm.

"I'm sorry," she wheezed. "I'm so sorry, Mr. Farnsworth, I don't always handle murder cases and it came on rather quickly."

"Oh, ma'am, I'm sorry." He was on his feet and running to the sideboard to fetch a cup of cold tea she'd put aside before they started.

"Here," he said, holding it out to her. "Drink this."

When her trembling hand almost dropped the cup, he

steadied it for her. The oxen man beside her then retreated like a shy schoolboy to the other side of the table. He watched her, and she observed the anxious eyes, using their blind faith in her and the innocence there to ground herself.

"I hope you aren't hurt," he said. "I told you, honest I did, but she didn't die straight away, I promise you she spoke to me."

"It's fine," she said. "I warned you it could be a little unusual, given the circumstances."

"Yes, ma'am." He fidgeted in his chair. She wanted to take pity on him and to say something that would allay his fears.

"She loved you so very much," Letitia said, straightening in her chair, giving him a warm, encouraging smile. "When that gimlet-eyed man talked to you, she knew he meant you harm, and she wouldn't let anything happen to you. Your father might have died in the war, but it didn't matter what the robber in the hat said, she didn't want you to die for some common criminal."

He took several deep breaths, broad chest heaving.

"Ma'am," he said, his thick Midwest accent endearing, "I didn't come about that. I wanted to know...I started that fight. And maybe if I hadn't—"

He screwed his hat where he clutched it on the table, his eyes misty, but he gritted his teeth.

Grown men don't cry, Letitia thought with a little irony. Except Mr. Farnsworth was only nineteen, and as much as he looked a man, great shoulders confined by the cheap suit, it wouldn't take long for one such as him.

"It wouldn't have mattered, Mr. Farnsworth," Letitia said. "You were everything to her, and she fought for the honors to be paid to your father's family trust. She wanted a bright future for you."

Letitia shouldn't say more, since the young man in front of her was dealing with enough as it was, but she couldn't stop the hand that reached across the table and wrapped around his wrist.

"I think she wasn't happy after your father died," Letitia

said, and he nodded, his eyes sliding shut.

"But she was...you know, all right? Didn't regret nothin'?" he asked, holding his breath.

"No," Letitia said, "she didn't regret it, not if it meant you could go on."

He got to his feet. "Ah, I gotta head out, let you get some sleep. It must tire you. And it ain't proper to have a gentleman in your room so late. I'll take my leave and thank you for the kindness you've just gifted me."

Letitia didn't have time to open the door. He was gone.

She wanted to go after him, but fatigue ate at her consciousness, and she sat for some time in the chair, recalling what had happened.

She was too tired, even as she did it, but she brought the scrying mirror down and watched the vision again.

"There..." she whispered. There was a figure, standing in the dim-lit halls of the bank, behind the fighting robbers and citizens defending their small wealth, but it didn't watch them. It was looking at her.

Where had she seen it before?

It was not the same figure as the one at the Driscoll's house, and she shivered at the thought alone.

Casting her mind back, the figure in the vision didn't carry the same malevolence as the figure in the Driscoll basement. Yet she *had* seen it before.

At the house with Joseph when the alcohol and concussion collided. Feet in front of Stephen as his heart gave out. But where else?

Behind Mr. Driscoll when she first met him. Beside Mrs. Quinn—Abby—at the café. No, it wasn't the same.

Was it the nuance of her gift that eliminated the overwhelming spitefulness in the figure?

She racked her brains, trying to understand what it was doing there if it wasn't the figure that haunted Finola.

The dark shadows were remnants of souls who couldn't

remember their physical form in life or even appear in such a way once they hit the veil. There was nothing left but what kept them here. They focused all of their energy on how they'd passed away in life—what had caused them to die and regret enough to stay.

Old Mother Borrows had said it was always worse for people who could see ghosts, such as Letitia, most of all when they were the target of the phantom's emotional connection to the world.

"*If you can see them,*" Old Mother Borrows said, "*you acknowledge them, strengthen them, give them a greater reason to stay. They could influence dreams, turn them to nightmares, drive you to madness.*"

Letitia's ability to see them was not what caused her institutionalization.

She had killed the figure that wanted to hurt her that terrible night when six women went to a witch who didn't know what she was doing. The foolish woman called upon dark forces, bringing something into this world that was never human.

The figure who had shadowed her before the séance had been vastly different.

But to tell them apart was to rely on instinct alone.

She'd loved her husband.

Daniel hadn't wanted to leave his wife and unborn child. He simply wanted to stay until the child was born, and then pass on. The goosebumps rose on her skin when she was alone in the house and heard her name called in empty rooms. A gentle breath in her ear whenever she'd touched her growing belly had driven her to distraction. She hadn't known she'd attuned to his presence with her own latent abilities. But the more she listened for him, the stronger he became until she sought the help of a woman claiming she could commune with the dead.

The witch opened a door, but she brought something far worse into the world than the ghost of Letitia's loving husband. Letitia killed it and the witch.

But it had cost Letitia her baby.

After the operation, not only had her powers grown uncontrollable but so too had her ability to see Daniel, who was nothing more than a dark shape weeping with his wife. He was responsible too since his presence drove her to the psychic.

After the event and Letitia's expulsion from the asylum, Old Mother Borrows guided her through the entire soul-wrenching process of conquering her fear of Daniel and saying goodbye. It allowed him to go beyond the veil, though it hadn't relieved Letitia of her guilt. And Old Mother Borrows warned her never to entangle herself with figures of darkness. Only Daniel's emotional connection to Letitia had allowed him to pass on.

Other creatures wouldn't feel the same way.

She hadn't seen another figure until Mr. Driscoll first stood in her doorway, the shadow looming over his shoulder. Had she attributed her fear of the shadows to the phantom's presence?

Letitia had no control over her panicked reaction.

Others would be dangerous, could cause her harm. Old Mother Borrows warning rang loud and clear, and Letitia remembered the lesson well. Not speaking to the soul that invited one in would cause it to lash out, being full of rage at its stolen life. Other souls lingered, attaching to people who could see them for far more malicious reasons, such as the revolting sensation of perverted joy Letitia had experienced when she'd sensed the phantom haunting Finola.

Shuddering, she rubbed her arms, thoughts drifting to the recent and persistent presence in her visions. Her patrons' loved ones had all passed on, so the figures weren't attached to the patrons—they'd been watching her. But how and when had this come to pass? Letitia needed to write it down, to sit and think. Her brain didn't plan on letting her though, and instead, she massaged her temples and walked to her room.

Her hand touched the knob of the door, and she perceived it then.

The same shiver on her spine. The tingle through her bones. The intense and uncomfortable fear that something was staring at her with such intensity it would stop her thundering heart in her chest if she cast a look its way.

Unsure what to do, Letitia realized she'd left the scrying bowl naked on the table, still facing the mirror. She couldn't stop herself whirling about, even as she raised her hands to fend off a blow that would hurt her soul and not her body.

There were no waiting shadows.

Letitia hurried to the scrying bowl, the open access point to the veil. She was quick to carry it to the window and throw the contents out into the garden. Her head leaned against the raised sill, and she breathed in the chilled air.

Her thoughts left her so distracted that she'd done the unforgivable in leaving a portal open.

She inhaled the night air. It was still the tail end of winter, but she could almost taste spring, the coming of new life, the end of a dark time.

Letitia wanted to believe what her senses told her, but as she closed the window against the dark, the creeping dread still lingered. Not about to let herself fall asleep without the relevant safeguards, Letitia defended her home the way Old Mother Borrows had taught her.

Tools cleaned and locked away.

Salt the doors and windows, even in her bedroom.

Doors locked against inquisitive hands.

A kitten wash of hot water from the iron kettle was all she needed as she'd had the long bath earlier that afternoon, though she dabbed juniper oil behind her ears. Using the remaining hot water to brew a soothing cup of chamomile, she got into bed with relief. Sliding between the thick flannel of her bed was a delight she relished for a few moments before picking up her book.

But as Letitia settled in bed, a page of her book open at random and tea by her bedside, she couldn't relax.

Her brain buzzed with a million insects, and she was unable to quiet them or focus on her book.

Cranky and exhausted, she instead switched off the light and snuggled into her mattress, hoping her tiredness would overtake whatever was making her thoughts dance like jackrabbits in the spring.

Letitia closed her eyes. Although she was weak with fatigue from the previous night at the Driscoll's, a prickling sensation remained imprinted on her skin. Her usual precautions on nights she feared nightmares would haunt her would be to drink lots of water and eat a plain dinner.

Tonight before her session, she'd eaten in the kitchen with Mrs. Finch, who hadn't minded Letitia's absence when she explained. But Letitia felt she couldn't say no to a dinner of baked fish and creamed potatoes. Letitia had returned to her rooms bloated and queasy. There were few times when she remembered being so exhausted.

Her thoughts now were not her own, and instead turned to the Driscoll house, to its cellar, and the typewriter there. She hadn't touched it, hadn't laid a finger on it, but her mind's eye created those strong hands typing out bills, hands that would later bend, break, and bash.

Finola hadn't been able to sleep, and now neither could Letitia.

She tossed, and heaving a sigh, turned the light back on.

It was a relief not to see any strange figure waiting to scare her half to death, for she wasn't sure if her heart could take it. Instead, she rose to her feet, threw a few logs on the dying fire, and set to watch the flickering flames.

Inside them was the heat she wanted from Mr. Driscoll, but its warmth was no comparison.

The way she'd fallen into the assumed safety of his arms—what a fragile and tangible comfort she clung to, her mind lingering over the press of his fingers against her shoulders.

Letitia had loved before. Her whole life vanished in a matter of months because of love.

Scowling at the memory, she picked up her case files and

messages as a distraction.

The case files she scanned for any similarity, annotating the ones with other figures lurking within. The only common thread was that they started appearing after Mr. Driscoll had first visited, and in each of those sessions she hadn't been afraid. She'd panicked at the sight, but the memory spoke something else to her, though she couldn't place her finger on why.

The figures in the visions were scary, but they didn't emanate the same emotions that Letitia experienced when she'd looked for the spirit haunting the Driscoll household. In fact, the longer she thought on it, the more she saw those figures as being like Daniel—they were trying to get her attention. They had nothing to do with the cases. They were there for another reason.

Confused about how to account for them, she turned instead to the list of phone calls missed during her absence.

Imogen had taken them, but Letitia hadn't looked through them yet.

There was one from a lady asking to see what happened to her late sister who'd died abroad and her death was being treated as a mystery. Another regarded a father who'd ended it all. The last one was a simple request for a call back.

It was Mr. Barkley again, and he wanted her to meet another family whose daughter had vanished.

The girl had been missing only forty-eight hours.

Chapter 13

"Mr. Barkley? It's Ms. Hawking. I'm sorry for calling so early, but I haven't been home and this sounded very urgent." Letitia clenched the phone, hearing the grogginess in Mr. Barkley's answer at the early morning call.

"Ms. Hawking." There was noise in the background, made fuzzy by the line, but there was a long moment before he spoke again. "I'm so glad you called. Would it be possible to appeal on your good nature and arrange an appointment this morning at all?"

Letitia hesitated.

She was still exhausted from the previous night's lack of sleep and had another appointment later that afternoon and the session in the evening. But the message had stayed with her all night—another girl, missing only weeks after Mr. Barkley's daughter.

"I have to tell you, Ms. Hawking," Mr. Barkley said, "I understand that I...that my dau—"

His voice broke off, and Letitia heard murmurings in the

background, indicating others were listening in on the call, and Letitia waited a moment before speaking.

"This is a terrible time for you," she said, voice as compassionate as she could make it, "but I must tell you I'd only be able to tell them whether she is alive. I don't believe that information is the most useful thing they need to hear, not while there is still hope they can find her."

"I know," he rasped, "but please, Mrs. Edwards is eight months pregnant, and the stress of what's happening make the doctors think..."

His voice drifted off.

Letitia's head dropped back, her eyes shut, and she bit her lips.

Taking one steadying breath after another, she dropped her tense shoulders.

"Please do not bring Mrs. Edwards. I will do nothing if she comes," she said. "But if there is a Mr. Edwards who would like to come by my address at ten, that would be fine. It shouldn't take long."

"Can he come by earlier? Say in half an hour?"

It was seven in the morning, but Letitia thought it would be far better to be done with it.

"Yes, Mr. Barkley," she said, "that will be fine. Please tell him to bring her picture and something that belonged to his missing daughter. I'd like to add that there will no compensation required. However, I cannot do this again. For anyone, Mr. Barkley. You need to understand I have to protect myself from people who don't believe me."

"I understand," he said, "and thank you so very much for your help."

Letitia heard him ring off, and she put the receiver down.

"What are you doing?"

Letitia gave a start, seeing it was only Imogen behind her standing in her doorway and still in her dressing gown. It was a beautiful peach silk with chrysanthemums stitched on the shoulders.

"Helping someone find out whether his daughter is alive," Letitia said.

"There's another one?" Imogen said, eyebrows raised in shock.

"Yes, and less than three months since someone took Mr. Barkley's daughter."

Imogen looked at her with wide eyes. "That's the gentlemen you didn't do a reading for because someone kidnapped her."

When Letitia nodded, Imogen shivered and rubbed her arms.

"How ghastly," she said. "It's a wonder the police don't do more. Have you thought about going to them?"

"And have them accuse me of being a con?" Letitia asked. "Or worse, involved in some scheme of blackmail or kidnapping?"

"No," Imogen said, "I suppose not. They aren't as strict about those things here, religion and such, as they are in England, but you have to admit, many people aren't..." Imogen waved her hand, giving up on the sentiment.

"Otherworldly gifted," Letitia supplied when Imogen struggled for a word. Imogen was comfortable enough with her gift, but not experienced in the terminology Letitia preferred.

"Speaking of abilities," Imogen said, spinning about and going to her rooms, "I have something for you."

Letitia walked into Imogen's apartment, a strange and theatrical taste dominating the sitting room from blood red Turkish rugs to large sunny prints of Parisian fashion, and oriental chairs and tables. It was far more flamboyant than the somber burgundy of Letitia's session room with its old furniture.

"Through here," Imogen called, disappearing into the bedroom. Letitia had visited the sitting room before but the room beyond was new to her. Letitia glanced inside to see racks upon racks of clothes. Scarlet taffeta was a splash of blood, summer's gold bringing dawn, green the hue of a nymph. Stitched on everything were glittering beads, gauze on every second item, chiffon hung so as not to crease. A rainbow kaleidoscope of color all vying for attention, spectacular in the tones and hues. She'd known Imogen's apartment was bigger than her own, but not by how much.

"Where on earth do you sleep?" Letitia asked, amazed at the mass of clothes.

"There's another little room at the back," Imogen said from among the racks. "Well, I say room, but it's a small corner I keep for myself. I bring home a lot of old things and find other uses for them, or if they're nice enough I keep them for myself. Ah, here it is!"

She came back carrying a dress over her arm.

Made of black silk that hung only to Imogen's knees, the dress was wreathed in copper and jet-black beads stitched in a swirling pattern that caught and distracted the eye with its intricacy. Threads dangled from the shoulders, covered with more beads, which flared out when the dress swished. Sleeveless and close cut, it was a magnificent dress, and far more than Letitia could afford.

"I can't take that," Letitia said, not sure whether her refusal was in protest at the hemline or the sheer wealth of such a gown.

"Nonsense," Imogen said, "you have to take it, I've already fitted it for you. Though you may need a snugger corset than normal, just to make it sit right."

"I wasn't expecting this," Letitia said, as Imogen brought it up to Letitia's reluctant hands.

"It will look divine on you," Imogen insisted.

"But isn't it indiscreet?" she asked, looking at the length against Imogen, who laughed.

"Silly, I'm a foot and a half taller than you. Hold it against yourself." She thrust the garment into Letitia's arms.

She held the dress to her front, and it hung down about her calves. She gave a little sigh of relief and Imogen chuckled.

"Heaven forbid *you* be improper," Imogen teased and grinned at Letitia's raised brows.

"Thank you, Imogen," she said instead. "It's kind of you."

"Feel up for going out for dinner this Saturday?" Imogen asked. "I know our plans were waylaid, but that's no reason not to do it at all. Perhaps we could go to a club afterward?"

"Yes," Letitia said, wanting to be gay and light and forget the last few weeks of darkness, "that would be splendid."

"How do you feel about company?" Imogen asked, and when Letitia looked concerned Imogen shook her head. "Not men. I mean a few of the girls I work with."

"Do they know what I do?" Many people frowned on what Letitia did, and she'd rather not have her evening spoiled.

"Actually," Imogen said, "they are curious more than anything. Expect a few questions but I will restrain them if it becomes tiresome."

"I can manage that," Letitia said with a small smile.

"Great, we'll leave here about seven, and make an evening of it." Imogen leaned forward, giving Letitia a quick embrace. "I'm glad you are coming. You've looked all out of fun, and I recognize the expression well."

Letitia knew it to be true, but hearing it made her soul weary.

"I'll go so you can get ready for work," she said. "Thank you so much for the dress. I am looking forward to an evening out."

Saying farewell to her neighbor, Letitia went back to her rooms and put the kettle on for the impending arrival of Mr. Edwards. With so little time she dressed and did her hair with haste, adding her heavy sessions veil. Having an anxious man visit her, another who'd lost his daughter, made Letitia nervous when she heard the urgent knock at her door minutes later. It was less time than she'd expected, and ramming the last pin into her veil, she went to the door.

Mr. Edwards was panting, his pale complexion reddened by what must have been a run up the stairs. A rotund waist showed too many dinners, but his weight made his face look younger than his years, though he'd hidden the roundness underneath a trimmed beard.

He brushed past her as she opened the door, still puffing, eyes darting about the room.

"Mr. Barkley said you needed a picture." He thrust out an image to Letitia without looking at her.

The rudeness shocked Letitia, but she didn't let it show as she closed the door.

"Have a seat, Mr. Edwards," she said. "There are some things I need to explain to you that Mr. Barkley may not have told you."

"I know, no compensation." He still searched his coat for a wallet, taking a wad of bills out and flinging them on the table. "And that's too bad because I have to know. I don't want to go home and tell Sally that our daughter is dead."

Every single word rose as he spoke, his worry transforming into an uncontainable rage.

"You must understand, Mr. Edwards," Letitia said, cutting through his anger with her coolness. "Rudeness won't be tolerated. I didn't ask for money because I don't know if I can help you."

Panic showed in his widened eyes, and Letitia knew he had a dread that he would leave without knowing.

"Now," she said, softening her voice, "I suspect you'd like to sit down and have a cup of tea. Perhaps talk about your daughter. It helps to know things about her."

Letitia waited, the seconds stretching past the uncomfortable awkwardness into an uneasy peace.

"That would be good." Mr. Edwards seemed to decide it almost to himself as he sat down and put the picture away. He left the money on the table.

"Tell me about your daughter," Letitia encouraged, making tea as he calmed and placing milk and sugar before him. He added both while speaking of his daughter.

"Cassy's a beautiful girl," he said, eyes distant. "She's delicate like her mother. Loves to paint watercolors of the sea, reads poetry, and wants to be a nurse when she grows up, but for animals. She's the sweetest creature on this earth, and I don't know what we'll do if I don't get her back."

Mr. Edwards met Letitia's gaze, and she saw what it cost his pride to let himself cry.

When the tears came, a part of him faded as he stared at her, lost, blinking away the wetness but not raising his hands to wipe it away. It was as though if he didn't acknowledge the tears, then they weren't there.

"The picture, Mr. Edwards," Letitia said, focusing him on why he was here. "Did you bring anything of hers?"

He brought the picture out again and a folded piece of paper, which he opened and laid in front of Letitia.

The girl was blonde from the pale tones of the photograph, dainty in a frilly dress, a shy smile aimed at the camera. Letitia's gloved finger stroked the edge of the picture as she examined the figure, and for a moment she wasn't sure. There was a glimmer there, but it was fading, the last flutter of a dying flame. It wasn't enough to confirm though, and putting the photograph aside, she looked to the paper.

It was a watercolor of the seaside, the view from a cliff along a beach to a lonely house on the opposite headland. The pastel colors had been added against soft lead lines of the scene, denoting that the artist was sure of her hand as she worked. The water was rich with color, distinctive from the gray sky painted above, darkening to the distant house on the far bluff.

"She painted it over the weekend," Mr. Edwards said. "Sally, I mean Mrs. Edwards, wanted to go to the ocean before she had the baby, and so we spent a day at the beach. It was too cold to swim, but we had a picnic on a headland, and Cassy painted that. She finished it when she got home. She…she disappeared the following day."

Letitia didn't know what to tell him. The sensation she had from the photograph was dim—a thread of life that could be cut at any moment. Wherever Cassy was, she wasn't safe.

Letitia pulled off her gloves and touched the watercolor.

The dark assailed her.

The smell of the sea whisked over her face before turning to the fetid aroma of rotting seaweed, the air cloying and sickening on the tongue as other scents filtered in. Earthy, but not clean, it smelled dank and unpleasant. It consumed all, the dark and the stench.

Letitia drew her hand back.

The same as Maisie.

Whoever had taken Cassy was the same person responsible for taking Mr. Barkley's daughter.

When Letitia reached out to pick up the painting again, she focused on the girl rather than the object, on how she'd felt when she'd drawn it. Letitia brushed the watercolor with her fingertips, and she knew without a doubt that this girl had been sad.

"She's an only child," Letitia said, "and she wanted one more picnic with just the three of you. It wasn't Sally's idea. It was Cassy's. Even if it was freezing, she wanted to go. To stay long enough to remember when it was just you three. She never thought you'd have another child."

Mr. Edwards' hands clenched on the table, so much it creaked, and Letitia stopped and put down the picture.

"Is she alive?" He hissed it out between his clenched teeth.

"Yes, Mr. Edwards," Letitia said, knowing she had to tell him the truth, but she feared it might not be for much longer. Mr. Barkley had been far better at receiving the awful news, but he'd had months to prepare. Mr. Edwards still had a chance, but Letitia became aware with a sickening twist of her stomach that while Cassy was alive, they would never see her again.

"I can't tell you anything about where she is, except it's dark," Letitia said. "I can only do so much, and I'm afraid to say if her kidnapper...progresses things, I cannot tell you much about what happened."

"You can damn well show me who took her!" He slammed his hand on the table, the frustrated rage turning his face an unbecoming shade of purple.

"Not unless I want to die, too," Letitia said, not raising her voice as he had but sitting still and composed.

"Mr. Barkley said you wouldn't look for his daughter if someone had murdered her, but my little girl is still alive!"

"Yes, and that means she still has a chance," Letitia said, "which is why you should look for her because I can't see where she is. It's all darkness. There are no clues. She is somewhere I can't see, which makes looking for her of no use to you. To do more would be dangerous enough as it is."

Standing so quickly his chair flew back, he came to stand and yell down at her.

"She needs your help, Ms. Hawking," he leaned over her, spitting his accusation. "An innocent girl is in the arms of a man who has taken over four girls in the last two years. Do you think God will forgive you if you sit in your chair, with your dramatic veil, and tell me you will do nothing?"

A sudden spike of animosity speared her and would not be contained.

Letitia ripped her veil off.

When she looked up at him, she knew what he saw and why he stepped back.

She'd had few patrons who behaved in such an uncivilized manner, and while she sympathized, she needed to not only protect herself from his brutish nature but from her own sense of guilt.

"Look upon me," she instructed, insinuating her voice with authority, and he took a step back but his gaze was fixed on her.

"The gray in my hair was from doing what you are asking of me," she told him, voice low and threatening, "and of which you have no comprehension. It even touched my eyes—I see the silver every time I look in a mirror or when strangers stare at me the exact way you are now. It's not natural, is it? Forced to age through an event I had no control over. God had nothing to do with it. I was left to fend for myself and couldn't save my baby.

Or didn't you wonder why I said I would not do this with your wife present?"

He fell back, the flush fading from his cheeks as Letitia glared.

Without another word he collected the things from the table and rushed out the door.

It relieved Letitia when he took the money with him, but worry over his hasty departure bit into her heart. Getting to her feet, she went to the hall and looked out the window. Mr. Edwards was running down the street.

She had meant to frighten him, but not to such extent. Mr. Edwards had already lost one daughter, and it had been unkind of her to remind him he might only have one left. Picking up the phone, she called the Barkley household.

"Yes?" It was Mr. Barkley himself, as though he expected Letitia's call.

"Mr. Barkley, Ms. Hawking again," she said, drawing in a breath. "I appear to have startled Mr. Edwards, though he was being rather rude. I think I may have stressed too much the nature of why I couldn't help him. Would you be kind enough to pass on my apologies?"

"Of course, Ms. Hawking," Mr. Barkley said, but she heard the disappointment in his voice.

"Thank you so much," Letitia said in relief, "and Mr. Barkley, I trust you will do as I've asked and not bring my name into conversation with any such people again. I believe it hurts more than it helps."

There was a long silence on the phone and then a sigh.

"As you like, Ms. Hawking," he said, "though goodness knows, you could help a great deal of people if you wanted to."

Letitia didn't answer, feeling the sting of responsibility in the wake of Mr. Edwards' accusation. These men had two daughters, one dead and one alive, and she couldn't help either of them.

"You mistake me, sir," she said. "I can die for your peace

of mind, or you can accept what little closure I can give you. In that, I think I've been rather generous."

Letitia rang off, not waiting for a reply.

Chapter 14

Furious at offering her aid and having things go astray, Letitia cleaned up, her stomach rumbling for breakfast. A quick tidying up around the sitting room did much to dispel her irritation at both herself, the angry Mr. Edwards, and the judgmental Mr. Barkley.

By the time she went downstairs, she was far more composed.

"Decided to join us?" Mrs. Finch teased, already sitting at the table, tea poured and a platter of bacon, eggs, and toast laid out. Letitia picked up the toast and buttered it.

"I'm sorry about the recent discrepancies in my attendance at the dining table," Letitia said.

"I miss your English manners," said Diana, one of Mrs. Finch's daughters, sweeping by to collect a cup of coffee up and not waiting for Letitia to respond. The young woman was a bane to her mother—sharp of wit, bored, and intelligent. She read at the store when she thought no one was looking.

"I'll ask her to teach you sometime," her mother shouted at her daughter's form retreating to the work room.

"Are you finished with the paper?" Letitia asked, staring at the discarded folds.

"Oh, yes," Mrs. Finch said, rising to her feet. "I best get this cleaned up."

"I'll do it. I want to have a moment to myself first," Letitia said.

"That's kind of you, for I have a lot to do this morning." Mrs. Finch downed her tea, placed the cup in the sink, and then went off to open the store.

Letitia returned the folds to the front page, and the front page's blatant headline glared in her face.

GIRL KIDNAPPED!

Letitia saw Cassy's picture and cringed.

She read the article.

Cassy had been dropping her father's lunch off to him on her way to school. He'd seen her off, but she'd never arrived at the school. They hadn't called the family until midday to ask why she wasn't in attendance.

A local search had revealed nothing as it appeared Cassy had used backstreets to make a shortcut. Police were calling for all parents to take care of their children and to contact them if anyone knew anything about the disappearance.

There was a follow-up article reviewing the missing Barkley girl and two others before her. For all the nuanced disavowal in earlier reporting that these disappearances had anything in common, it appeared the papers were no longer prepared to abide by the police department's reassurances. Instead, they raised the concern that another girl was taken less than three months after the previous one, indicating the kidnapper might strike again...

Slamming the paper down, Letitia moved to clear the table. She ate her breakfast while doing the dishes. She needed something that got rid of the uselessness creeping over her skin. Mr. Edwards' accusation and Mr. Barkley's disappointment prickled at her.

Worse still, she knew that wherever Cassy was, she would not be alive long.

But what was Letitia to do?

If she reached out to the girl, all she could do is sense the girl's fear and whatever fate lie in store for her. Like Maisie, Cassy was somewhere dark that smelled of the sea. It could be the western seaboard for all she knew since she had no other information, nothing but what the girls were seeing, which wouldn't be helpful to the police.

To look for them, and going in blind, was a risk Letitia dared not take.

It wasn't worth her sanity, or her life, to be dragged down into death with them.

She couldn't help them. She'd only suffer the same fate.

The reasoning chaffed more with every reassurance she uttered to herself. Little white lies telling her she helped Mr. Driscoll, so why not these girls? But it was different. She could see Finola's enemy. These girls were trapped in the dark and could tell her nothing. They would only sweep her into their own dread-fueled deaths.

Ignoring the newspaper, Letitia wiped the table clean and went upstairs to gather her purse and coat.

She wanted fresh fruit. She was intent on buying an orange—something rather than sit in her rooms.

Back in her session room, a box caught her eye.

The present Mr. Driscoll dropped by when he returned to pick up his things. She hadn't opened it. She'd even thought about returning it, but she didn't know where he bought it and didn't want to ask him. Picking it up, she placed it on the table and unwrapped the surrounding ribbon. Lifting the lid, she saw it was a rather flat hatbox.

Nestled in the tissue paper a black cloche sat, peaked on one side and dropping to the other. A small swathe of chiffon hung down over the eyes, which would leave the rest of the face bare. The veil was pinned to the sides by two green and copper collections of stained crystal. It was gorgeous, fashionable, and well crafted.

When she looked at the maker's label, she put the hat down.

It was Italian, from Milan, and a name she recognized. He must have paid a small fortune for it. Letitia had never owned a designer piece before and scarcely knew what to do with it. Yet her fingers brushed the silken folds. She guessed it would fit her to perfection.

Of all the things to buy her, he'd chosen the mask he appeared to so loathe.

Not that it mattered now.

She'd have no idea where to return it, and as her fingers brushed the soft wool of the cloche, she knew it didn't matter because she would keep it. A small reminder of him.

Whatever anger existed at their last encounter faded under the kind gesture.

She took the box to her room, and with a small amount of vanity, put the hat on and looked at herself in the mirror.

The chiffon veil came down to just cover the tip of her nose, making her jawline and mouth stand out. The effect made her seem mysterious and knowing, as the judgmental eyes of the figure in the reflection roved over the lines of the cloth.

Letitia never thought of herself as dramatic but couldn't shake that this was the impression Mr. Driscoll had of her—that it was slight mockery as much as a well-meaning gift. It would be why he'd bought the hat with a veil rather than some other gift of apology.

Letitia couldn't imagine that he'd ask for it back. She hoped perhaps he would so that she might explain herself better than she had at their parting.

Rather than hang it with her other hats, far more drab by comparison, she put it back in its box and put it beside her wardrobe. The colors he'd chosen still called to her and picking a hat for the day from her normal ones, Letitia resolved to make another similar to it. She'd collect the materials today, and when she had the time to update and amend the hats she had, she might even stitch up a new one. The chiffon rather than lace or other sheer materials made it far easier to see, but she'd never thought to use it quite as they had on the cloche.

Adding a detour on her list of tasks that morning, Letitia collected her coat and purse and took to the stairs.

"Ms. Hawking." Mrs. Finch was coming through the kitchen toward the back door. "There's a letter come with the post this morning for you."

"Thank you," Letitia said, taking the letter. "Do you need anything from the market?"

"Are you going to Chinatown?"

"Yes, I need some things," Letitia said.

"Could you pop into the apothecary and see if they have any new oils? I'm thinking of something to get into the swing of spring. See what you can find?" She held up a wad of money, but Letitia waved it away.

"I'll get it in exchange for a single soap with the new oil," Letitia said.

"Oh, very well then," Mrs. Finch said with a smile. It seemed to thrill her that both Imogen and Letitia liked her products, even to test them, and she didn't hide it. Imogen loved the makeup kits Mrs. Finch's other daughter, Norma, created. Letitia had one too, but it went untouched.

For Letitia, it was the scented soaps Diana and Mrs. Finch made that she loved.

She enjoyed bringing them the odd scents she found at the stores she visited, so much more exotic than lavender or vanilla, though those soaps had their place, too.

Letitia resolved to get something that wasn't quite roses, perhaps with citrus or a rare lily. Picking something to challenge the girls gave her something to look forward to after her unpleasant morning. Walking into the sunlight, Letitia was optimistic, the worst of a terrible situation behind her.

The feeling diminished when she approached the corner

store with its newspapers out front, which reminded Letitia that perhaps she hadn't done all she could. The headline of the missing girl haunted her.

She was considering visiting Mr. Edwards, but to visit Cassy's parents risked repeating the trauma of the mother losing her baby, or being confined to the asylum, or worse.

The bitter memory should have been more than enough to reassure her that Mrs. Edwards was not the same as Letitia, who'd done all she could.

Watching out for her safety and protection sounded fine when she remembered those events, but it didn't change that there was another frightened girl out there. Locked in a basement, in the dark, at the hands of a depraved and jaded soul, and for what purpose didn't bear thinking about. He would take other girls and wouldn't stop unless caught. Mr. Edwards' hasty departure sent a wriggling nervousness through Letitia of what he may do because she didn't think she'd seen the last of him.

Letitia didn't like the direction of her thoughts and instead turned to the letter she still hadn't opened.

Keeping an eye on other busy pedestrians making their way through the streets, her gloved fingers struggled for a moment to open the envelope, ripping the paper by accident as she plucked the letter out.

Dear Ms. Hawking,

I can only excuse my rudeness in offering you compensation as a result of what transpired in the cellar and as a need to recompense the immense sacrifice you made for my daughter, now that it's clear to me. It's one thing to hear about spirits from another person, but to see for myself shook the foundation of my fears. My offer was to atone in a way that I could, as I know now what it is you faced. I'm sorry to have caused offense.

I feel we left on bad terms and would like to find

another way of making it up to you. Not only the act of your complete generosity and selflessness in helping my daughter, and in keeping my secret, but also for acting with such compassion and dignity. It has been both traumatic and healing for our family.

Abby would also like to extend her gratitude to you, as Finola was doing well in less than a few hours after ridding the house of that item. It will please you to know I took it out on a boat myself and threw it into the sea. It should trouble no one further.

I would like to renew our acquaintance on friendlier terms if you are amenable to doing so. Would you deign to dine with me this Saturday evening? This is by no means a way to reimburse you; I found your conversation and intelligence becoming. I would no more lie about my intent than the darkness that came to possess our house. Please know that should you not reply, I will consider my proposal rejected, and trouble you no further, despite any temptation to do otherwise.

Yours Sincerely,

Alasdair.

Letitia's feet had halted on the sidewalk and she glanced around as though the man himself would be right there. Walkers passed her, one with a scowl for stopping in his path, so she stepped into an alcove to reread the letter. Ignoring the sense of guilt for spying, she slipped off a glove to lay a trembling hand over the cream letter. She could see him, thoughtful as his pen traced across the paper, written in his sunlit study yesterday afternoon. Seeing him in her mind's eye, it was as though he touched the paper with the purpose of imprinting himself onto its surface.

The impression was so strong she even heard him say her

name.

"*Tisha.*"

Not even Daniel had called her that. Letitia's cheeks heated at the sound of Mr. Driscoll's voice, and she clutched the letter, a quivering in her chest catching her breath. Delighted and afraid, Letitia put the paper in her purse, and even then, the feeling wouldn't fade.

She couldn't accept since she'd already agreed just that morning to go out with Imogen on Saturday. Having canceled on Imogen when she'd fallen ill, it would be the height of rudeness to do so again, even if she only changed the date. Still, a part of Letitia couldn't banish the way Mr. Driscoll whispered her name. With fondness and longing...

Walking through the stalls of the market, Letitia picked up several oranges. Brought from further south, they were a little bruised but would do. When she arrived at the Chinese market, she went inside her favorite apothecary.

"Good morning, Mr. Chen," she said to the elderly gentleman behind the counter. It was impossible to guess his age. The old man's distinguished hair was pale gray, combed to fall down his back, and a long beard far darker than his hair gave him a contrasting appearance.

"Ms. Hawking, so nice to see you again." He came around the counter, holding out his hand to her, arthritis and age bending the limbs as he hobbled with a walking stick. She took his hand, and then they both turned to the shelves.

"What do you desire today?"

"More juniper oil," Letitia said, "and something for spring. Mrs. Finch does so enjoy getting new scents from you and they are making the soaps for the new season."

"Ladies need to embrace the budding flowers, just as they too are blossoms." Mr. Chen's hands drifted over the brown bottles, moved by memory alone. His daughter and her husband kept the shop stocked, and helped when needed, but Mr. Chen appeared to know what everyone wanted when they came in.

Plucking a bottle off the shelf, he held it out to her.

"It isn't common, but I think you may like it," he said with a shrug.

"Cherry blossoms?" Letitia asked, taking it. "I didn't know you could make an oil from that."

"It is not, in fact, from China but comes from Japan. They have the most beautiful cherry trees there, and in the spring the blossoms are a sign of renewal. Life is short, Ms. Hawking, and we must not let it pass us by while we wait in the shadows."

Letitia studied the old man, pausing before sniffing the oil herself.

Opening her abilities, she felt a stillness and peace, the scent of freshly dug earth and oncoming rain soothing her senses. If he was perceptive of her assessment, he gave no sign, but he stood there with a gentle smile.

"You said more juniper oil," he said, turning about after her stare became scrutiny.

"Please," Letitia said, and on impulse, she snatched another bottle of the cherry oil, "and I think I'll take two of these."

"That will be two dollars, please," Mr. Chen said, wrapping them in paper.

"I believe it's five with the cherry oil," Letitia said, "it says so on the label."

"You are correct," he said, and Letitia counted out the notes and then took her package.

"Thank you."

"Take care, Ms. Hawking," he said, the words enunciated and slow, "and should you need anything that might be more difficult to acquire, please just ask."

It was an odd thing to say, but then there had been more than one comment that morning that had made her believe he might be affected by his age.

"Good day, Mr. Chen."

Giving it no further thought, Letitia went to a few other stores, guided into picking cloth and ribbons in green and bronze as she remembered the hat Mr. Driscoll gave her. She would have to call him and make her excuses, but goaded by Mr. Chen's comment, she decided perhaps she could meet him for lunch tomorrow instead.

It wasn't a bad thought, and it encouraged her as she made her way home.

The back door was open wide, and voices spilled out onto the street.

Mrs. Finch spoke to someone, voice high and stressed. Whoever it was, it was clear they weren't welcome. Letitia used the oil as an excuse to walk in, perhaps to help Mrs. Finch.

There was a man there she didn't recognize.

Mrs. Finch's arms were folded, and when she saw Letitia her face fell, eye darting between Letitia and the stranger who regarded her with open curiosity.

"Ms. Hawking, I presume?" He was clean-shaven, dressed in a decent but inexpensive suit, and holding a hat in his hands. Blue eyes the color of forget-me-nots scrutinized her despite the veil on her face.

"Can I help you with something?"

"Yes, you can," he said. "I'm here because of Mr. Edwards."

Letitia's heart plummeted through the floor.

"I can do nothing further to help him, for which I am very sorry," Letitia said, but the man held up his hand.

"I think perhaps you misunderstand why I am here, Ms. Hawking." He stood inches from her, and for a moment she let herself feel the icy gust of his personality. She stepped back at the chill, flakes of ice almost striking her.

"What's your name?" she said, taking another step back.

"Andrews," he said. "That would be Detective Andrews."

The policeman looking after the cases involving the missing girls. Letitia felt the blood drain from her face and the world sway as she stared at him, regretting her terrible error in not chasing down Mr. Edwards.

"Mr. Edwards thinks you may be able to help us with our

inquiries," Detective Andrews said. "I thought you and I could take a trip downtown to discuss how he believes you are involved in the kidnapping."

Letitia heard Mrs. Finch gasp but could do nothing, standing there in shock.

"But I can't help him," she blurted out. "I don't know anything."

"It would be best to come with me," Andrews went on, "before he outright accuses you of doing the deed yourself. After all, such a crime is punishable by death."

Chapter 15

"How does American law work regarding an accusation of kidnapping?" Letitia asked as Andrews sat opposite her at the police station. "My understanding is that I do not have to speak to you without legal assistance."

"You aren't under arrest," Detective Andrews said, the litany becoming tiresome, "and we've already tried to get in touch with Mr. Driscoll. He isn't in his office or at home. It would be best just to tell us what you told Mr. Edwards."

"He came by to ask me to help find his daughter, and I couldn't help him," Letitia repeated.

"That's strange," Andrews said, lifting up a file over an inch thick from the desk, "because he says you knew things only the family would know. That you must have been watching them. You have to admit that from what he told me it sounds very damning."

The small grin he gave her was belied by the blast of ice of his persona.

Letitia didn't need to read his personality. Andrews would

take any chance to find out what he could on this case, even if it meant badgering her until she broke.

He'd even made her take off the veil.

Letitia shifted on the hard chair in the dingy room, the only light a single bulb that cast shadows in the corners. Another man leaned against the wall behind her, a Detective Smith, and glowered at her. She could feel his stare, but the questions fired off by Detective Andrews caught her off guard. Letitia hadn't dared talk about her abilities to this man who had eyes like flowers and a warm disposition but who smiled like a cat with a canary.

Andrews had taken her straight here and she'd been made to wait for over an hour before he came back to talk to her. He'd offered her plain black tea or coffee and she'd declined both, asking instead for water. She'd need to use the bathroom soon but felt as though she could not ask. Their intense gazes, their doubts, and the room they'd locked her in were eating at her confidence and raising old memories of being trapped and cast out of the known world.

"Would you like more water?" Andrews asked, and when she nodded Smith brushed her as he collected the glass and walked out.

"You see, Ms. Hawking," Andrews went on, as though they had been in mid-conversation, "when a woman approaches a man whose daughter is missing and tells him she knows the girl is still alive, it raises many questions. You wouldn't know that unless you're somehow involved. Or is this the...occultism Mr. Edwards was talking about?"

Letitia's hands gripped the edges of her chair, sweat beading down the back of her dress, shoulders so tight they hurt. She was pressing her legs together as the ghostly sensation of blood came trickling back. She wanted to cover her ears. She didn't want to hear this again.

A policeman questioning her, while she lay on a bed, drugged out of her mind, bleeding, not dying but watching the shadow behind him.

There was none here, but she couldn't shake the sensation away.

"That's very blasphemous," Andrews said when she didn't answer, his tone turning to sympathy, "but these days few people are as God-fearing as they used to be. I know. I did my time in the war—I ran supply lines to the front. Not glamorous, but I had a knack of getting into tight spots. Of being able to get behind or around enemy patrols. Did your husband die in the war?"

"Yes, he did," Letitia said, raising her head, trying to hold on to her composure. Andrews was relentless—this was the second time he'd tried this tactic. Always returning to what it was she did, what she knew of the girl, and the subtle undertone mocking her abilities.

"Did you try to contact him?" Andrews pressed. "Your dead husband?"

Letitia couldn't speak, couldn't do anything but fight the tears that clogged her throat, and when Andrews' observant eyes scanned her face, there was a glimmer there and a twitch of his lips.

"Mr. Edwards said you made a merry song and dance about that." The detective leaned back in his chair. "Told a father you knew where his daughter was but wouldn't help him because you had something bad happen to you. What was it?"

The door opened and Letitia started. It was Smith. He held no water glass in his hands but a bowl. Her scrying bowl. From the locked box in her rooms.

Letitia stood, outrage pouring through her like molten lead. "How dare you!"

"I thought you might like to do a trick for us," Andrews said, as Smith placed the bowl in front of her. "Isn't this how you do it? Look into the water and tell people what they want to hear?"

"You are a vile man," Letitia snapped, "and you do not understand what you speak of. You have no concept at all."

He smiled.

Shocked that she was speaking of her services, her mouth clicked shut, and she covered it with her hand.

"Take a seat, Ms. Hawking, please." Andrews gestured to the chair, and when Smith lumbered over, she sat down, fuming at their behavior but unable to see a path clear.

"If you could help us return a little girl to her father," Andrews went on, "you wouldn't only be saving her life, you'd be helping us to put whoever took her behind bars."

"Not if you think I had something to do with it," Letitia said. Rage simmered within, burning the fear, turning it to charcoal ash in her mouth. The bitter taste ate away at her senses.

"We only want the truth, Ms. Hawking," the detective said, and he leaned forward, staring at Letitia with an intensity about to resolve itself on some great truth. "There is a little girl out there, and she hasn't been the only one. We want to be sure that whoever is taking them is stopped. Can't you understand that?"

Letitia's teeth pressed together so hard her jaw ached, a twinge in her cheek protesting the pressure, but it was better than allowing herself to speak. Andrews waited for a while, and after a glance at Smith, the other detective left.

They were alone.

"My mother was an Irish Catholic you know," Andrews said. "She hated the English, and I suppose she was right to after all she'd been through. I never cared much for her politics, but there was one thing she always said that stayed with me. No matter how much another person's opinion differs from your own, some people forget the right thing to do to hold true to their opinions."

"Do you think that's true, Detective Andrews?" Letitia held back the mocking laughter at his faux speech. The fury seethed within her—that they'd invaded her home—rising above all else, even her fear.

"I think a lot of us imagine that we're right in our own way, no matter if it hurts another," he said.

Letitia stared at him and decided that if Smith wasn't here, what happened between them would be Andrews' fault. He wasn't panicked like Mr. Edwards had been, and she would gain far more from it than he would.

"Give me your hand, Detective Andrews." Letitia was about to give the detective a dose of his own medicine. She'd prove her tricks went far beyond her parlor and read from him what she could to get herself out of this situation.

Without knowing how far away Mr. Driscoll was, if he was coming at all, Letitia decided to see how far she could push Detective Andrews.

He was amused as he laid his hand on the table. Andrews wasn't afraid of her.

That was his mistake.

She had already been searched for weapons by a cautious but thorough policewomen, and while she was not handcuffed, she suspected that there were several officers outside in addition to the glaring Detective Smith.

Letitia pulled off the glove of her right hand and opened herself, preparing for the arctic blast of his personality. There was a gentle drift of snow, and after a moment she saw that the rampart part of him was not focused on the cat-and-mouse chase. He wanted to see the trick, to call her out.

"Are you going to read my palm?" If he meant to offend, despite the neutrality of his tone, he didn't succeed as she ignored him and placed one finger in the center of his palm.

Scenes rushed by her eyes, paper, and blurred photographs, the snarling faces of the underworld, the sleepless nights as someone found yet another body. Andrews was not in charge of kidnapping cases. He worked in homicide and was good at it. This case, however, had been going on two years, and there was not a tally of four girls but in fact seven.

Letitia gasped, snatching her hand back.

"You found one," she gasped. "You found a body by the docks."

He didn't react as she expected. He left his hand on the table, eyes fixed on her. "As the killer would well know. I believe he wanted someone to find it. A declaration to the world of his power. Do you know, fish ate the little girl's body and we could still see what he'd done to her before she died?"

It was meant to shock her.

Letitia knew it was not enough, and with a deep breath, she reached out and grabbed his hand. It took a matter of moments to sift through the memories, but each one etched onto her what he'd experienced. Fresh though it was only yesterday. She heard him curse, but he didn't pull away.

"Oh, my Lord," Letitia said, weeping, "you saw the body, you knew who it was, you knew the parents. He was a police officer...a sergeant who you'd worked with for a long time... Leavitt. You worked with him for years. You had to tell him it was his daughter. There had already been four other girls, you knew there was something dark and ugly in the city, but when you told the commissioner he told you..."

Letitia stopped, aghast at the exact words. Andrews was gripping her hand now, eyes intense.

"Say it," he whispered. Soft, but hissed between clenched teeth.

"He told you not to say anything," she said, hating every word, "and made you cover it up. You thought if there was a public announcement about the killings you could catch the killer, make people more aware. Someone must have seen something but all this while the commissioner has pulled you back. And if you don't do as he says, he'll...he'll...oh, God." She tried to draw away, seeing what drove Andrews to keep her in his custody when he had no direct proof, why he was breaking the law with his inquisition. She tried to let go, but he held her fast now.

"What, Ms. Hawking?" His hand was so tight on hers it was turning pink, even as his was white with the strain as he clenched her in his viselike grip.

"He'll take you off the case. He'll fire you for incompetence. He will make you a scapegoat for the public outcry. This isn't about saving a little girl. This is about the city's politics."

He let her go.

Letitia drew her hand to her chest, massaging life back into it but the vivid welts he'd left would bruise her skin.

"Only the commissioner knows that," he said, "and I doubt he told you." He gazed at her, time stretching onward, but he left his hand on the table, perhaps in the hopes she would touch it again, but she'd rather touch a snake.

Letitia knew more about him than he'd ever want her to know.

"I am not a killer, detective," she said, "but your case is going nowhere, and it's not aided by the fact that your superiors want you to be quiet about the entire affair. How many more little girls have to go missing before you ask for my advice?"

"Nothing but vague and meaningless clues. And when you wouldn't offer any to Mr. Edwards?" He chuckled at her. "I think not."

"I can't," Letitia said with helpless exasperation.

"Withholding information is a criminal offense, Ms. Hawking."

Letitia understood then. It didn't matter what she saw, because he would use her to take his place as a sacrificial lamb.

This situation was out of hand, and without someone there to protect her, Letitia needed an edge.

"Then why don't we talk about something else, given neither of us is getting what we want," she said, "and perhaps you'll believe that I'm telling the truth. I can find things out, but I can't find those girls."

"What truth do you know?" he asked. "You've just made good guesses so far. I'm not that impressed."

Letitia gritted her teeth. "Then let's talk about you. For example, how did your mother die? Alone in an expensive New York hospital that took the family fortune. It should have allowed a man of your intelligence to go to university, but you did the noble thing and sacrificed it all for her well-being. She took years to die. You have a kind enough soul that you don't even resent her for it. Much."

Andrews' arm swept across the table and sent the scrying bowl spinning, spilling water across Letitia's dress and face before the bowl smashed against the adjacent wall.

Letitia caught her breath, a tiny part of her breaking with it and disappearing as though it were nothing.

Old Mother Borrows had made that bowl for her.

The door was flung open and Mr. Driscoll stood there, greatcoat on, white scarf about his neck, hat, and briefcase in hand. His eyes roved over the scene in a second—the detective's raised hand, the black glass shattered on the floor, the water staining her clothes, and the bruised hand still held to her chest.

When he looked at the detective, fire burned in Mr. Driscoll's eyes.

"Detective," Mr. Driscoll drawled, and only the intensity of his glare denoted his fury, "I require you to leave so I may speak to my client alone, please. We can work out how on earth the commissioner will pay my client for the infractions on her person. Or did you think invading her house without a warrant would be ignored?"

"Mr. Driscoll," Andrews said, getting to his feet and sending a grin to Letitia that was more a baring of his teeth, "the accused is all yours."

"Accused?" Mr. Driscoll asked. "What has she done?"

"Withheld information in a critical case. Collaborated with another to kidnap young girls for unknown purposes, one of whom was found dead." The detective turned and stood between Mr. Driscoll and Letitia. "And she will stay here until she tells me what she knows."

To Letitia's surprise, Mr. Driscoll laughed.

"I will make a call, detective," he said, "and explain to Judge Lindsay how you've invaded this young lady's home, and as far as I can determine, avoided giving her the legal help she asked for. Then there is the matter of assault. Do you think progressing with this case is the wisest course of action?"

Mr. Driscoll was a good head taller than the policeman and he gazed down at Andrews with the lazy arrogance Letitia was familiar with.

"You know she can help us find this girl." Andrews lost his composure, stomping a foot down as he took a step toward Driscoll. "She's just a coward for saying no!"

The comment stabbed Letitia like a knife, the guilt compounding until every heartbeat hurt. It burned brands of shame on her cheeks, her tongue a wooden block that couldn't voice her protests. She couldn't look at either man, her gaze instead drifting to the broken pieces on the floor. It represented all Old Mother Borrows sent her out to accomplish. To make the world a better place...

"If she's told you or that idiot Edwards anything," Mr. Driscoll said, "then perhaps you best use the advice, because she will not offer it again."

Mr. Driscoll pushed past him, taking the coat she'd laid to one side with her handbag and hat. He helped her to her feet, wrapping her in the coat. She didn't bother pinning the hat back on, since there didn't seem to be any point in covering her face.

His hand was warm on her arm, and he was about to lead her out, but Letitia paused. After a moment, she knelt and picked up the pieces of the bowl. Some shards were too small, but she gathered what she could in her hands, and Mr. Driscoll pulled out his handkerchief so she could lay the sharp edges against the cloth rather than risk cutting herself.

When they stood his eyes met hers, and she felt herself crumble.

He placed the handkerchief in her hands with the utmost care, and she did not miss the sneer on his face as he turned to Andrews.

"Damage of personal property, Andrews?" Mr. Driscoll said.

"You best believe the judge and the commissioner will hear from me."

Letitia let him escort her out while trying not to clutch the shards to her chest, the precinct a blur. Then they were out on the street, and she got into his car. He closed the door and they rumbled away from the station.

She laid out the handkerchief in her lap to look at the shell of what had been her grounding force. Her one hand that was still bare brushed the surface. She liked to touch them with her skin and to see the work Old Mother Borrows had put into making it for her—for her alone.

Nothing resonated from the pieces. They were calm as Old Mother Borrows had been.

But even now the sensation was fading to nothing more than echoes.

"Where can we get another one?" Mr. Driscoll was beside her, almost leaning over her lap to study the broken pieces.

"Scotland." Letitia's voice was devoid of emotion.

Mr. Driscoll cursed long and with eloquence. "I will buy you another."

"It won't be the same," Letitia said, numb to the words that spilled from her mouth. "This was made by the woman who helped me regain my sanity after I was institutionalized. She taught me control and how to use my abilities for the better. It was my penance for what I'd done. She didn't agree, but she made me the bowl. I used it to give grieving widows and families the chance to say goodbye to those that they loved. The chance no one gave me..."

Letitia shivered. Mr. Driscoll drew her close under the crook of his arm.

"I'll fix it," he vowed in her ear, the conviction there as his breath brushed her hair.

"Once something is this broken," Letitia said through stilted words, "nothing can erase the marks left behind."

"Don't be ridiculous, Ms. Hawking," Mr. Driscoll said. "You

fixed my daughter after we'd given up hope. You let my sister know that at the end the only man she ever loved was thinking of her. You showed me the dark, and you were unafraid. I broke, Ms. Hawking, and you were fearless."

The words were a lie to Letitia, and denial was a shield to stay true to her convictions.

"I'm not," she gasped. "A man came the same as you, and asked me to save his little girl, and I couldn't do it."

She shook her head. The guilt grew with every second Cassy was out there in the hands of a monster, and Letitia couldn't face her fear to find Mr. Edwards' daughter.

"Tisha," Mr. Driscoll said her name as though it were a prayer, "you have to stop blaming yourself. I've been down that path, as have you, but you have never veered from it."

"You don't know," Letitia said, her whole story coming to the fore. She had to explain how wrong he was about her.

"You weren't there, you don't know what happened, how this could go wrong. Did go wrong. The woman at the séance... she promised to find my husband. His spirit followed me for months after his death, worried about us—the child inside me. I sensed his presence but didn't understand it. When I had the chance, I went to a séance to find him, to see why he haunted me. The woman, the witch, was a fake, but because I was there, reaching for Daniel, I made it happen. I opened myself to Daniel, but something else came through. It tried to possess me, and I couldn't let it, not with Daniel's baby inside me. It took the witch instead and used her body to kill my baby!"

She was bending over, shards in her lap digging into her stomach where she gasped through the memory of similar pain. The confession was an admittance of her guilt, and she deserved the agony scarred onto her soul.

"Sweet Jesus," he said, enveloping Letitia in his arms.

"I can't look for another lost soul." She wept against his coat, clutching it as close as she could, even as she heard the delicate threads tearing in her hands. "You see that now, don't you? I can't!"

"I'm sorry, Tisha, I'm sorry I even asked." He squeezed her tightly against him, running his hands down her back, threading to the nape of her neck, holding her as though she were the most treasured and careful thing. Inside she was as jagged as the glass shards in her lap.

They were the fragmented promise she could no longer keep.

She had sworn she would offer true aid and closure to those who needed it like she herself had sought when the tides of the veil had turned against her in her naivete.

Her chance at giving peace to others ended with the shattered bowl. The inquisition by Detective Andrews was a knife wound to her bitter memories.

She cried through them all as Mr. Driscoll swept her away.

Chapter 16

"You'll be safe with me," Mr. Driscoll said.

Letitia set the phone down. She'd canceled her next week's appointments. The explanation of her continued illness was the only excuse she could think to tell them. Most were kind enough to state they could wait. One humorous man said his wife would not get any deader. Letitia gave a polite reply but otherwise didn't respond.

It was as though she had exhausted all of her energy in the car.

Not even embarrassment trod upon her as she glanced at Mr. Driscoll.

He leaned on the doorjamb, having listened in on her conversations and not leaving her side for a moment. They hadn't spoken of what had passed between them.

"The house is huge," he said, "and you are welcome to stay as long as you like. I don't believe the police will come by again, but I don't trust Andrews."

"I suppose it's for the best." Letitia stared beyond him at the mess.

After what they'd done to her apartment, she didn't want to be there.

The police had ordered Mrs. Finch to open the door after Andrews had taken Letitia away. They had opened drawers, combed through her things, taken some of the case files on her desk, and pried open the hazelwood box, and taken her scrying bowl.

Letitia had broken down again at the invasion, and the hatred toward her things. The violation of it all.

Mr. Driscoll had set her down in her chair by the fire, made tea, and done what he could to straighten her things.

When he finished and she was calmer, he'd given her the appointment book and told her to cancel her upcoming meetings. She'd followed his instructions in a daze, unsure of what else to do.

Beyond exhausted, she didn't have the energy to be afraid anymore.

It didn't aid matters that Mr. Driscoll wore an expression that didn't bear defying.

There was something about him that was disconcerting, though it wasn't directed at her. It had haunted his eyes since the police station, but if she caught his gaze, it vanished under a slight smile, only to return within moments when he didn't know she studied him.

"I've packed you a bag," he said. "While I don't imagine they will come back, it would be better to be out of the way if they do. That you had your address book in your handbag means they don't have all the information on your prospective clients. Detective Andrews is convinced you can help him, and he will keep pursuing you."

"I know," Letitia said, hand resting on the phone.

She loved it here. The routine she'd developed was still so new that it hurt to have broken it.

"Tisha." He took her listless hand. "I will run this down to the car and come back. Can you collect what else you want to take with you?"

She nodded and walked through her rooms.

There was nothing she couldn't replace in here, though she took some of the oils—sandalwood, lemongrass, and rose. There were others, but the names on the labels were a blur as she turned away from the destruction and entered the bedroom. Far less violated, it still bore signs of the unwelcome entry. Letitia glanced around at the desk, but since the files were gone there was nothing else of note.

Mr. Driscoll had already collected her copy of *Pride and Prejudice*. Her closet was for the most part empty. The rest didn't matter.

It struck her then how little she possessed. How fruitless her life had been if only to give closure to others, and she now no longer could. She stood in the middle of the room, absorbing the last few months. Had she made a difference to many people? Had it been worth it?

She turned at the sound of footsteps.

Imogen was there.

"You're home early," Letitia said.

"What on earth happened?" Imogen raced across the room and wrapped her arms around Letitia.

"The police," Letitia said, as though that should explain everything.

"But they can't do this." Imogen let go of Letitia's unresponsive form to bend down and meet her gaze. "It's illegal, and you need to find a lawyer."

Mr. Driscoll was there behind Imogen, studying Letitia.

As though waiting for permission.

She'd never thought twice about asking him.

"I have one," Letitia said, and Imogen turned around, startled to see him.

"Mr. Driscoll," she said. "Thank goodness you are taking care of her. How did this happen?"

"Ms. Hawking was helping a client," he said, "and the client took the information to the police, who seem to think Ms. Hawking has something to do with the missing girls."

"But she can't," Imogen burst out. "She's not a hurtful bone in her body!"

The truth that Imogen didn't know landed heavily among Letitia's other evasions. Of secrets she hadn't confessed in her grief during the car ride with Mr. Driscoll. The people around her weren't aware of her past, and it was in self-defense, but Letitia knew she was capable of harming someone.

She could kill if she wanted. If she had to.

"Be that as it may," Mr. Driscoll said, "Ms. Hawking has been in the country only a few months, and this case appears to have been going on for much longer than that. They are grasping at straws and looking for scapegoats, and they will not find one here."

"Can she stay with you, though?" Imogen asked. "I know you were here while she was sick, but we would look after her." There was more than a ghost of censure in Imogen's voice, and it caused Mr. Driscoll's lips to twitch as he gazed at Letitia, who took it upon herself to answer.

"I'm fine," Letitia said, struggling to find her voice. "There is Mr. Driscoll's sister and her daughter at the house. Besides, it has already damaged my reputation. I will need to move to another city." The concept of having to leave and of figuring out where she would go clenched her stomach hard. Letitia stopped herself from cringing.

"I'll come visit you, if I may?" Imogen said. "I don't think you'll feel much like going out, though."

"Actually," Mr. Driscoll said, "I think it would be a wonderful idea. Ms. Hawking has had little chance to let her hair down these days, and I suspect she could do with an outing. But only if she feels like it."

There was an insistence there, but Letitia didn't much care.

"Well, that's settled then," Imogen said. "I'll come by Mr.

Driscoll's house tomorrow afternoon at least, and we can take tea and go from there? That is, if you'll please give me the address, Mr. Driscoll?"

"Certainly." He rattled it off, watching with amusement as her eyebrows rose at the prestigious location. "I'll arrange for a car to pick you up at about two in the afternoon. It's a long way to take a cab. The address is just in case you or Mrs. Finch are worried or would like to visit. You are more than welcome."

"That would be very kind of you." She smiled before turning back to Letitia. "You will be all right, won't you?"

"Yes," Letitia said and nodded in affirmation when Imogen's smile faded. "I'm just quite shook up is all."

"I don't blame you. I'd lend you my place as a hideout, but it's not very good."

"And full already," Letitia reminded her, and Imogen grimaced.

"We should leave," Mr. Driscoll said. He didn't need to say why.

Looking about, Letitia collected a few of her favorite hats, the materials she'd bought to make more, and the hatbox he'd gifted her. "I'm ready."

Mr. Driscoll came over to take the box out of her hands, a warmth in his eyes when he caught sight of his gift to her. It was brief, only a sliver of eye contact, but it did much to dispel her unhappiness.

"I'll see you tomorrow," Imogen said as they left the apartment. "If the police come by, I'll tell them what for."

"Don't do that—" Letitia started, but Mr. Driscoll interrupted her.

"They have no right to be here without a warrant. Call me straight away if they dare show their face here."

Even Imogen's eyes widened at the heat in his voice. "Straight away."

"Thank you," Letitia said, "for everything."

"You are most welcome." Imogen embraced her again and

then drew back.

Letitia went down the stairs and into the kitchen, already taking her purse out.

Mrs. Finch was making dough and covered in flour, but she looked up as Letitia entered the kitchen. Her eyes were red, face pale, and the smile she attempted trembled on her lips.

"Oh, my dear girl," she said, waving her hands about, sending gusts of white powder into the air. "I couldn't stop them. I only let him in because he said he'd break down the door."

"Which one was that, Mrs. Finch?" Mr. Driscoll asked, putting down the hatbox to take out a notepad from his suit pocket.

"That Smith!" She snapped his name, detest in every syllable. "Tried to insinuate our Ms. Hawking was a con, and that she was going to prison. I knew they wouldn't find anything like that. She's the honest-to-God real thing, and the people who visit here are made whole again!"

Letitia was already shaking her head. "Not all that," she said, derision coating her words. "Nothing like that."

Mrs. Finch shook her finger at Letitia.

"That first couple you'd seen, the one whose brother died," she said, coming around the bench to stand before Letitia. "He felt as though he should have died in the war with his twin. It was destroying their marriage, their chance at a future. I heard them outside on the street, I was in the garden. He was apologizing to her, saying he would be a better husband, reopen the shop. You gave them back their lives."

Letitia stared at her. "I only meant to give them closure…"

"They weren't the only ones you helped. Far more could leave their grief behind because of you." Mrs. Finch reached her hand out for Letitia's, but she drew it back at the flour there. "More than one step was lighter on the stairs as they left—I heard them all—and was glad for it and for them."

Letitia swallowed against the constriction in her throat. "Thank you."

"Well then, there you go," Mrs. Finch said. "Now, you've paid me three months in advance just the other week, so you put away your money. Let's just see where we're at in a few days. And as for that policeman, if he comes back here, I'll set my daughters on him. See if I don't!"

"Please call Mr. Driscoll," Letitia said before Mr. Driscoll could speak. "Don't get in their way. I'd hate this to hurt your business."

"I've kept it alive during the war," Mrs. Finch said. "Not a bit of gossip will stop me. That cherry oil you left has pleased the girls, too. Can't say I'm going to like it much with you not here to do that."

"I promise to come back, even if it's to deliver scented oil," Letitia said.

"Well, then," Mrs. Finch said with a sniff and watery eyes. "Be off with you. You look like you're in capable hands."

Letitia had forgotten Mrs. Finch would still assume Mr. Driscoll was her intended.

"Yes, and thank you," Letitia said, blushing, before they took their leave.

Out on the street, the car was waiting, and Letitia was unable to ignore the sense of persecution at departing, as though this were England and she was running away again. The world was her choice then. Now she had only one, but she was grateful for it as she slid into the car.

Mr. Driscoll got in beside her, and they drove out to his estate.

She glanced over her shoulder as they drove away, a pang in her chest at what was to her an ideal and safe place. But no longer.

Following fast on its heels was a burning resentment toward Mr. Edwards. The doubt she'd failed him faded under the assault on her person by the police. While her heart was heavy in sympathy for the lost girl, ire grew at both Mr. Edwards and the police at what had been done to her private things. To her life.

Her numbness faded to rage, and she fumed on the long trip to the Driscoll house.

"It's perfectly normal to be angry," Mr. Driscoll said beside her, looking down at her clenched hands on her dress. She smoothed the material out. If he noticed her shaking hands, he said nothing, and Letitia was glad he didn't comfort her again.

She needed some measure of distance when her interest in him was rekindling.

Letitia could no more say no to his aid than she could stay for an indeterminable time at a hotel. She needed his legal help should the police come back, and to flee now would invite suspicion. His unwavering kindness was more than because of her help with his daughter. There was something restful about the assured way he'd taken control of the entire situation.

When the car pulled up at the house it was nearing sundown. Mr. Driscoll helped her out, but rather than go inside he took her around the side of the great house.

"I thought you could use some sunshine," he said at her puzzled frown.

"I suppose," Letitia agreed, taking a deep breath. "And I've yet to thank you for all...this." The enormity of what he'd done was sinking in, and she hastened to extend her gratitude. "I don't know what the legal fees will be, but I have quite a bit put aside—"

"And you had the hide to say I only thought of money." Rather than harsh, his tone teased and she glanced at his amused smile.

"It's hardly the same," Letitia said, consternation in her tone.

"Isn't it?" There was a warning in his low voice, a question with a barb inside.

"The kind of trouble I might be in could bring you much embarrassment," Letitia rushed on. "Not to mention that I am staying at your house. Won't your colleagues or some such find it inappropriate?"

"It may surprise you to know I'm a very private person," he said. "And I have no intention of telling anyone where you are unless you wish it. You are no more bound to my help or hospitality than you want to be, but I am here for you, without any other expectations despite what I said in my letter."

He held fast to her arm when she would have drawn away. Her breath caught for a moment, seeing the sun on one side of his face, the auburn waves of his hair threaded with silver and glinting in the light. All the while his green eyes were bright, burning away any doubts she might have had with regard to his honor or intent.

His hand brushed strands of her hair aside. "I think you have difficulty allowing yourself the luxury of letting someone else take care of things for you. And I would very much like to do so. Not because you need me to—never that—but because you want me to."

Words died on her tongue, but rather than be answered he swept her away across the gardens. The grass was lush green under their footsteps as they left the stone terrace, and after a time she let go of his arm.

"I need a moment." She glanced up at him, and ever amicable, his hand touched hers before he let go.

"Walk for a while," he said. "Think on my offer to stay, and if it doesn't suit, I'll do as I promised and take you home or anywhere else you'd like to go."

Letitia's hand tightened on his for a moment. "But I can't go home, can I?"

"It isn't wise," he said. "But there are a number of other places that shouldn't be too fiscally taxing if you'd prefer. You are, however, more than welcome here."

Any answer she wanted to give sounded foolish, prideful even, and she needed some safety from the law.

She needed to think and to undo the damage Detective Andrews had inflicted.

Without a word, she let go of his arm and entered the garden.

Winter's spell withered the leaves of wizened roses, thorny barbs leaving no sign of the oncoming blooms. The bedded gardens gave way to rolling grass and trees, lush as any English garden. Letitia walked under bare trees beginning to bud for spring, and all the while she thought about what had transpired, Mr. Driscoll was never far out of sight.

For once it was welcome, never intrusive, ever watchful, so she didn't mind that he followed as she strolled through the chilly grounds. The breath of spring ghosted through the air in the sun's weakened touch, but without glancing back she knew warmth was only a few steps behind.

Somehow, she sensed she wouldn't be free without wrenching something from herself, and her capacity to hold her swaying emotion toward him faded with every backward glance.

No amblings across the grounds gave her answers as to what to do now, and every time her eyes met his, her resolve crumbled until she returned to where he waited.

She couldn't dwell on what to do from here, and he was a welcome and supportive distraction.

"Better?" he asked.

"Yes, a little," she said, tugging strands of loose hair from her eyes, his gaze following the gesture. She dropped her hand, thinking of his fingertips on the curve of her ear moments before.

"What about some tea?" he said.

"That would be delightful," she said. "Thank you."

When he offered her his arm, she took it, sliding her chilly hand around his elbow, and when his warm hand covered hers, she couldn't help but think of when she'd absorbed his essence on her sickbed, and how it sunk down into her bones.

She wanted that warmth again.

As though he was the one who could read thoughts his hand tightened on hers.

"I don't mind," he whispered to her. "I'd be honored."

Letitia's hand tightened on his arm.

"It was a mistake—"

"Will you fight me at every corner?" His amusement returned. "Is this what I am to look forward to?"

"Borrowing someone else's essence isn't one of my strong suits," Letitia said, and unbidden another confession came spilling out her lips. "It's why I worry about Finola. I have such a dark past, and you aren't aware of the worst parts. But Old Mother Borrows is safe. She has far more control and ability than I could ever hope to possess."

He was silent a long moment, accompanied by the wind in bare trees and the rustle of their steps over the lush lawn.

"That is why you wanted me to take her to Scotland," he said. "So you wouldn't hurt her."

Letitia breathed a sigh of relief. "Yes. I know this is a subject you aren't familiar with, but simply because I recognize and could help get rid of the phantom doesn't mean I can do everything."

"And here I thought you were without flaws," he answered, though the corner of his mouth curled.

"Don't lay false platitudes at my feet," she said with a reprimand. "I do what small part I can to stop others being hurt, though it does not sound like the truth today."

"No," he said, voice harsh as a whip crack. "They scorned you and your abilities and had no right to do so."

"But can't you see," Letitia said, slowing her pace, "how easy it is to do so when you don't understand?"

Mr. Driscoll's head dropped. "I'm not doing this to ask for your forgiveness either. But you are precious, just as Finola is, and you fight things no one else can see or touch yet haunt us still. To my eyes, at least, it makes you braver than any soldier."

Letitia swallowed against a sudden well of tears. "I think that's one of the nicest things anyone has ever said to me."

"And I hope it will not be the last," he said, taking her to a table laid out with tea things.

She poured, and he turned the conversation to the gardens

and house. The air filled with his subtle banter and her witty replies.

The day's unimaginable sadness diminished to the farthest corners of her mind.

Whatever misgivings she had about Alasdair Driscoll's interest in her, he was now her friend. A part of her wondered how much she'd like to be more than that, any trepidation she might still have melting with each of his devilish smiles.

Chapter 17

L etitia stood before the mirror, criticizing her dress.
The color she thought as forest green should have made her dark hair shine. The lace at her cleavage was a little old and faded, and there were a few places the beads were falling off. She turned, watching it swish about her ankles before adjusting the waistline to a better height. Letitia tried to believe she looked something other than drab.

But then she'd hadn't cared for years what anyone thought of her clothes.

Sighing, she eyed the beaded dress of copper and jet black that still hung in the wardrobe. Tempting as it was to swan down to dinner in the garment, Letitia discarded the idea.

She would save it for another time. Anything else implied putting herself on display, and the thought alone was distasteful. It was also not what interested Mr. Driscoll in her, which she discovered after spending the afternoon letting him take away the depression of her day.

Resigned to the ordinary dress, Letitia had a pang of guilt

when she opened the cosmetics kit she'd packed with the rest of her toiletries. Applying a light amount of powder, rouge, and lipstick, Letitia felt her reflection at least looked confident enough to withstand Mr. Driscoll's charms.

When she arrived in the drawing room for predinner drinks though, she discovered she'd arrived first.

"Where is everyone?" she asked the footman, whose name she couldn't recall.

"Mr. Driscoll is on his way, madam. Can I offer you a drink?"

Letitia had no idea what to ask for. She'd never been in a house with servants on hand. The footman seemed to sense it and looked at her with kindness.

"Does the lady like soft liquors or something harder?"

"I don't know," she said with a self-deprecating chuckle. "What do you recommend?"

"Let's start with something easy, perhaps a Bee's Knees." He crossed to the side bar and began mixing her a drink. Letitia walked around the room, admiring the dark furniture against pale yellow wallpaper. There were even a few portraits, but they appeared to be older family ones rather than more recent renditions. She looked for a picture of Mr. Driscoll as if staring at his photograph would prepare her for the strength of his personality, but he was not there.

He reminded her so much of a desert she'd never visited, a potentially dangerous place. While Letitia walked along its edge, she couldn't help being drawn to the heat.

"Here you are, madam." The footman held out a silver tray upon which sat a rounded glass filled with cloudy yellow liquid. She took the cocktail and sipped it, pleased at the tang it left on her tongue.

"That's wonderful, thank you," she said, taking another sip.

"Gin, lemon, and honey, ma'am," he said. "They make it with bootlegged gin, but with the right gin is palatable."

"Are you giving Ms. Hawking bootlegged cocktails, Horner?" Mr. Driscoll stood in the doorway, and Letitia felt her breath catch. He'd dressed for dinner, black tie and all, sophisticated in the elegant suit. Regret at not wearing the prettier dress flittered over her mind, her hand brushing the material of her dress as he came in.

"No, sir," Horner said, "a proper Bee's Knees."

"Quite the underground drink," he said, returning the grin Horner gave him. "Pour me a Scotch."

Horner went to the bar, while Mr. Driscoll crossed to Letitia.

"You look beautiful." He took her hand and kissed it.

"Thank you," she said, stopping herself from dismissing his flattering of the out-of-date garment. "Where is your sister and Finola?"

"Gone to the theater," he said, letting go of her hand to take his drink from Horner, who then disappeared. "She thought Finola would like it, that it may take her out of herself. Finola's been cooped up here for months, and Abby didn't want her to rejoin social circles if crowds will be a problem."

He was frowning and drew away to sit on the couch.

Letitia sat opposite, leaning forward, as it appeared there was more to his story.

"Is she not doing so well?" she asked. "I would have thought she would fare better without the nightmares."

"I thought it best not to trouble you," he said. "I see now why it might be of concern. I've already made arrangements to take Finola to Scotland."

Letitia was surprised. "When does she leave?"

"There is a boat in two weeks leaving New York," he said. "All I need from you, Ms. Hawking, is a letter of introduction."

The formal address and request made her laugh. "I can most certainly write one for you, although one look at Finola and Old Mother Borrows will know what to do with her. She will be so overwhelmingly strong."

"Thanks to you," Mr. Driscoll said.

"And please," she said, "call me by my first name."

He paused for a moment. "I'd like that, and I invite you to

do the same."

Letitia covered her growing blush with a sip of her drink. "So now, Alasdair, will you tell me about Finola?" She didn't miss the curl in his lips when she said his name, but he sighed when thinking on her question.

"Yes," he said, with a cant of his head. "Her thoughts are much stronger, but she's taken what you said very much to heart. She's protecting herself from seeing what others think. I can't describe it because she can't, but she says you surrounded yourself in light, and the bad thing went away."

Letitia hadn't realized Finola had garnered that much in their short and somewhat traumatic meeting.

"Really?" Letitia said. "I didn't know she'd read that from me."

"Finola understood what you did, though," he said. "She sees a bubble, like one made with soap. Covered in rainbows and light, harder than steel. She says she's imagined it around her, too. It doesn't make much sense to me, but the last three nights she's slept like a lamb."

"I'm glad she's come away from it not too traumatized," Letitia said. "She's quite a gifted young woman."

There seemed to be something else. He stared at the carpet, not meeting her gaze.

"Does she do anything else?" Letitia asked. "Such as not like to touch people or look them in the eye?"

"She draws, as though ridding herself of the nightmare," he said, stroking the rim of his glass. "They are dark images. Nothing profane, but still horrifying. But she says they help, or they will help. She's convinced the pictures will matter."

"To whom?" Letitia asked.

"I don't know," he said, "but I am convinced by her belief."

Letitia nodded, sipping the cocktail. "A woman once told me that expressions of art to process traumatic events was a credible way of relieving the grief in one's heart."

"And what's your creative expression?" He asked, and the

sudden change made her shift uncomfortably in her seat.

"I used to—well, you know, it doesn't matter, I don't do it anymore, and it was silly anyhow." She gulped half her drink, coughing as the gin hit her throat. Alasdair leaned forward, chuckling, something of a predator about him as he rested his elbows on his knees.

"Nothing about you strikes me as being silly."

Fiddling with her glass, Letitia found herself confessing. "I used to write poetry."

Though his eyes twinkled, he treated her creative endeavors with respect by asking an intelligent question. "An understated talent. Are we speaking of the tales of Edgar Allan Poe or perhaps less American?"

"William Blake, or Emily Dickson, rather. Of death and the passage of time," Letitia shrugged. "I wrote to release the anxiety of my soul."

It was an intimate thing to say. But by now she was at ease talking to him, though perhaps Horner had been too generous with the drink. She wouldn't have minded another. Initially nervous at spending the evening alone with Alasdair, she was now embracing whatever was happening between them.

"What about you?" she said.

"I don't mind poetry, but I like novels, too," Alasdair said. "I was always a fan of Oscar Wilde. Not the depravity of his writing, or the flippant and meticulous insults, but the greater condition of a soul that had sinned."

They were treading on dangerous philosophical ground.

"Rather flamboyant a choice?"

"Would you rather we discuss Jane Austen?" The taunt was meant to poke at the book on her bedside and Letitia's blush returned. She wanted to point out her lonely childhood, but it would spoil the mood, and instead, she put her empty glass down.

"Do you have something to say on the matter of romance?" she asked before her courage could leave her.

When she met his gaze, there was a glimmer within that was more than amusement or interest—it was almost proud.

The gong rang before he could answer, and he stood and offered his arm as the pocket doors slid apart. She walked beside him into the dining room, set for two, and he pulled out the chair for her to the left of the head of the table. He took his place, and a footman came forward to lay a napkin over their laps before the first course was brought out.

Surprised by the strength of her appetite, she devoured the beef broth laid before her. The broth was followed by lamb shanks and then a rich chocolate flan. Each course was accompanied by a different wine, all of it part of a world she had never known. Conversation floated around the food, but was superfluous at best, and evolved to literature and music. She asked what Abby and Finola had gone to see at the theater.

"Much Ado About Nothing," he said. "Innocent enough for Finola, and a fun and confusing play."

Letitia's eyes widened in delight, and before she could say something suitably appropriate Alasdair's countenance changed to amusement.

"Would you like to go?" he asked.

"It would be divine," she said.

"I'll take you to see it next week and then we'll have dinner," he said. "There's an Irish place downtown I like to go to with private dining rooms. A little rough around the edges, but I suspect you'll keep your English primness."

"A lord in his castle is hardly in a position to question my manners," she retorted, "especially when his conduct has a questionable past."

Alasdair surprised her by laughing, not remotely offended, until Letitia echoed him.

Alasdair then told stories of Ireland and of legal cases, always seeking to entertain and never letting the conversation fall short. She answered in kind—how she'd grown up on the west coast of England, not within sight of Ireland but explained that she always wanted to go there.

They talked of their families. Letitia had none, and the extensive Driscoll family lived all across the United States, though its roots were still firmly dug into Ireland.

He asked her about what she did during the war, and she regaled him with schoolyard antics before he told some of his own.

Letitia's cheeks hurt from the laughter he coaxed from her, and he was never far from a devilish grin that made his eyes glimmer with his misdeeds. Letitia felt the perpetual tension seep from her shoulders. Everything was pleasant, as though she were on a cloud.

"Coffee in the drawing room, sir?" Horner was there, the meal gone, and Letitia was full and far happier than she had been in a long time. She had stopped drinking the wine, feeling a little light-headed but hadn't taken leave of her senses.

"Yes," he answered. "Though given Ms. Hawking's disdain for coffee, I suspect she would prefer tea. Is that right, Letitia?"

"Tea would be nice," Letitia said, flushing at the casual use of her name as he escorted her to the room they'd spent the sleepless night in. The grand piano was open with sheets already laid out.

"Do you play?" he asked as she eyed it.

"No, the best I manage is choir from when I was a schoolteacher, and they were all so dreary."

"Perhaps something by an American composer." Alasdair smiled and sat at the piano. He began to play, and with far more expertise than Letitia had imagined of the broad hands. A bright and sudden tune, it matched their conversation and spirits. It was pleasant on the ear, and Letitia lost herself in the melody. Alasdair stroked the keys, softening the tune until it became a trickle of intrigue and a pleasant apprehension.

"What seductive nonsense," she said when he finished.

"It's Gershwin," Alasdair said. "I learned to play when I became frustrated with Chopin, and I find some of these new jazz players relaxing, but with poignant points."

"I had no idea you were so talented," she said, surprised at his ability.

"I'm not just a lawyer," he said, playing a riff at random but not looking at her. "I have other passions, you know."

She did want to know.

Letitia had never been surer of anything in her entire life.

"What else can you play?" she asked, coming around the piano to run her fingers over the keys.

It was the first time she'd deliberately come closer, and from his sudden stillness, he'd noticed, careful in his movements as he turned to her yet remaining on the bench. She sat beside him, letting her fingers stroke the keys, indenting them to play the mournful and jarring tune at random, every note a chance to create something more.

"I'd play Chopin if I thought it would please you," he murmured, and she gazed at him, too close and somewhat intoxicated, but still her whole self, eyes wide and waiting.

Her lip curled up at one corner.

He captured her hand on the keys, the other cupping her cheek as he leaned down to kiss her.

Chapter 18

Letitia's face was aflame, heat pouring from him into her, searing through his lips and on to her own.

The kiss burned with an intensity that rippled down her body, and she couldn't—and wouldn't—have stopped it for anything. The sensation of him gusted over her, hotter than she could imagine, the depths of the desert chasing away the echoing dark within her soul. He became the air she needed, the link to the life she had let fade. It was her own; she'd become lost in her past, and he was her future.

She wanted nothing more than for him to keep kissing her.

There was a bang in the hall, closely followed by a shriek.

"Alasdair!"

He broke away, getting to his feet, but a tentative squeeze of her hand and a promise in his eyes assured her this was far from over. Letitia was so lost in his gaze that she jumped as the drawing room door was thrust open.

Abby stood there, pale but for two pink spots in her round cheeks. She darted her gaze between them.

"Oh, Letitia," she said, "thank goodness you are here."

"What is it, Abby?" Alasdair was striding across the room.

"It's Nola," Abby panted, face pale. "She was fine when we left here and had dinner with Patrick and Suzette, but when we got to the theater, she started to get nervous, twitching and starting at every little sound. I thought it might be the crowd of people, but she said it was something else."

"What else?" Letitia said, coming over, and Abby shook her head.

"Alasdair, I don't know what happened." Her hands covered her face. "Nola's gone!"

"What do you mean, gone?" Alasdair asked.

"We were at the theater." Abby gulped between sobs. "Everything was fine during the first act, but at intermission, I went to get lemonade, and when I got back, she'd disappeared. I don't know where she went. Someone saw her walk to the restroom, but I don't know how she left the theater. Nobody saw her leave."

"Did you call the police?"

"Yes," Abby said. "The theater manager did, but I came straight out to get you, because I knew—" Abby broke off, staring at Letitia.

"He came to take her..." Letitia whispered, a terrible apprehension overwhelming her. "She escaped from him, so he took her to finish what he started."

Letitia broke off as Abby grabbed her arm, pinching it to the bone.

"Do you know where she is?" she said, voice whisper-thin. Nails dug into her skin, but Letitia didn't need Abby's reaction to become riddled with dread.

"You're hurting me," Letitia said. Sickness was filling her, a revulsion itching to make her ill on the carpet as fear cascaded over her. Fear—and realization.

Simply because she'd removed the spirit didn't mean another entity wasn't out there.

One she hadn't predicted.

"Help me find my daughter," Abby demanded, shaking Letitia's arm as she grimaced. "If you think he's got her, you have to find her now, you have to!"

"Let her go, Abby. *Now*." Alasdair snapped, taking his sister's arm and drawing Letitia back. He was careful to hold Letitia to his chest and to usher her to the sitting room.

"I made a mistake," Letitia whispered with horror. "I think I've made a terrible mistake."

"What mistake?" he said, sitting her on a couch.

"I-I think I'm going to be ill."

"You'll do nothing of the sort," he said, brusqueness in his tone as he rose and retrieved a drink from the sideboard. He returned to thrust a tumbler into her hand, and she didn't touch it, so he brought it to her lips, sure to see her swallow the contents. She coughed against the burning liquid in her throat.

"He's the one," Letitia said, feeling her teeth chatter. "I've been so stupid. The spirit haunting Finola—I never thought of him as anything other than a spirit. But the specter, whoever he is, he's not gone. He's found a way to enact his will. The typewriter wasn't enough..." Her voice drifted off, her mouth opening and closing in horror as it occurred to her what she would have to do to save Finola.

"I have to find out where she is," she said. "Scry for her, search for her somehow. Right now, before he—"

"Don't you dare say that, you can't let him. You have to do something," Abby screeched, coming to stand in front of Letitia, who shrank against her seat.

"You aren't helping, Abby," Alasdair said in a clipped tone, and she stepped away as though he'd struck her.

"You don't get to back away from this," Abby said. "This all started because of you."

"If you can't be civil, then get out—now!" Alasdair shouted, and Abby whirled about and fled the room, eyes filling with tears. Alasdair looked after her, but after a moment his shoulders sagged, and instead, he turned to Letitia.

She gritted her teeth. "I need to find another way of reaching out to her. I need to find her and where he might be holding her before I can't anymore."

He stilled. "What do you mean?"

"I have a horrible fear that whoever has taken her knows the spirit's wishes," she said. "That they mean to do to her what they only hinted at in her nightmares."

"You mean the violation—" Alasdair choked off the word.

Letitia nodded morosely, clutching the now empty glass to her chest. "Maybe I should have searched harder before this happened, taken the chance, and seen for myself who he was, even if it meant opening myself to his evil."

He came before her to fall to one knee, grasping her upper arms and giving her a light shake.

"No, Letitia," he said. "Don't do that to yourself. You have to stay collected. I need you to find her before that happens. Can you do that?"

Seeing the conviction in his green eyes, she nodded.

"Good," he said. "What do you need?"

Letitia forced herself to take one breath and then another. "I'll start with something of hers. An object, something that belonged to her."

Alasdair drew back, the slow movement drawing her attention.

"Like a picture?" he said. "One she drew, that she said would be important?"

"Yes," Letitia breathed the word, and when he stood and held out his hand for hers, she took it. They climbed the stairs, rushing past Finola's bedroom to the adjacent room. It was a studio of sorts, lined with books and cupboards with a large table against one wall. In the center stood an easel.

Paper and drawings lay like discarded leaves from a tree, all in charcoal black, of darkness and figures, hands reaching out.

Letitia bent to pick one up without thinking, and a jolt

ripped through her hand.

Flung into darkness, she felt someone grip her thigh hard enough to bruise. She couldn't see them, but their strength pinned her down. She couldn't struggle against the chains on her wrists, and she felt the cool breeze of her nakedness as another hand grasped her.

"No!" She snapped out of vision and dropped the picture.

"What did you see?" Alasdair was at her side, staring down at the images with disgust.

"Nothing," Letitia assured. "It wasn't real."

She panted, fearing the worst, but as the sensation receded she could see it was only a memory. But the answer lay in the pictures here and Letitia needed to find it.

She left the ones on the floor and went to the picture on the easel, full of blackest shadow.

There was so much on the paper that at first, it was hard to distinguish what Finola had drawn, but beneath the charcoal lines came a sketch in silvery lead. The outline of a door, with columns at either side, gaping white holes becoming windows. But in every window a figure stood looking out, hands to the panes of glass, beseeching, all while the doorway had the ragged edges of a gaping maw.

Hovering over the sketch, Letitia's finger traced them, and she saw within the anxiety of the picture itself. "She drew an old house..."

"Goddammit," Alasdair muttered, and Letitia looked over her shoulder at him. "It's the hotel. She's drawn the old hotel."

"The one you took her to when this first started?" Letitia asked, and he nodded, studying the drawing.

"Whatever I did, I didn't get rid of him," Letitia said. "He's still there. And it may be where she is."

Alasdair spun on his heel to leave.

"Don't," she called. "I'm not sure yet where he's holding her. We can't go until I know where we should go."

"What do you suggest, then?" The tone was sharp as glass.

"We have to be certain," Letitia said, swallowing the fear clogging her throat. "There is no point running out there blind. After all, the spirit saw me, knew me as a threat. It's insidious and clever, and we must take every and all caution against it. I'll have to do a scrying to find Finola, to see where he's taken her."

"But you said before it's a risk," he protested. "What do you think you'll garner by going into a vision where you can't see?"

"I'll be able to at least say whether the old hotel is right," Letitia said, "or tell you if it's somewhere else. It hasn't been that long, and we should check before going in the wrong direction. They might not have reached it yet." Though fear wanted to make her curl away, rising guilt at the great disservice she'd done Finola for not ensuring the spirit was gone prevailed.

"Can you do this?" Alasdair asked, and she heard the indecision in his voice.

"I will be fine, Alasdair," she said, saying his name with purposeful confidence. "Arrange for a bowl of water, and a photograph if you have one. But first I need to be alone with the drawings, I need to...try and sense her."

He nodded and then disappeared down the hall.

Letitia focused on the picture, bringing an unbidden memory that was not hers. Someone else had seen this house, but she couldn't figure out who it might have been. There was only one way to find out, and she did something she promised Old Mother Borrows she would never do.

Ungrounded and with no safeguards, she touched the paper and opened herself to the vision—and stepped within.

Letitia stood in front of the old hotel.

Peeling paint and dust aside, it rose three stories above her, a tower in the center adding a fourth room with wide windows looking out to sea. Against the white weatherboard, the windows were dark and open like eyes. Columns along its wide front porch may as well have been teeth for the menace emanating from the hotel. A snarling grin to welcome her.

The wind whipped through her hair, pushing it into her

eyes, but she still studied the hotel. There were figures in the windows, and the sense of watchfulness within them burned her skin. A sullen resentment thrust out at her, but it was nothing compared to the darkness of the doorway to the hotel.

It was the figure from Finola's nightmare.

It didn't seem to want Letitia, but she sensed the phantom's hatred was goaded by her strength. Gone was the mild observance, and in its place was a growing aggression that crawled over her skin, burning her like a forest fire, ash stinging her eyes as the figure drifted from the doorway ever closer.

As she stepped back, the figures at the windows raised their hands. For a moment she believed they were threatening her, too, before she comprehended the desperation. They didn't want her to leave, reaching out even as the figure at the door tried to banish her.

"You're trapped," she said, staring at the windows and recalling the unsettling figures in her visions. He wasn't the only one seeking her. "It isn't only him—you're stuck in the hotel, too."

There was a scream, a cutting noise that was so loud it struck her like a physical blow, but it had not come from the doorway. It had come from under her feet, the shocking pain in that voice frightening Letitia. It rippled through her skull and the old hotel swam before her eyes before fading away.

The vision slipped and she found herself on her hands and knees back in Finola's studio. Her legs trembled as she got to her feet, hands visibly shaking as she raised them to her hair, which was still pinned in place.

Sitting back and avoiding touching any more of the drawings, Letitia remembered another drawing.

On a headland.

A great tower in the middle, a front balcony that looked like teeth, and a dark doorway.

Letitia removed the picture from the easel with the barest flick of fingers to avoid touching it before she replaced it with a blank one. She was no artist, but she drew from memory another building, one that had been drawn on a headland.

"What are you doing?" Alasdair was behind her.

"There is someone in the old hotel," she said, hearing her own tremulous words.

Alasdair stepped over the scattered drawings to lay a hand on her shoulder.

"I know," he said. "I just don't know how to get rid of a spirit."

"No," Letitia said, gaze drifting and then returning to the picture. "I think someone is using that hotel now. This image isn't from Finola. One of the girls who went missing, Mr. Edwards' daughter Cassy, drew this before she was taken. On the day before."

"He's the one that reported you to the police." Alasdair said it tentatively, but Letitia shook her head.

"It doesn't matter, Alasdair," she said. "I think that girl is in the old hotel. I think that whatever this *creature* is, just as it attached itself to Finola, what if it...what if it was possessing someone? Say, a man?"

Alasdair scowled at the drawing.

"No one goes there but me," he said. "I've had a few tradespeople through it to quote the work that needs doing, but I haven't been back for as much as two months now."

"None of them are doing any work?"

"No," he said, "I canceled it all and locked up the place after what happened with Finola. I didn't know what it was then, and at the time a few of the workers were making comments about odd things happening around the hotel."

"Such as?" Letitia pressed.

He shrugged. "Things going missing, hearing whispers, the sound of running. Finola was there with me a few times when I visited, so sometimes they thought it was her. To be honest, they didn't always know I brought her with me. It's a very large hotel."

"That's not it," Letitia said. "I think we're missing something. You never found anything there, did you? Any sign someone was using it?"

"I was only doing maintenance and upgrades," he said. "Some of the work myself, but I was the only one with keys—"

His voice cut off, face pale.

"What?" Letitia said.

"I didn't have all the keys," he said, anger growing with every word. "Because Calbright had another set."

"The seller?" Letitia clarified and Alasdair nodded. "He was in your office the day I first went to you. Not the father but the son. I thought he wanted to sell it?"

"He also made it a condition of his signing that he kept a copy of the keys," Alasdair said. "Which didn't alarm me because we hadn't finalized the titles."

"He's using it," Letitia guessed. "Or perhaps the spirit is using him. The keys would be the connection between the two... how the spirit is attaching to this Calbright. Just like with the typewriter and Finola."

Alasdair's hand clenched the doorframe, wood groaning from his grip.

"It's where they've gone," he said. "I'm sure of it."

"Maybe, but we can't go in blind," Letitia said. "The old hotel is full of ghosts, not only the one that found Finola." Letitia rubbed her arms as she said it, studying the picture. "It isn't common, having it stalk her like this. In fact, Old Mother Borrows confessed she only ever saw something like it happen to me, a spirit's ability to move from the place it haunts to people and objects. But what if a spirit in the hotel possessed Calbright? What if it's wielding him through its will?"

"Then we must leave—"

"Not before I've scryed," Letitia reiterated. "If Calbright has taken her, then he might be somewhere else. This is simply where the spirit has come from. We have to know what we're walking into, and nothing is going to help Finola if we can't work out…" Her voice drifted off, the sentence unfinished. She couldn't bear to think Finola already dead, let alone say it.

Alasdair opened his mouth, to deny or yell at her she didn't know, but he closed it at her hardened expression.

"We need to scout his territory," she said when he didn't speak. "It's the only way to be sure we can get her out alive. You don't know what these things can do, what lies beyond death, what can come from behind the veil. I do. I need to take all precautions or none of us may get out of there."

She dropped the papers, and he enveloped her in his warmth.

"Tisha, I…" he paused, and Letitia let herself relax against his chest. He didn't go on, and she didn't prompt him, but when he let go she didn't give him the chance to do anything more. She turned to head toward the stairs.

"I need to know more," she said. "I need to understand what is happening here. The only way I can do that is reaching out for Finola."

He didn't protest, and when they had descended and returned to the parlor, Abby was finishing her brandy.

"The police telephoned," she said. "They've had no sign of her."

Abby crumpled in her chair and Alasdair went to her side.

"We'll find her," he said, embracing her. "I promise I'll bring her back."

"She's all we have left," Abby sobbed. "Do whatever it takes, Alasdair, but bring my little girl home to me."

Letitia withdrew to a chair in the far corner. A bowl already lay in place in the center of the table. Not sure of where her handbag or any other tools were, she found a nearby lamp, taking out the wick and dropping several splashes of oil in the surface of the bowl.

Alasdair had been thoughtful in his selection of a terracotta-stained bowl, its dark varnish giving the midnight hue that so helped her visions.

As if sensing her mood, Alasdair led Abby to a waiting maid

and shut the door to give them privacy. He came to sit before her in the other single chair.

"Tell me what you are thinking," he said. "What did you mean upstairs about the hotel and those missing girls?"

Letitia adjusted the bowl, trying to stop the shaking that seemed to have taken over her. "I think the...phantom who haunted Finola has attached himself to a man. Whoever he is, he is living out the deplorable desires of the old hotel manager."

Alasdair was silent for a long time.

"I know how it sounds," Letitia said, confused herself. "I don't know enough about how malevolent spirits work."

"It's a delicate topic for you," he murmured, "but this happened to you once, or nearly happened."

"It wasn't the same," Letitia said, leaning forward. "The spirit was Daniel, and he loved me."

Alasdair's face turned blank and Letitia saw her error but plowed on.

"But when I opened myself at the séance to reach him, an evil creature came through, one that wasn't ever human," Letitia said. "But the old hotel manager was once human. It may be forcing someone or possessing them into taking small girls to satisfy its urges. We need to investigate it thoroughly because I think the girls' souls are trapped there, too. And I feel stupid not to have realized sooner that this was a possibility."

As soon as the words were out, she knew it was true, even if she hadn't meant to say it.

"You couldn't have known." Alasdair's assurance fell flat.

"I still don't, and it doesn't matter anymore. I have to be sure and to do so I have to seek Finola out in a scrying bowl."

Alasdair stared hard at her, and she didn't flinch or waver.

"Do you want me to leave?"

"No, but I don't know what I'll face there or what I might find. I need you to be ready for that."

"You mean if he's hurt her," he said in a dark and dangerous whisper.

"Y-yes..." Letitia said, licking her lips. "But I also don't want you to be angry with me."

"What do you mean?" He had stilled, eyes narrowed, and she couldn't go another moment without expressing the depths of her fear.

"Do you understand that I could lose?" she said, hands clenched on her dress. "The last time...the last time I fought such a thing I killed someone."

There it was. The confession and the ugliness of it.

"You did what you had to—"

"No," she said, swallowing past old fears. "A woman was possessed with an evil spirit and I beat her to death over what she did to me. Do you understand how out of control these situations can get? I spoke of risk before, but that is what I truly fear."

Letitia had refused time and again to help those girls so she could save herself, given that they were already dead. She had feared falling into that darkness or worse—inviting a monster inside of her again.

And for Finola, she would break every rule, even lie to herself about why she was doing it. Though she cared for Finola, she'd risk it all for the man across from her, the man begging her to save his daughter's life. She couldn't tell him now that she was head over heels in love with him because she didn't want him to know he'd cracked the walls around her heart.

But he had to know everything about her past, and what may come, before she tried. She would not lead him blindly into the darkness.

"I don't have the right to ask..." he said, enunciating each word as though dragged from his mouth.

"I've already said I'd do it," she said, one hand drifting to touch his hand on the table, and she sighed in relief when he returned her grasp. "No matter the cost. I must know, if not for you, then for me."

He was quick to kiss her hand. He let her sit before the bowl and fall into it, and though it was nothing like her treasured bowl from Old Mother Borrows, there wasn't a moment to waste.

Letitia leaned forward and reached out for Finola.

Chapter 19

Her jaw hurt.

The gag stopped her from speaking. He didn't like her to talk, not when she knew his thoughts.

It was her only weapon.

"My dad and Tisha are going to find you, Mister Calbright." She thought it as loudly as possible, pushing with all her might. She saw him start in the driver's seat, head turned toward her, and knew she'd pushed too hard again when he leaned over the seat to slap her face. It stung, but she was ready for it—she had the memories from her nightmares to prepare her.

His father had such soft hands, ones that handed out sweets to good girls who smiled for him, kind eyes crinkling at the corners, and always gave seconds.

Mr. Calbright's son was a bastard.

Angry face. Reedy hair, thin lips, narrowed eyes.

Pale as the moon and watery as a pig with diarrhea.

She projected the last thought and Calbright ran a self-conscious hand through his hair.

BEHIND THE VEIL | 213

Light glinted off it, slanted from the street, and flickered as he drove away from the city toward his lair. She knew his filthy mind, but not until too late. She thought the spirit that haunted her dreams was elsewhere, distant. She sensed it in the theater, knew he would come for her, and she went to the bathroom to throw up the nice dinner she'd had. She could not let Abby worry. Wiping sweat from her brow, she was focused on returning to the foyer when she walked out of the restroom and bumped into a stranger.

No, not a stranger, a man who worked with her father. He had a smile for her. Only when she looked into his eyes did she see what lay within. The nightmarish phantom was somehow inside Mr. Calbright.

She wasn't as astute as Tisha.

He'd hit her, hard, darkness spinning in her head as she fell into his arms. He'd taken her out a back door to a waiting car and shoved her inside. They'd driven for a while before he pulled over and tied her up. The rough rope on her legs and hands roused her but all of her struggles had done nothing. When she screamed, he took a cloth and tied it about her face.

When he looked at her now, she didn't see the phantom. Her fear faded, only to be replaced by the revulsion of Mr. Calbright, the things he'd done at the forefront of his mind.

She'd wept, shaken her head, drew away from him.

And he'd smiled...

Her only hope was that Tisha could find her and get her father to help. Nola knew now that Alasdair was really her father. It didn't matter. She'd known for some time before Tisha came along.

All she could do was listen to Mr. Calbright's thoughts and hope they would find her in time...

Geoff was anxious. He didn't know what to do. He cursed the psychic for finding the spirit—the spirit who bade him stay, to run to the hotel, to hide, to take one final victim before the end. He didn't want to die, couldn't yet. He was on the cusp of great wealth...help his father die and take the money and go somewhere no one would find out about him.

If the girl was right, then someone else knew. No, not someone, that bitch Driscoll hired to fix his damn niece. They knew. They were coming for him for what he'd done...

It made Nola's skin crawl, and she could face no more of his thoughts.

Nola wanted to taunt him some more, see if she could convince him he would be caught and that her father was coming for her.

But something bade her still, a sliver of awareness prickling over her skin. She forgot the outward thoughts of Mr. Calbright and looked within...

There was a familiar hand on her brow, a tentative touch.

But she saw nothing in front of her face but the back seat of the car.

The hand was familiar. Nola remembered that cool hand from another nightmare, a presence that she knew. Tisha...

Where was she? Where was Nola!

That was more important, and she glanced up at Mr. Calbright. She could tell the lights from houses were fading in the distance. She lifted her head, fighting the bonds to glimpse out the window. They were on a darkened road, driving north—the sea on the left-hand side. A disused road along the coast, not one she recognized.

Her leg cramped and she curled back in on herself, muffling a whimper at the tight muscle in her calf she couldn't touch.

Blinking away the tears, Finola refused to acknowledge panic as she twisted against her bonds, agony warring with her relief as she tried to see more. The features were shrouded in night's form, but after a while something emerged against the skyline, dark and terrible.

The old hotel.

Finola was very much alone with her kidnapper.

Time, time, time.

Finola heard it—Tisha was trying to speak to her—but they had none left.

Geoff glanced over the car seat at her, blue eyes aflame, thoughts of the secret place he'd hide her before attending to his needs. He'd leave Finola's battered and broken body on the cold floor and run for Canada.

Help! Finola called through her connection to Tisha, the last reserves of her courage wilting to nothing as the reality of her nightmares came to fruition.

When Geoff touched her to pick her up and carry her to the hotel, she struggled.

They're coming, she screamed in his mind, falling back on the car seat as he flinched away. They are coming for you, they know what you'll do, and you won't get away with this if you hurt me! She'll hunt you down to the ends of the earth, and there is nowhere you can go where she won't find you!

The raging whirlwind of her thoughts assaulted him, battering him, invisible fists he couldn't stop.

He hit her.

"They just got to the old hotel!" Letitia shouted, squeezing Alasdair's hand so hard she heard the bones crack. She was back in the living room, head spinning as she rose to her feet. "She's going to try and bide us time, but we have to go, and we have to go now."

Alasdair rose to his feet. "I'll get the car."

"Don't think about leaving me behind," Letitia said. "But we'll need what precautions we can gather."

"The car has lanterns for breakdowns," Alasdair said. "The electricity is unreliable out there."

"Get more. We may need them."

Alasdair called down the hall for a manservant, but Letitia brushed by and headed for the kitchens.

At this time of night, they were empty. The stove was turned low, but Letitia went straight past it to the pantry.

"Salt, salt, salt," she whispered to herself, examining the lower levels. There were two bags, and she grabbed both, ducking out of the pantry and trying to think of what else they could bring that might help. As an afterthought, she ran to her rooms and retrieved a vial of juniper oil and her gloves. Best not to get drawn into an unwanted vision, either by touch or by accident.

When she arrived back at the hall Abby was arguing with Alasdair.

"I want to come with you," she said.

"And I said no." He held a rifle in one hand and Letitia saw a pistol on his hip.

"You have to call the police," Abby insisted. "If you know where she is, then this is dangerous, and she'll need all the help she can get. What about doctors or transport to a hospital?"

Alasdair glanced over Abby's shoulder at Letitia, who shook her head.

"There can be no one else there," Letitia said, rather than make Alasdair say it.

"Don't you want to see Calbright arrested?" Abby spun on her heel.

"We are going into the lair of the creature that possessed your daughter," Letitia said. "It's night, it's dark, and we have to do it because we cannot afford to make Finola wait for daylight."

Abby's hands clenched by her side. "I cannot sit here and do nothing."

"And I can't take you," Letitia said. She didn't even want Alasdair coming, uncertain as to what she would face. "Anyone else there may be at risk, and the fewer people I have to think about the easier this will be."

Abby's eyes slid closed. "But you know she's there? That she's safe?"

"For now," Letitia lied. "We must hurry though."

Abby paused and then stepped aside.

Without a word, Letitia left the house, Alasdair by her side. Lanterns sat in the back of the car, and she placed the salt down beside them.

"Something to break chains or locks," she said, thinking of the specter's habits.

"There are bolt cutters and a crowbar in the back of the car on the floor," Alasdair said, laying the gun over the rear passenger seat. Letitia slipped into the front and settled in for the drive.

Alasdair got behind the wheel and the vehicle shot off into the night.

"You can't shoot him," she said after several miles had passed.

"Why ever not?" Alasdair bit out.

"He has to pay for what he's done," she said. "The families of the girls who were taken have as much right as you."

Alasdair clenched the steering wheel, and Letitia studied his profile, waiting for the tightness to fade and for him to acknowledge what she'd said.

"It will clear your name, too," Alasdair said. "Though I cannot confirm he'll arrive at the station without a beating."

"He deserves much worse." Letitia grabbed onto the seat and door at his fast driving. "But we have to focus on the greater threat. Any spirit able to manifest in such a way is going to be the real danger here."

Alasdair gave a clipped nod. "What do you want me to do?"

"Do as I say," Letitia said, not sure herself. "But if I am not myself, then you must leave me."

There was a long silence as Alasdair's gaze fixated on the road.

"Alasdair?"

"No." The terse answer denoted his feelings, but she pressed on.

"You do not understand what can and might happen," she said. "Finola must be our priority. She is ill-equipped to deal with this. She will need you, and you need to do as I ask you so

I can ensure that happens."

"For God's sake, Letitia," he said, head snapping about to glare at her. "You aren't a martyr or a prophet. You have no idea what's going to happen. There is a man who has my daughter and that is all. I shouldn't have let you come."

Anger sparked inside Letitia. She tried to curtail it, but it slipped into her voice.

"Do not think you know what it will be like," she replied, "or how bad it can possibly be. You've never faced anything like this before, and no gods or guns will keep you safe against a creature such as this!"

He didn't answer, and she sat back against the seat, staring out the window and watching the landscape blur under his driving. The speed was reckless to be sure, but for every mile, they passed a sense of urgency pressed down on her until she stared out into the night willing the old hotel to appear before them.

"You have to keep yourself safe," he said, clearing his throat. "I don't know about all of this...mystical stuff, but I know it is real enough that I'm glad you are with me. But please, don't let yourself get hurt."

"I won't," Letitia was quick to answer, and when his hand reached out for hers, she took it, squeezing it between her own.

Their touch made the wait bearable as Alasdair drove.

Letitia closed her eyes, willing strength to come to her and imagining herself and Alasdair protected by light. Now that they were hurtling through night's shroud it was more important than ever to hold on to the image, to keep it in her mind, fresh and present.

A sliver of her wanted to reach out to Finola to offer the same protection but without the bowl, she couldn't reach her.

She had to hope that Finola would hold on and keep Calbright busy or distracted.

What else might have happened didn't bear thinking on, but if Calbright knew they were coming she had to hope it would be enough to stay his hand.

The hotel loomed before them, and Alasdair didn't slow or stop his approach but drove the car up to the front of the building. Headlights illuminated the gaping maw of the old hotel's front door.

It didn't lend itself to invitation, but it mattered not to Alasdair, who grabbed a lantern and the gun and headed for a car parked to one side of the hotel.

With the lights of the car shining inside, there was no need for additional light, but Letitia took a lantern and the salt as something caught her gaze.

Not in the hotel but out on the headland.

All should have been indistinguishable, but it was not light or movement that caught her eye.

When she straightened and gazed out over the gorse-covered hillside she sensed someone out there. In the distance, a storm's approach flickered with distant lightning, but stark against the sky was a figure wreathed in shadow.

"Alasdair," she called, and the examination he made of the other car ceased when she repeated his name. He came to her side.

"There's someone out there..."

"Finola?"

"No."

Letitia lit the lantern, and with unsure footsteps walked out across the sandy headland to a figure revealed only by the oncoming storm.

The wind beat at the grass, rustling loud, but through it carried the sound of sobbing.

The man's shoulders shook as he stared out at sea, hands on either side of his face.

There was a click, the cocking of a gun, and Letitia had no time to tell Alasdair to be silent.

The man whirled about and Calbright faced them.

Letitia searched his eyes and found no sign of the specter

within, but it didn't bode well for them.

"Where is my daughter?" Alasdair said, weapon held aloft.

"He has her," Calbright whimpered. "I did as he asked but I could not stay down there, not a moment longer, not when he wants me to...wants me to—"

Calbright released a howl akin to a wounded animal, snarling, spittle flying from his mouth. "I am not about to end things the way he did! I will not bow down to him!"

Nearing panic, Letitia took several deep breaths, trying to figure out a way to reach Calbright.

"I don't want you to," Letitia said, putting down her lantern and the salt. She approached him as though he were a dangerous animal, making him focus on her. "Did he make you do things you didn't want to...?"

Calbright's gaze dropped as if considering the question before the rage faded. "No, it's how he found me, you see, or rather, we found each other."

"How did you meet?" Letitia asked.

"I was doing an assessment of the assets," Calbright said. "My father is dying. He wanted everything done before that happened. He wanted to be sure I had a bright future. It didn't include this place."

He gestured behind them at the hotel, but Letitia kept her eyes on him.

There was something wrong with the darting gaze, suggesting a madness or perversity within, but none of it mattered when Calbright had Finola.

"You didn't want to be like him?" Letitia asked, trying to find out how possessed Calbright was or if there was any part that detested what he'd done.

Calbright scoffed. "Hide in the shadows as a servant to others? Not likely. No, the only appeal of what he did was that it would never be found..."

Letitia swallowed at the glint in his eyes, weakness fading from pitiful creature to arrogance that made him stand tall.

His gaze drifted over Letitia's shoulder to Alasdair. "I never would have kidnapped her if he hadn't made me, but you see, you made him angry with all of your refurbishing, the work you were doing to the hotel, and you interrupted our plans. Both of you."

"Finola was his pet," Letitia guessed. "And you had your own collection."

"I never did understand his fascination with her," Calbright said. "She's almost too old."

"That's enough," Alasdair hissed, but Letitia's hand shot out, a growing dread at why he was simply standing there rising within her stomach, his words churning a deep-seated fear.

"You weren't after her," she said, and Calbright shook his head. "Finola is fourteen. The other girls were younger."

"He didn't mind..." Calbright shrugged. "Our tastes are similar enough he was happy as long as they were kept in the dark and they screamed."

Alasdair cursed. "So help me, I'll shoot him right here."

Letitia stepped back to put her hand on his chest. "No, stop, listen! He isn't lying or hiding what he's done, but he's out here. He could have taken the car and run, he could have left, but he didn't. There is something wrong."

Letitia's palms on Alasdair's chest were enough to stop him approaching Calbright, who rather than be relieved grew secretive. His long, slow smile stretched his face into a macabre grin in Letitia's lantern light.

"Where is Finola?" Letitia demanded, stepping in front of Alasdair, and taking another step and another until she was part way between them, and yet one more until she was just out of arm's reach from Calbright.

He wasn't much taller than Letitia, and attractive enough, but she would have passed him and thought nothing of note or out of the ordinary, except the evil lingering in his eyes that he didn't bother to hide.

"Locked away like he wanted," Calbright said. "You need

to go and stop him torturing her, and when he's distracted, he won't be thinking of me. I won't be trapped here. I can run."

The frank confession of what he wanted her to do stilled Letitia. She gritted her teeth, knowing that Finola was trapped and that she had to make one of the hardest decisions of her life.

If Finola was only antagonized by the spirit, then they had time—it was nothing Finola hadn't faced before, and callous as it was, it gave Letitia the capacity to focus on Calbright alone.

"You did nothing to her?"

Calbright shook his head. "I like them awake, and she—"

He broke off, and Letitia nodded, trying not to show her disgust. "I saw. She can shout at you without saying a word, and it hurt you."

"You're very clever," Calbright said. "Aren't you?"

He slid his hands into his pockets and studied her, and she didn't move from her spot or react to the condescending question. "I can't let you leave."

Calbright's upper lip peeled back in disdain, and before Letitia could say a word he lashed out, snatching her dress and yanking her to his chest. Metal pressed to her temple as she stared up into his eyes and saw that while no specter lay within, another monster altogether had ensnared her.

"Not that clever," Calbright sneered as Alasdair shouted her name.

"Please," Letitia said, struggling not to fight against the hold on her dress front. "Let me go. I am no threat to you."

"Oh, no, but he is." Calbright's glance shot past her face to Alasdair, who Letitia couldn't see while Calbright kept his grip on her. "You're not nearly as smart as you think if you believe he won't kill me the first chance he gets."

He jerked Letitia forward to whisper in her ear. "But here's the thing...I'm not a sallow specter hiding in the shadows, happy to shovel other people's shit and think that my virtues excuse my sins."

The spirit that resided in the hotel. She'd remembered the

vision from her first contact with Finola.

"But I have to give it to the bastard," Calbright went on, "he's sneaky and clever. He knows just where to strike and when. He guided me through the streets, found the girls alone where no one would see. Made it easy when no one can see him unless he wants them to. All I had to do was wait and bide my time. It's a shame he got greedy and when he got caught decided to—"

The words cut off, and fine trembling overtook Calbright as he gazed down at Letitia.

"Mr. Calbright?" she said, but there was only a gasping answer before the gun was under her chin and forcing her head back. When she locked eyes with Calbright she could see it was no longer him.

The blue eyes were the same but within their depths, Letitia didn't see the arrogant young man who'd gloated over his decrepit taste. Instead, a fire burned there, unholy and evil as it sought her end.

"No!" Letitia screamed, wrenching away, heart leaping in her throat as the gun fired. A burning stung her face, but she'd pulled back, terror driving her to shove Calbright as hard as she could.

As she fell to earth there was another gunshot, but none of it mattered. Calbright staggered back, taking one pace too many, and toppled over the cliff's edge.

Chapter 20

"He's gone," Letitia whispered.

Alasdair fell beside her, hands running over her face. "I know, I shot him."

"It didn't matter," Letitia whispered, staring out into the night. "Not when I pushed him over the edge."

"You aren't to blame," he said, drawing her up. "But we have to go and find Finola now."

Letitia nodded, a part of her numb, another part relieved the bullet had missed her face, but dreading what awaited them in the hotel.

It sat against the skyline, gloomy and forbidding.

They had to find Finola and a way of ridding the hotel of the spirit that haunted it. Nothing less would do than its eradication, and given it wasn't tied to the old hotel, Letitia wasn't sure how to do that.

Despite the creature's presence in Calbright's eyes, nothing remained now, but she was ever wary of its malevolent gaze.

Alasdair came up beside her where she studied the hotel,

and she fought the inclination to take his hand. She couldn't lean on him now, not while the spectre lurked in the hotel. She could sense nothing, but that didn't mean it wasn't there.

The hotel faced the ocean, but the drive came to curl up one side. There were old oak trees at the back, their spindly limbs scratching at the windows.

When she was close enough, she could see what Finola had drawn, and Letitia stopped.

Standing before the building, she took in the view. It was everything she remembered in her vision—brighter with the headlights of the car, but the darkness of the windows made her gaze dart to each one, fearing a looming shadow within.

Her gaze fixed on the doorway of the old hotel.

Alasdair reloaded the rifle, and Letitia flinched at the sudden sound.

"You'd best leave that in the car," she said. "You cannot shoot a ghost."

"I'd rather have it," he said with a grimace, "and not need it."

The comment reminded her of the salt, which she retrieved along with the lantern. "You have your tools, and I have mine." She fetched the other two lanterns, handing one to Alasdair. "Light them all," she instructed. "We'll set them about the house to dispel shadows and fear."

He nodded, lighting the ones from the car and setting them down on the porch before picking up his own and the gun. Letitia opened the salt and poured some into the pockets of her dress.

Thus armed, she stood before the hotel, but her steps slowed to a standstill.

Finola was inside, but the absence of the spirit settled apprehension deep inside her.

"There is no purpose to our hesitation than to build up our fear," he said, placing his hand at the small of her back. "I thought you were the one who wanted to face this monster. Don't lose your spine, Ms. Hawking. We have to get Finola."

She scowled as she climbed the worn stone steps to the

wooden veranda, shaking off the trepidation that sunk into her like steel hooks.

"You don't know what may work within," she said, still clutching the lanterns and salt. "Fighting this thing isn't as easy as it might appear."

"I never thought it would be easy," he said, as the tumbler clunked over in the lock. "It's why I'm glad you're here." There was more pressure on her back, not so much a push as the firmness of his touch before his hand returned to the gun, which he used to push open the front door.

It swung inward, and there was not even a squeak of the hinge or an ominous shadow, and Letitia let out her held breath.

The car's headlights illuminated a slant across the floor, a pale beam like a knife upon the floor. It darkened the gloom within, more sinister than an unlit building. The shadows grew thicker even as Letitia lifted her light to penetrate them. She didn't want to take any chances, not with the menace she knew pervading in the old hotel, even if it hadn't made its presence known—yet.

"Ready?" Alasdair asked. He took one of the lanterns and placed it inside the door.

"No," Letitia said with honesty but stepped through the great frame before he could tell her to stay behind. The front door was wide enough for two to walk abreast, and the entrance hall lofty and open all the way up to the third floor. Wooden floorboards were bare in patches and needed sanding and polishing. Scuff marks from where people had walked left trails throughout the foyer.

Two sets of double doors on either side gave way to a sitting room and a dining room, each extending the length of the building. Furniture was piled against the walls, rotted, broken, and useless.

A square staircase climbed to each floor, opening to the ceiling above where a great tiered chandelier hung, crystals glinting from the car's headlights.

Under the staircase stood a reception desk with cubbyholes behind it and hooks for keys that were no longer there, making the space reminiscent of the hotel it had once been.

"He sat there," Letitia whispered. "That's where he typed the bills."

She licked her lips, pressing them together as though that would ease the tension curling in her chest and the scream ready to burst out.

Alasdair came to stand beside her. "That wasn't where I collected the typewriter from, the one you found in the basement."

"Which is where we should search first." Crossing to the reception desk, she let her hand touch the wood, though she was protected by her gloves. She didn't dare take them off here if this was the ghost's haven. Instead, she set the glowing lantern down on the desk's surface to light their way back to the car, and she took the other one Alasdair had left on the porch front.

"Where is the basement?" Letitia said, and with a grimace, Alasdair led the way.

"Tell me about the hotel," Letitia said as he took them behind the lobby and down a corridor to the kitchen.

"Why do you want to know?" There was an edge of impatience in his voice.

"Because it may help me figure out more about this being, and a way to undo him." She shrugged at his backward glance, but he still told her.

"It was run as a hotel for nearly ten years during the gold rush days of the 1870s by a man by the name of Grant Harlow. He financed it, in any case, to take care of invalids and those who needed assistance. Many older folks came to stay here to be taken care of, but the place shut down, Mr. Harlow stating financial causes. Thinking it was a steal, the elder Calbright, then a much younger and naïve man, took it off Harlow's hands. He didn't see that without the gold rush he wouldn't get people out here to staff it. Harlow robbed him."

Letitia studied the wall paneling outside the kitchen doors, tasting the name in her mind. "Maybe he shut down for other reasons, ones he couldn't be public about. If he was no longer the caretaker or ran into trouble, how long did he stop offering the services of a hotel?"

"He wasn't the caretaker."

Letitia paused. "Then who was it?"

"At the time it was a Robert Lynwood," Alasdair said, and Letitia sensed it then, at the utterance of the name—a prickling along her skin.

"Don't speak his name," she said, even as she knew it was too late. Something observed her presence, as unwelcome as a spider in one's bed. There was something more sinister behind the perusal and although she turned about, there was nothing there but the shadows. She stared hard at them, but they did not waver.

"I didn't imagine that, did I?" Alasdair asked. "Someone is watching us."

"Yes," Letitia said. "Don't say his name again."

Alasdair's brows came together in confusion. "Why not?"

"Because names have power."

Letitia didn't say more, prodding him on toward the kitchens.

Down a corridor to the rear of the hotel, there was a long, low room, which was full of stone benchtops and a great black stove that could have cooked for a hundred people. Letitia stopped to place the bags of salt on the table.

"This way," Alasdair said, and Letitia accompanied him as he opened a door and started to descend.

It was not the cellar of the Driscoll house with its stone archways and wooden beams.

Here they'd used brick. Pylons interspersed the extended darkness. Their lanterns cast shadows into the distance, but all was bare floor and there was nothing to indicate the lair of a deviant.

Alasdair took several steps into the place, scanning the

shadows. "There is nothing down here. It held a lot of furniture at one time, but I had the hotel cleared out about six months ago when I first gained access to the keys."

She acknowledged his words with a nod, but her senses stretched out around them, seeking the specter. Apprehension crawled over her at its silence as her inability to sense where Finola might be sent goosebumps over her skin.

They walked around the pillars, Alasdair striding ahead and calling out Finola's name.

There was no answer.

"She isn't here," Alasdair said with a frustrated growl. "No sign of her or where Calbright might have put her. Do you sense anything?"

The question was angry and impatient, but Letitia's growing dread smothered his rage as he waited for her assessment.

"It doesn't work like that, but there is something down here." She walked around the room and stared at every pillar, every corner, every crevice.

With all of her experience, there should be some revelation, a feeling or a sense to show Letitia a sign of the girl's presence, or even physical evidence of the other girls—corpses tied to the floor, stains suggesting they'd been killed here. There was nothing but the dusty brick and an overwhelming sense she was missing something important.

"Where else could it be?" Alasdair asked, studying the walls. She followed him almost in a daze.

There was a simple way she could find Finola, but while she was brave enough to come here, Letitia wasn't sure she was ready to scry for such a being within its own residence. But the longer she couldn't feel the spirit's presence, the greater her terror at what might have befallen Finola.

She felt as though she were on a precipice, afraid to look over in case the enemy was looking right back. She would know where it was, but it would know her position as well.

Letitia whirled around, staring at all the shadows and

seeking out the phantom that had tortured Finola, but there was nothing in the dark of the cellar. Nothing but her and Alasdair.

"Something isn't right," she said, frustrated by her helplessness.

"If it's not here, then we should try somewhere else," Alasdair said. "You haven't seen the creature, so this isn't where Calbright left Finola."

Letitia turned to him, trying to explain why her doubt was building like a rising tsunami, slow to start but once she recognized it for what it was, she couldn't help but spin about to look at every shadow.

"Alasdair, this is wrong. I know it's here." She focused on the darkness. "It's somewhere deep and dark—that much I remember from the other visions. It's down here somewhere."

"Then we must look for it," he said, striding off through the cellar. "We'll check all the walls. I'll give them a kick, and we'll make sure none of these bricks are loose."

In uncomfortable silence, she watched as he examined the walls of the extensive basement, seemingly with actual construction experience rather than guesswork. He made comments as to the work involved in building the original structure and its integrity and craftsmanship.

"I didn't know you were a builder," she said.

"You have to know the material you are working with before you decide to buy," he said. "And if it has strong foundations, you are mostly going to be fine."

He slapped a palm against the brick of a pillar thicker than the others, and something in his expression changed.

Alasdair stood, one hand still resting on the stone, the other holding the lamp loosely, but his glance slid to her. It began on her shoes, roving up her body, and in its wake, she shivered as though more than his gaze touched her. His mouth was tilted in a wicked smile that caught the lantern's light, flaring the ember green in his eyes. She was as hypnotized as a mouse before a cat.

She took a step back, not so much afraid as wary, but her

pulse hammered in her throat when he took an answering step forward.

"Running, little one?" he chastised, and Letitia caught her breath.

"I'm not running from you." She shook her head even as her eyes stayed locked to his.

"Aren't you?" he asked, with a mocking lift of his brow as she took another step back, and then again when he moved toward her.

"I think you're scaring me." She licked her lips as she searched his eyes, but she saw only Alasdair within.

"Liar," he drawled, and she knew it was true. Enraptured by his eyes, she wanted to run, wanted him to catch her and push her down to the cellar floor and show her how clever those wicked lips could be. *On more than her mouth.*

Letitia gasped at the thought.

It had been so insidious she hadn't realized it wasn't her own.

"Alasdair," she snapped, holding up her hand. "We need to leave. We need to go now."

But it was already part of the game. Even as she moved to the stair, he blocked her path.

"Is it?" he said, "I thought it was one you were enjoying."

He'd stolen her thoughts. The gift of his daughter was open to him, through him, and was not his own.

Lifting her lantern, trembling with a rush of dread as she did so, Letitia looked into Alasdair's eyes.

They were black.

It was not him.

Alasdair was on her in a moment, grabbing her arms to thrust her back against a wide, square column. The lantern was roughly discarded to the side, its flame flickering out. Both his hands were about her wrists, which he pinned above her head. His scent was there, the warmth burning her skin, but it was too hot, too intense.

"Please," she whispered, trying to free her hands.

"Say it again," he said, mouth coming to nip her ear. "I enjoy hearing that tone in your voice."

"Alasdair Driscoll!" Letitia called, putting as much power as she could into her voice, but it wavered as his hands touched her. "You are *not* yourself!"

"I'm a man inflamed by a mysterious woman who taunts me with her juvenile blushes and evasive answers." His fingertips flicked the buttons of her coat, parting it with his free hand.

"I didn't mean—" She broke off when she felt his lips on her throat, the slight sting of his teeth softened by the lapping of his tongue. Letitia couldn't describe the lustful lethargy the action spread over her skin, even as she struggled against him.

"Do you ever mean?" he countered. "You are not innocent, but there is something delectable about your naivete, Ms. Hawking." The sound of her real name gave him pause, but the moment vanished as his palm brushed the buttons of her dress.

Letitia's eroticism started to fade as his hand became desperate, wrenching a panel of her dress aside, the popping buttons skittering over the brick work.

"No, Alasdair," she said, aware of his intent as he brought his body to press against hers, nudging his hips between her thighs to press against her dress. The heat of his personality flooded her, reaching into her soul to warm the chilly depths within. She fought not to arch into his touch, not to give in to his desire as desperately as she wanted to. To drink him down until he filled the bottomless pit within her.

"Why not?" he said, looking down at her, arrogance and lust painting his face with wicked delight. His eyes were green again, but something within was not him.

"Do you think I don't mean it?" He said and reached above her head to where one hand still held both of hers. "Why don't you feel me like you did before?"

He did know her thoughts, and he took a secret lust and goaded her with it.

"Don't!" she cried, writhing against his hold.

Alasdair tugged off her gloves, and Letitia was afraid of what she might learn or what she could see, especially when she wasn't even sure it was Alasdair she was speaking to.

He wasn't controlled in the true sense of the word, like some hell beast crawling across the floor toward her. Alasdair was a man restrained by convention to mere words, and they were fading fast under his desperation to possess her body.

The gloves fell away, their palms touched, and an urgent hunger flooded Letitia.

A crawling desire was within him to simply push her to the floor and take her. Hear her whimper in his arms as he put himself inside her. She shuddered at his elation of this fabricated imagination. She wasn't immune to it, lusted after him too, her growing adoration turning to desire under his evocative touch.

But in the dark of that thought, a figure lurked, one who wanted Alasdair to lose control, to push, to take advantage, to make Letitia a thing to use.

She struck out with the light around her, but the darkness swallowed it. She'd taken a piece of Alasdair inside her, and now the specter used it as a doorway. The light vanished, and she couldn't recall it—she could only feel Alasdair's hot hands on her body. The inevitable taking was shrouded in revulsion because it was not Alasdair but the ghost.

"No!" she screamed, and he stilled.

"You weren't that scared a minute ago," he said, hand coming up to cup her face.

"Alasdair, look at me," Letitia said, eyes wide and breath panting in her chest, fluttering her with panic. "Don't do this!"

"You were never afraid before," he said, but she heard the doubt and clutched his palm to her own.

"Alasdair Driscoll," she said, taking only a small moment to regret what she was about to do. "I'm sorry, but I need you to be yourself and to remember we are here to find Finola."

The name returned his own fear long enough for her to

strike back at the spirit's influence on Alasdair.

She already had a connection to him, built since he took her to the sickbed and she sucked the warmth from him. It was just a touch, but she needed now more than ever to take away what was driving him. It was not her best skill, but Old Mother Borrows had shown her how to take away guilt and anger and to pull away sadness when it became too much. She never practiced the skill since she never intended to use it when it could be so dangerous, and so intimate.

She used it now to remove his covetousness.

Her fingers reached for the pulse on his wrist where he touched her, and she took it all away.

Adrenaline, excitement, the thrill of having her under him.

Like a tidal wave the warmth rushed into her, but rather than feed it back she replaced it with her fear. The growing terror of the single lamp and the burgeoning noise of the storm overhead and the panic that someone she trusted would violate her.

It flooded into him, smashing against the will of the spirit invading him, snatching away the compulsion to take her.

Letitia had never been the spirit's target. He didn't need her when he could take someone far stronger and bend an already growing attraction into something vile.

Dread that he would lose her, break her, take away something he didn't yet have the right to ask filled Alasdair. The horror of what he had nearly done overtook his body, and he leaped back, shaking his hands as though they'd been stung. When he took in her appearance—dress torn, gloves cast aside—he flushed. She could feel his burning shame as he dropped his gaze to the floor and shook his head.

"Letitia," he cried. "Oh, God...what have I done?"

Letitia couldn't answer him. She leaned against the wall, panting, eyes on the shadows for any sign of the figure's perverse voyeurism. They were alone.

Whatever strength the spirit possessed appeared to weaken after bursts of intensity.

It was one small mercy.

She held a hand to her torn dress, and another fell by her side to touch the brick wall, to ground herself. As her bare hand brushed the stonework, the impression on the stone struck within her, sending her spinning into a vision.

Letitia was falling into an abyss, opening to swallow her whole. She felt the roaring of the sea in her ears, the darkness filling her throat to drown her. She was tossed on the waves of insanity, which ripped aside her carefully constructed walls to wash into her with its taint.

She could do nothing but scream.

Hands were holding her too tight, the sense of dread overwhelming her senses as the dark ate at her mind. The cliff's edge was before her and she was poised to fall into an unimaginable hell.

Shaken like a rag doll, she batted at arms that trapped her own to her sides. Too many hands were on her, grabbing her skirt, squeezing against her chest, pinning her to the floor. A leg between her legs, forcing them apart.

Curling in on herself, Letitia searched within to forces no one person was meant to control. It burned in her, silver bright, the power to hurt back, and she lashed out with it. The hands recoiled, but she sought them out, struck at them with her power, livid whip lines that lit up the dark.

"Stop!" It was a voice in a panic, pleading with her, and she hesitated, unable to see. No one touched her.

The dark of her eyes faded to the gloom of the cellar. One lantern out, the other was rolling behind a pillar. Alasdair lay before her, propped up on his hands and backing away from her. His suit was cut with great ragged tears, crimson in the dim light of the forgotten lantern. She and Alasdair were halfway across the cellar floor from where they'd been, and Letitia had no idea how they got there.

Alasdair panted, one hand upraised as though to ward off a blow—from her.

"Are you hurt?" she cried out, falling to his side.

"I'm fine," he assured but didn't reach for her though she examined his wounds.

Whip lines marked his chest. "But how did this happen?"

He sighed, relief and tension expelled in his breath. "I want to berate you for nearly slicing me to ribbons but under the circumstances, it's only fair." Alasdair's charm was there, but there was also a tremor of doubt. He was afraid of her.

"Did I do that?"

He didn't answer.

Letitia sat back, both astonished and alarmed. She'd cut him with her mind.

Chapter 21

"We need to go," Letitia said, pulling Alasdair to his feet. "We are too much under his sway here in the cellar and it's not where he's keeping Finola. He can't hurt us so he's turning us against each other."

"Before we go any further," he said, getting to his feet, "I must apologize."

"Can we please go?" She picked up the remaining lantern and used it to light the one she'd dropped.

"But I—"

"It wasn't you!" Letitia yelled as she headed for the stairs.

"Yes, it was," he said, swinging her to face him. "I've wanted you like no other woman in over a decade. I tried, time and again, to find love and gave up after more than one night's dalliance. The monster saw the monstrous part of me."

He was begging forgiveness, and they could ill afford the time.

"And what about me?" Letitia said. "I only stopped you when I saw it was goading your actions, that it wasn't of your doing. If you were to...love me, for the first time, would we do it here on this dank floor?"

His hand was tight on her arm, though he was silent.

"You wouldn't ever," she said, taking his hand to soften his grip on her. "I know you would treat me better than that."

"I've been insufferably rude, and I'm not sure I deserve your forgiveness," he said, drawing away. Picking up her gloves, he handed them to her without another word.

"Oh, you are an infuriating individual," Letitia cursed, snatching the items and leaning forward to place a firm but chaste kiss on his mouth. "When we are through this, we will discuss our mutual affection, until then kindly keep the self-deprecating nonsense to yourself."

"That was a tad harsh," he rebuked, though there was a sliver of his roguish smile back.

"Don't you see?" Letitia said. "We were lured into a false sense of security, meaning we are close to seeing what is really here."

"And what is that?" Alasdair asked, stretching his neck and rolling tension from his shoulders.

"Look around you," she said. "Where are we?"

"The cellar," Alasdair said, scanning the darkness.

"And what does it have?"

He threw up his hands. "I don't know—pillars, the floor, the ceiling... nothing else."

"Except that one," and she pointed to the pillar they had leaned against before they both lost control. It was far thicker than the others. When Alasdair beckoned her over with the light, Letitia lifted it higher for him to better study the pillar.

He traced his fingers over the markings of stonework. "This part is from the original foundation, you can see it meets the bricks here," he pointed a long line down the column. "But the rest, a good five feet worth, isn't part of the original design."

"What's above us?" Letitia asked.

"The foyer."

Circling the column and surveying the brick work, Alasdair couldn't determine anything else from it, and so they left it to go upstairs where the storm was ready and waiting. Rain came in a torrent down the glass panes, washing the dust from the surface, and the crackle overhead grew at every gust of wind. In the entrance hall, Letitia paused, not sure where to start.

She was drawn to the reception desk, but when she went behind it there was nothing but the floorboards, pigeonholes for keys, and a few cupboards, along with pencils, a letter opener, and other odds and ends scattered about. Alasdair placed the lantern she'd left there on the floor to study the grooves of wood, but nothing showed a trap door of any kind.

Letitia turned to the desk itself, putting down her lantern to open drawers, one of which revealed an old ledger book marked by an oddly flat key. She put the key to one side and with gloves on flipped open the ledger. The soft lines of lead denoted guests from years ago, though little was entered against them. At least at first glance.

"Do you know this book?" Letitia asked as Alasdair examined the panels.

"It's just a relic. I didn't want to throw it out in case it could tell me what the blasted key was for."

The key was flat and made of brass, and the shaft was a narrow strip of metal with uneven segments cut from the end.

She checked the ledger, noting the entries. They meant nothing to her until she got to the end. There was a different slant to the handwriting for the last few entries, and what drew her attention was not the names but the numbers against them.

12.

11.

13.

12.

11.

10.

12.

Seven figures in all.

"The same ages as the missing girls," Letitia said, her mouth curling in disgust as she noticed they even had check-in and check-out dates. Someone marked the last one for yesterday. Letitia dropped the book on the counter.

She wanted to walk away, to throw up, to be anywhere but here, but there was also an anger firing within her at the numbers. The little ledger was a sign of a revolting appetite, but it was also proof of her theory.

"Look at this," she said, trying to stop the roiling in her stomach.

Alasdair leaned over the counter where he'd been measuring the floor of the foyer, and she observed the moment he understood what she had found.

"So, Calbright did bring them here," he said with revulsion.

"Yes, but where?"

Alasdair didn't answer, resuming his study of the floor. Letitia put the book aside, and she scanned the woodwork for something that would show her what the key was for. It was here, close at hand, and all she had to do was work out where it went.

They searched the area, but nothing stood out.

"I've been over this hotel more times than I can count," Alasdair said. "There is nowhere but the cellar that's dark and underground." He was almost shouting his frustration at the walls, and Letitia guessed where his thoughts lie—with Finola in the dark, and he with no idea of how to reach her.

But Letitia had one.

"I can try something..." Letitia said, her words trailing off.

"What?" Alasdair said, striding toward her.

"I can scry for her," she said. "But Finola may not know how she got to where she is now. She might have been unconscious, which leaves me with only one option."

"You can't." Alasdair stopped when she gave a slow shake of her head. He must have seen the fear in her eyes, and he guessed her intent. "I can't let you do that."

"Do we have a choice?" she asked. "If I scry for him, he might show me where he kept the girls...and where Finola is right now."

"But isn't that dangerous?" he said. "If Lynwood knows you're looking for him—" Alasdair broke off with shock, but it was too late.

The hotel groaned around her in protest at the storm, but there was something else in the air as well. While the weather raged outside, inside the air was heavy and pendulous.

It was laden with animosity.

He was coming to strike them, but she didn't know where or how.

Letitia lifted her lantern, studying the halls and walls, and as though Alasdair sensed it, too, he stood with his back to hers, lantern aloft, while they stared at the ominous shadows.

There was a creaking noise and the windows by the front door shattered. Rather than fall to the floor, the shards spun through the air, tearing toward Letitia, who stared at the oncoming glass yet couldn't move.

Alasdair's arm encircled her waist, jerking her to the side, and pieces of glass smashed into the wall, thudding into the wood and breaking apart. More debris flew at them, driving them back down the corridor and into the kitchen. Alasdair dragged her along as she covered her face.

He let her go and slammed the door shut, and Letitia snatched the salt from one of the bags, pouring it across the threshold. Alasdair was quick to catch on, doing the same to the cellar door before bolting it shut. Letitia went to the windows, liberally spilling salt over the sills.

They stared at one another, panting at the sudden display.

"Was that the spirit?" he said. "I didn't know it could do such things."

"Yes," Letitia panted. "And he doesn't want us to find him."

"We're trapped here," Alasdair said, staring around as the

realization dawned on him. "If we go out there..."

"He could kill us," Letitia answered. "Which is why I must find the lair."

She went to the ancient stove, looking for anything to light a fire in the old hearth to give them light and warmth against the pressing dark.

"Let me." Alasdair was there, grabbing old, discarded newspapers off the kitchen table. A bucket of dry wood sat beside the stove, though Letitia doubted it would last the entire night.

While Alasdair made a fire, Letitia dug through the shelves to find an appropriate dish. There was an old metal pot, which would hold enough water, and she retrieved the vial of juniper oil from her pocket and placed it on the table. At the old sink, the hand pump wouldn't budge until Letitia put all of her weight against the handle, forcing dirty water to splash out. She waited until it ran clear before she filled the dish and carried it to the table.

By the time she was done, Alasdair had managed to find some coal in a hidden box beneath the stove and used it to feed the flickering fire.

"What can we expect?" he asked, as he watched the flames.

"More moving objects, perhaps voices outside, the same paranoia and anxiety we experienced when we've seen him before. As much fear as he can muster. He likes to terrorize his victims, even if we aren't his preferred type." On the latter point, Letitia's voice trembled, and she had to close her eyes to force herself to think. "Imagine yourself surrounded by light if you can, and if you feel your thoughts stray, pinch yourself or something worse, but do not let your thoughts wander or fall out of focus." She stood behind the chair before the pot of water, fighting the terror within at what she was about to do.

"Are you sure this is the only option?" He ran a hand through his hair, eyes darting to the door as though the spirit might appear before them. But this wasn't something Alasdair could fight. It was Letitia's battle.

"I can do this," Letitia said. "I will seek him out and find the lair, and there is a good chance that during it he will be enthralled. If I can follow him in his own memories, he'll be distracted for a time, perhaps long enough to find where he's hiding Finola."

"You said the last time you did this that something possessed you, tried to come through and take you." Alasdair's voice rose, hand falling on her shoulder, and Letitia turned to him.

"I am not as naïve as I was then," she promised, "and we cannot stay here. He will be crueler, make you do far worse than in the cellar. Anything to stop us reaching Finola."

It was a lie. A cunning and deceitful lie, and though he stared hard at her, she did not waver or flinch. She did not know how to fight or stop Lynwood. It was like nothing she'd faced before. But she had no other choice. It was the only way to find Finola, and she would be damned before she left the hotel without doing everything within her power to save the girl.

"I don't want to lose you." His confession should have been sweet, but she couldn't afford the vulnerability.

"Would you rather wait for him to kill us?" she said, her tone harsh. "He's already proven he can slip into your mind and possess you. Not much, not as bad as I've seen, but remember what happened in the cellar. Remember what he truly enjoys. What if he made you do it?"

She shot the question off, hammering with the truth, and his hand withdrew from her shoulder.

"Don't trust your thoughts," she went on, sitting at the table. "And don't leave this room. Not until I know for sure where he's hiding."

"How long can you last?" he asked.

"Not more than twenty minutes," she said. "Less if he's waiting for me. I will try to tell you where the lair is during the vision, but I may not be able to until it's over. Alasdair—"

She broke off and chewed at her lip, hesitating over her

fears, but he waited for her to finish.

"If something happens to me—if I'm not myself..." she said. "Don't trust what I say or do."

"You mean if he takes you." Alasdair's hands clenched on the table.

"Y-yes," Letitia said, swallowing against her pulse rising in her throat at the thought of an entity like Lynwood making its way inside her. The power she contained was no small thing and was regularly exercised with her readings, but there was no telling what a creature like Lynwood could do with all she possessed. Lynwood borrowed Finola's gift of reading minds from her connection to Alasdair, but there would be no telling what he'd do with Letitia's gifts.

Letitia took a deep breath, trying to remember all of Old Mother Borrows' advice, but on the heels of it was the certainty that this was what she had to do.

"I'm going to...insert myself into his vision and the final moments of his death," she said. "That will make me more than an observer. I will be a participant in his memories, but it makes me vulnerable to what happens inside them as well. If this doesn't go well, you have to promise you'll leave. Let me fight it on my own terms, but don't make yourself a tool of its arsenal again."

She held his gaze, and after a moment he nodded.

Knowing the time was at hand, Letitia leaned forward, surprising him with the briefest kiss.

"To remind me of what to come back to," she said and drew away to stare down into the water, seeking out the spirit of the old hotel.

"Thank you for staying at the Santa Barbara Seaside Estate," *he said to the disappearing customers, who gave quick glances back as they hurried away.*

They were the third customer that day to cancel early, and he was distressed.

Had the sheets not been clean, the food not excellent? The sea made it difficult to grow much, even if the oaks protected the garden from the worst of the weather. It was the salt air, but that's what guests came for—a seaside retreat.

He tried to think back and recall slips of any kind.

The elderly couple who'd come for a restorative stay while their son ran an operation out in the new gold-mining district had been hastily collected by the son and his wife that morning.

He'd only had a note and the remainder of a paid bill left on a man's bed. When the maid told him, he'd dismissed it as an emergency of some kind or an early train.

Instead of worrying about the cancelations, he instead finished writing up an account on his beloved typewriter before he toured the public rooms.

It was a regular activity, pointing out any little inconsistencies to staff in the otherwise pristine service the hotel offered. It was what his financial backer demanded, and he did his level best to make sure every room was occupied, everyone wore a smile, and every account was paid.

Now, though, he saw the darting eyes. The unfriendliness of the place he had come to call home pressed on him from all sides. Dropping the account book, he yanked a bill from the typewriter, shoved it in the guest's pigeonhole, and went to the dining room.

Tables were scattered throughout, each with a cream tablecloth that would have done an English restaurant proud. Silver service was denoted by the cutlery and pristine plates on every table, ready for dinner. Crystal glasses lit the tablecloths in rainbows, one for each type of wine. Towering over them were bouquets of seaside flowers and grasses, a colorful array for the oncoming spring.

He checked every table, measured a few, but otherwise it was as perfect as a lord's house.

Walking to the library, he found a book lying on the floor, but no one nearby who may have been reading it. Shelving it, he went to the rear drawing room that looked to the north. There was no one there either. It was eerily quiet, and he was quick to stride across the hall and into the kitchens.

The cook was gossiping to the butler.

This wasn't an unusual affair, he was used to it, but when the cook's gaze slid to him and her eyes widened, the first real dread settled in his chest.

"Is the dinner menu ready?" he asked, ignoring her reaction to him.

"Yes, sir." She answered slowly, hands clutching at her apron. "Just like you asked for."

The butler said not a word, but his gaze penetrated. A kindly old man, the look reflected there was of a disappointed father.

Letting the door close, he continued his rounds, questioning here, directing there.

Each time he found the staff jittery, their normal subservience lost in nervous glances.

He wasn't here to be liked, but he knew well enough that they at least respected him and the work he did.

In an uncharacteristic action, he climbed the top stairs to go to his room, perhaps make sure there was nothing untoward in his appearance. The maids, with the beds made and nothing much to do until the servant's dinner gong rang, were collected in the servant's hall and didn't notice his stealthy feet upon the stair.

"It's all over Santa Barbara," one girl said. "Someone saw him with that little girl, the one that went missing. That's what I heard. Alice, that was her name."

The world was ripped out from beneath him.

He'd been found out.

Someone had seen him. He could deny it all—it had been dark and quite early in the morning—but not without speaking to the police. They'd ask for an alibi, which he didn't have, and they'd come to the hotel and ask questions. The idea of them traipsing through his sacred space was abhorrent.

Abruptly turning about, he saw a woman on the landing below, staring at him.

"Who are you?" he said, surprised at her quiet presence.

"Oh!" she said, startled by his sharp tone, "I'm looking for... my maid."

"What's her name?" Lynwood asked. He didn't recognize this woman, but some of the guests had checked in while he'd been busy.

"Jane," she said quickly. "Yes, Jane. Can you call her?"

He stared at the odd woman a moment and then turned to look down the hall.

"Is there a Jane here?" he called. "Your mistress is looking for you."

A single head peeked around the corner at him after a long moment.

"Ain't no Jane here, sir," she said. She withdrew when he asked no further questions, but when he turned to tell the lady that her maid was not upstairs, she was gone. Frowning at the rudeness, he ignored it, remembering instead what the girl had said. The way she'd looked at him.

With revulsion.

The police were coming.

Lynwood wasn't sure what to do. A part of him had always known this day would come, and yet he had found such happiness here. It had been a delight, living his dual life, excelling in and relishing both.

It dawned on him then that he couldn't let the police take him. He couldn't fall victim to their public inquisition. His affairs were intensely private and he—

Stopping on the stair, he caught sight of the woman who'd been looking for her maid. She studied him now, eyes wide, mouth grim, but her gaze was so intense it took him several moments to take her in.

Within the hazel eyes were streaks of silver, and as he focused on her, a floor below, he couldn't help but feel it was a mirror of himself. Something about her was intriguing, and he had to speak to her. He hurried down the stairs, but she ran, too. No guest paid her any mind, even though she was pushing past them down the stairs.

Who was she?

His mind was not driven by anything other than the mystery of her person, and the more he tried to remember her face the more he found that he couldn't. He saw only her eyes, burning brightly, her penetrating attention propelling him.

She was not a woman he would have lusted after—too wide in her hips and breast—but he found himself aroused all the same. Not from her body, but what he would do to it.

When he rounded the last corner of the stair and stood in the foyer, the woman was gone.

He scanned the room searching for her, whatever drove him to find her goaded by the oncoming paranoia of police involvement. They would be arriving any moment now, so there was no time to waste.

Striding behind the receptionist desk, he took a key out of the drawer.

No one but him knew what it was for or where it went. With another glance around the room to be sure it was unoccupied, he turned and placed the key in the lock hidden in a miniscule hole between the panels. Further along the wall behind the reception desk, a seamless door swung inward at the key's turn. No one would ever know it was there without tearing down the panels.

There was a gasp, a noise he hadn't expected, and he turned to see the woman from before at the door's entrance. Almost a ghost as she glanced at him, she ran down the secret stairs.

She was invading his hallowed sanctuary.

Lynwood had to stop her, and while he paused to light a spare lantern, he discovered he couldn't find the key. She must have taken it.

She'd left the door open behind her, and with another glance around the empty foyer, he climbed through the opening, sealing the door behind them. No one would find them. The stupid woman had just walked into the best of traps.

Humming to himself as he descended, he was irked that his final victim might not be of his taste, but when the police came it wouldn't matter, he'd have time at least to add something to his collection. It would be a new experience to accompany him to the afterlife.

No place was like this place, he knew that now, and he'd rather die in here than on the run.

But first, he'd enjoy his last victim.

Neither one of them would leave this room alive.

Lying with a woman with hair between her legs. Feeling that ample soft body.

A part of him was revolted, wanting the smooth clean lines of a young body, but another part was intrigued. And it was better than nothing at all.

He traced his hand along the wall, feeling every stone, hearing the song echo off its surface as he admired the masonry and skill gone into building the spiral staircase.

The site had originally been a house with a cellar that had a cave beneath it. A long, rocky passage led down to beneath the headland, and in all the nooks and crannies guns had been stored during the Civil War. But after his uncle died and the war ended, all of that had been useless. It didn't change what an excellent hiding place it was, or how strategically located.

But Lynwood was penniless aside from the land. He needed a reason to be there. Picking up and discarding dozens of ideas he didn't have the funds for, one finally became obvious. The far headland was a frequent picnic and scenic spot for travelers between Santa Barbara and Los Angeles. Lynwood had been quick to discount a restaurant, but a hotel?

Lynwood approached Harlow, a wealthy man from the

gold rush, to finance the idea. He'd accepted. Lynwood need only hand him the title documents and Harlow would build the hotel. Lynwood already knew what he wanted to do, even if it cost him his pride during the day. He'd been an integral part of its development and shown Harlow he was a capable manager. Onsite, Lynwood had bribed the bricklayer to incorporate the spiral stairs from the old house into the new hotel. It wasn't on the plans, and Harlow had never known it existed. Lynwood just wished he'd had more time. It had taken two years to build the hotel, and another ten to have it perfectly operational.

None of it mattered if he could finally indulge his fantasy.

He wondered what would happen to the place now. The police would undoubtedly shut them down.

As he thought of his collection, he didn't care.

There were sixteen locks of hair on the walls. Sixteen reams of skin. Sixteen bodies taken through to the little alcove where the seawater came out of the bowels of the cave. He could hear the tide pushing water through the rock, see the water moving. It never came up above the lip of the cave, and no waves came in and out. When he'd jumped in, he'd found it was about waist height and that there were other underwater caves leading away into the dark. He'd never dared to venture through to see if he could reach the shore. No, his purposes had been far more particular.

He used the water inlet to weigh down the remains of the bodies and let the fish eat their fill, and if anything came back up, he buried it under his makeshift bed.

Lynwood liked sleeping down here.

Sometimes he could only sleep if he could hear the live ones whimpering.

Now though, it was silent, and he listened for the sound of the woman's breath. She had run in here, and he scanned around his castle looking for signs of her. The light glimmered over his home, but she was not there.

The more he searched, the more confused he became. She

couldn't have gotten out, there was nowhere for her to hide or run. He started to become nervous and offended by her uncontrolled presence. The feeling grew, urging him to anger that she had somehow escaped, that she had brought the police, and that she was going to tell everyone!

"Where are you?" he asked, not expecting an answer when even the light showed no one there.

"Did you think it would be like this?" A ghostly voice called.

Something grabbed his thigh. Hard enough to bruise.

"Are you as afraid as they were?" she whispered.

His wrist burned, and he shook it, using the light to see what had been done, but there was only a faint pink mark.

"Did you think it would be easy?"

"Where are you, witch!" he snarled into the dark. Mocking laughter floated in the gloom.

This wasn't right. This was his domain, his place of refuge, his secret...

Lynwood stopped.

"It wasn't like this," he said aloud, and the voice was silent.

He walked around the cave, knowing every crevice, every stone, every cage...

Whirling about, he looked at the wall of trophies.

There were more than sixteen.

He'd been tricked.

There was someone else in the cave. Someone who danced in the shadows and had tried to make him afraid. He smiled as he sensed her presence and became aware of it as a growing aggravation and not another lamb for the slaughter. A woman with ghosts in her eyes and a stain on her soul that opened wide for him...

He reached out. "Got you!"

Chapter 22

His hands were around her throat.

She was thrust face down in the bowl of water, his invisible hands pinching at her neck. The tureen was far deeper than she realized, and no matter how she battered at it, it wouldn't move. Violent struggling brought on panic—the need to breathe, the splashing water filling her mouth as she fought to push away from the table.

Hands wrapped around her arms and with a wrench she was torn backward into Alasdair's arms.

Letitia coughed the water out of her throat and lungs, blearily wiping her eyes.

"Are you all right?" Alasdair cradled her. "Answer me, Tisha, are you hurt?"

"No," she sputtered. "But I know where he is, I know how to reach Finola—"

She stopped at his indrawn breath and turned in his arms to scan the room.

Everything in the room floated.

Pots, pans, buckets, skillets, chairs.

Hovering ever so gently in the air.

There was a vibration, the hum of a string pulled taut and ready to snap.

Letitia remembered the glass shards. Instinct drove her to roll under the table, and Alasdair was quick behind her as everything came crashing upon the cupboard they'd just been leaning against.

The noise of smashing pots and breaking furniture was deafening, and she threw her arms over her head, Alasdair using his body as a shield as the shards flew everywhere. She was pelted and shards scraped against her clothes, but all fell away to nothing. For several moments she lay curled in a ball, afraid to move, as a hush descended. Alasdair's arms let go only when the last noises died away.

Letitia lifted her head, looking around for a new threat, but there was nothing.

Then there came a sound, distant at first, like the noise of an approaching train.

Under the table, her view was obscured, and as she warily looked over its edge, the table jerked above them. The legs lifted from the floor and then came hurtling down on them.

"Move!" Alasdair shoved her toward the door.

She scrambled to the exit, his hand on her back urging her on. The table flew at them, though it was too wide for the door, and instead landed with a crash against its frame. Letitia staggered to her feet and ran into the foyer, Alasdair close behind her.

As they tumbled out into the corridor all stilled behind them.

They held one another, panting. Letitia was shaking off the vision's haze and readying for the next attack. But there was silence.

"I think...I think he stretched himself to his limit," Letitia said. "Spirits have finite power."

"Did you find her?" Alasdair asked as she rounded the receptionist desk to retrieve the key from its drawer.

"Yes, I think so, but we have to hurry." She found the key in the drawer and returned to where she'd seen him in the vision.

The wood was older now, the beautiful polish dried and flaking.

Letitia focused on the latch that held the little door closed between the open reception and the foyer. She unhooked the latch that held the half-door open, closing off the reception area. She now faced the paneled wall beneath the stairs. As she scanned its surface, her gaze dropped to the metal latch that held the small reception door back. There was a narrow opening under the latch.

Letitia didn't dare breathe as she slid the key inside and turned it.

There was a click to her left, causing her to jump. A door in the wall popped open, the gap enough to slide her gloved hand in. She thrust the panel back to reveal a set of stairs leading downward. This is what they were searching for.

"Alasdair..." she said, and he collected the lantern from under the receptionist's desk, safe from the spirit's rage. He held it aloft, ready to enter but she grasped his arm.

"This time," she said, "we must not fall into his trap. He is using whatever he can to distract us so he can gather his energy. He's proven he can overcome our defenses, but I'm not sure what else he's capable of."

She didn't want to hurt Alasdair, to have what happened in the cellar occur again, but one look at his stern face told her there was no negotiating with him.

"I go where you go, Tisha." It was said with kindness, and with a quick sigh, she nodded and turned to the doorway.

There were no railings, and the stairs were barely wider than her shoulders. Alasdair would need to turn his body to enter. She took the stairs with care, one at a time, turning ever downward into the dark. It might be a subcellar, yet still, the staircase went on until she became dizzy with the turns.

"Any sign of the blasted bottom?" Alasdair asked behind

her.

"No," Letitia said, the confines of the walls pushing at her senses, fear curling in her throat. Onward they went into the dark, the spiral around her like a net she couldn't see. Only the tender flickering flame of their lamp eased the pressing shadows.

Letitia knew its game then. It was using terror trying to choke her, made every step about the one after that, and the one after that, each harder than the last.

She tried to curb her fear of the dark and of falling, but as she stepped down something far worse pressed on her senses.

She could smell the rot of brine and the stank of seaweed, and underneath it was a far more harrowing scent. Blood. Urine. Death.

Letitia's lips trembled with a useless prayer before she made it to the bottom, terrified of how far they had come and what she would see when she descended into the cave.

Yet there it was, the dirt and sand floor, stretching away to the edges of the light, and for a moment she thought she heard the rattle of chains.

"Good God," Alasdair said, holding his kerchief against his mouth.

"This is it," Letitia said, without having to look. "This is the lair."

Her eyes were drawn to the far side of the room. Three wrought-iron cages were buried into the rock, solid as the walls of the cave itself. They were empty but for the chains strewn on the floor, rusted and worn with use.

No, not empty.

A bundle lay within one of them.

"Finola!" Alasdair rushed forward, grabbing the door but it was padlocked shut.

Calbright had dumped Finola inside, her temple bleeding.

"Oh, God." Letitia wept, her hand going to her mouth to cover the revulsion.

"I'll get her out," Alasdair said, seeking something to break open the lock.

"Finola?" Letitia crawled over the rock to reach out for the girl, but like that night in her room, she didn't respond. Finola was shivering with the unknown touch, lost in a nightmare.

"Hold on," she called to Finola. "We're going to get you out—just hold on."

There was a grimace in the dark. Alasdair uttered a curse before he came back to the cage with a file in hand.

"It will take me a few minutes," he said, focused on his task. Letitia nodded and rose to scan the room and learn what she could of it or what might be useful for stopping Lynwood.

There was a rocky center, almost a platform, with bolts through the stone. Melted candles adorned the stonework around the four chains, and when she drew closer, lamp light illuminated the stains of blood across the macabre temple.

Unable to stomach what the vile things had been used for, she turned away and instead focused on Alasdair's back. He was methodical in his rasps on the chain. Letitia didn't want to know where he got the file from, but something drove her to search the cave to try to comprehend the depths of Lynwood and Calbright's depravity.

A cul-de-sac made into a working room showed benches and tubs, a chopping block, and working tools, all gleaming sharp from a whetstone that lay on the bench. Letitia's gaze followed the bench to the far end until she was drawn to the back wall.

Bits of hair and leather hung from racks upon racks, some of it incredibly old, others gleaming with youth and vitality. A wavy brown set of locks. A curling set of blonde.

Letitia recognized it from a photograph.

She turned away, rupturing her stomach's contents all over the sandy floor as she came to terms with what was hanging on that wall of horrors. The sheer amount of variety festooned there and the disgust of it all spilled up from her guts in a font of bile that burned her throat and tongue.

"Easy." Alasdair was beside her, holding her.

"Sweet Jesus," she uttered, as her stomach threatened to heave again.

"Just slow down and try not to move," he said.

"We need to get the police down here," she said. "That lock of hair belongs to Cassy...Cassy was here, only days ago. That's her *hair*."

Letitia waved to where she meant, but he grasped her hand.

"I need to get Finola free," he said. "Will you be all right?"

"Yes," she said. "Go back to her."

He handed her a kerchief and helped her to her feet.

Her task was not done here, though. She needed to find a way to stop Lynwood from hurting anyone else.

She hesitated, drawn to the little alcove that Alasdair had left.

"Letitia, you don't have to look," he warned, and she waved him off, nearly stumbling forward. As she walked on unsteady feet over the dirty surface of the cave's floor, she scanned the other section. Inside sat a desk and a small bunk with a figure curled up on its side away from the light.

It was a skeleton in a suit covered in a blanket.

Curiosity, morbid to say the least, drove her to take one step after another nearer to that small and huddled figure. But as she drew closer the old scent of rot and decay assault her senses, and she wrinkled her nose, staring at the huddled figure and unable to stop reaching out to it.

She gripped the edge of the old blanket, every second stretching into eternity as she drew it back. Something stuck to the thick wool, and she tugged at it until a dark head of hair showed, along with a loose woolen suit down to thin legs and brown shoes.

There was bone gray in the gaps.

Between the collar of his shirt and his hair.

Around his ankles.

Where there was a glimmer of the bone of his hand at one end of the suit's arm.

This man was dead—had been dead for more than fifty years. He had come here, laid down, and died.

But that couldn't be all there was to it, and so she reached across and touched his shoulder, the form stiff, the resilience in a pose that had been held for decades. She yanked it around to face her.

A wide-open skull greeted her, mockingly, with empty eyes and rotted teeth. Letitia knew it was Lynwood.

At the same time, she sensed his growing resentment, the essence of him filling the room. He'd gathered himself once more, and he was coming for them again now that she'd found all of his secrets.

Here was the key to defeating him. The refuge was within his body.

"Alasdair..." she said, tone rising with a warning.

"Almost done," he panted, sawing through the lock, the vestiges of rust giving way with a snap. "There."

He flung open the door. That was the last straw.

Wind filled the cave, a whirling sound so fierce that Letitia turned with dread to the room full of tools.

"Run!" she called out, and Alasdair needed no goading, sweeping the unconscious Finola into his arms and running for the stairs.

She was fast behind him as hurtling metal ripped through the air to strike at the stones around her, but with every turn of the tunnel's upward climb, they clattered uselessly onto the stairs.

As they neared the top, Letitia knew it wouldn't stop the spirit, the open space dangerous since they now held his prize.

Letitia had to keep it distracted.

"Run to the car," she yelled at Alasdair. "Don't stop. You must get Finola away from the hotel, out of range, and you must do it now."

"Don't you dare stay behind," Alasdair shouted over his shoulder as they fell into the foyer.

As they reached the front door, the warmth of headlights vanished as an infinite blackness swallowed the space beyond, forbidding them from leaving. Letitia didn't dare approach it or let it in.

"This way," Alasdair called as he headed for the rear of the house, but as he ran Letitia did the unthinkable—she stopped running.

Within her, the white light that had been so useless before rose once again, and she imagined it filling her and exploding outward, stopping the creature from reaching through the hotel to where Alasdair escaped with Finola in his arms.

It was only a second, a few at most, but enough that a scream on the wind rose, wrath pouring from the void in front of her as she fought to exhaust the spirit once more.

"Is that all you have, monster?" she yelled, panting in exertion, adrenaline filling her with false confidence as she backed into the foyer. "I defied you, like none of those girls could."

Letitia shouted to the empty corridors and rooms, putting as much power into her voice as she could, filling her chest until she could no longer contain the sound.

"You are powerless!"

The darkness vanished into the true night once more, the scream dying with it.

The absence of so much noise brought a clanging to her ears. There was no rain, no wind, no thunder or lighting. Letitia stared around warily, watching each of the shadows and wondering from where he would strike next.

The longer the silence drew on the more she wondered if he hadn't lost his power and dissipated. Letitia wasn't sure how much strength he had or how long he could keep attacking her. But as the silence continued, she became concerned. Nothing moved.

She had one last task to do before she could be sure Finola would be safe, and she had to do it while Alasdair was outside the confines of the hotel.

Returning to the foyer, she walked around, looking up the stairs and watching every piece of furniture, her mind guarded but ready. Letitia had to drop her shields to be sure the spirit wasn't present.

Every nuance of its personality was gone. She sought it out and found nothing.

Thinking it exhausted once more, Letitia took up her lantern from the reception desk and readied herself for what she should have done without hesitation down in the lair. There was no time to regret that she hadn't acted sooner, but now she knew what to do, despite any fears.

She hurried to the top of the cave's stairs.

The figure waited for her.

It lunged out of the darkness for her face.

She dropped the lantern, and the wick sniffed out.

Letitia couldn't see.

She stared as hard as she could, focusing on vague shapes in an effort to recall where things had been, wondering what shadow settled about her sight. Nothing touched her face or eyes but a blackness far more infinite than night covered her vision. In her blindness she felt a prickle on her skin, the horror tingling the hair up all over her body until it itched.

It was trying to possess her.

It hadn't moved. It watched her—it was right in front of her and Letitia was too terrified to move, too frightened to breathe, too scared to blink.

It sought a way inside her and Letitia could only push her thoughts outward and not dwell or think on what lay within her or what would happen if it were to take her.

Tears gathered in her eyes and filled them with pressure, forcing drops to leak down her cheeks as she refused to blink.

Her thoughts drew unbidden to that painful night, the closest to death she'd ever come.

Whatever this spirit had been, it was no longer a man, and

she had forced it into revealing its true nature, its indomitable will, and it was going to tear her apart from the inside.

It had found a way in.

It was going to take her.

"You hold no dominion over me," she whispered to it, her voice trembling as she heard the lie.

Because it did. It had found the dark stain of her soul, and it was coming to possess her.

In the dark of the veil she couldn't pierce, it struck her.

Chapter 23

etitia was falling.

Down she went until she landed on her hands and knees. She ached so much, the kind of pain that starts with the smallest of twitches and grows into a wave that washes into unconsciousness. Her abdomen pulsed, echoing her heart, but with every thud it faded, growing softer. Her hands were covered in blood, mixing with the tears that fell as she stared at herself in horror. It was nothing compared to the blood spilling into her drawers, sliding down her thighs, thick with mucus.

She could see it now, see the soul inside her, watching, unable to move, as the little life slipped away. It was all she had left of Daniel, the spirit who had lingered over her, caressed her skin when she hadn't been looking, wanting to hold her and their newborn.

Anything was better than the desperate agony of being burned alive on a sinking ship. His pain and regret brought him to Letitia, who'd sought his spirit in her grief and created a bridge she couldn't control. Instead of Daniel, a creature that had never been human came through, drawn by her power as she'd parted the veil between life and death.

Letitia tried to stop it, but she'd only banished it to a weaker mind.

It had taken the witch instead.

The creature struck out, using the witch's body, scaring the other women into fleeing as it spat out its vileness at Letitia's prone form. Letitia's body broke under the witch's attack. The little child within her gave a sharp twist of pain, and Letitia couldn't do anything to stop it. It was too late.

Letitia threw back her head and screamed.

For all the world it sounded in her ears like the desperate cry of a dying animal. There was nothing human in the sound and it wasn't enough.

She roared her pain.

Howled until her throat bled and she could not draw breath.

Blood pounded in her head, leaked out her body, rocking with agonizing misery.

The creature used the witch's voice.

"You'll be mine," it taunted. "You haven't escaped yet. I can still take you."

A fury spurred her into lashing out at the older woman's body. Letitia raked it with clawed hands, tore clothes and hair, brought her hands to fists, and hit again and again until she could no longer hold up her arms, striking until her knuckles were bloody, one hand spasming with tight, painful pinches. And yet the body still moved, still watched, still laughed.

Letitia didn't even recognize what was left of the witch's body by the time she ceased.

She fell back, leaving it in the corner, watching it twitch as the final breath left the body.

And then it giggled.

Soft at first, then it grew, mocking Letitia as it sat against the wall laughing.

"You're dead!" Letitia screamed at it.

The body jumped to its feet and danced about the room before it fell to its knees in front of Letitia and she gazed into its eyes.

Black, completely dark, blood oozing into its eyeballs and it didn't even blink, didn't push away the scalp of hair dangling over its face, didn't care about the broken jaw as it spoke.

"You'll give in to me in the end," it whispered. The grin was stretched wide over its gaping teeth, lips cracking and drooling blood.

It was savoring her growing fear, feeding itself on her horror as the darkness left the corpse and hovered over Letitia.

She wanted to look away, to run, but her legs would not move. Everything hurt, and the thread that had been holding her to life was starting to stretch. What did she have left to defeat something she couldn't kill?

"You'll survive," it promised, "and you'll help me into the world."

"I won't let you," Letitia gasped, unable to move.

"But you will. I can exist in you," it said. "I can exist...in here." Its hand drifted to Letitia's belly.

Bile climbed up Letitia's throat, but she couldn't move away for her tired body wouldn't obey her commands. Tears beyond grief poured down her face as silent as the grave as she stared in wide-eyed revulsion at the monstrosity before her.

The body slumped to the side, strings cut, maniacal grin still in place as behind it a shadow rose.

Shapeless as smoke, darker than night.

It wafted above the witch, rising higher to loom over Letitia. She couldn't stop herself staring into the eyeless face of the creature as she was washed in its true malevolence.

A shadowy hand reached down to cup her cheek and stroke away her chestnut hair, the other hand coming up to hold her face into position, almost sweetly, before burying its thumbs in her eyes. Letitia felt a stabbing pain so cold it burned, slicing down into her mind, cutting through to her soul. Real and not real, her eyes were there but a part of her was being ripped to shreds, every nerve ending struck as though the thing had truly plucked out her eyes.

It danced along her nerves, agony following in its wake, and the thing was inside her, in her veins, the pumping blood of her heart, and it buried itself in her before extending outward. Seeping through her body, a drop at a time, it coursed through her, flexing the fingers that were Letitia's. She trembled as she fought for control. She was jerked to her feet, limbs moving as though pulled by a puppeteer. She danced around the room as the witch had been made to do, spinning about until it brought her to a halt in front of a mirror.

The thing clumsily used her hands to pull the ringlets back into place, streaking blood over her pale cheeks, forcing the same macabre grin on her lips. Her mouth hurt it made her grin so much, and she tried to lick her lips before her teeth clacked down over her tongue, biting hard. Stinging pain spread through her mouth, and she cried out against the feral smile still in the mirror as blood spilled down her chin.

"Yes," it said, but this time it was through her mouth, patting her distended stomach. "You're pretty, and when this heals, we will fill it up again!"

Watching herself speak, seeing the mad smirk and black eyes, a part of Letitia wanted to scream but could not utter a sound.

No...Letitia had no voice to speak with, no tongue to say the words, no eyes to cry her pain.

"Yes, we will," it laughed. "We'll fill you up with the spawn of a demon's get. The right man will be enticed to lie between your thighs and rut upon you until he dies! Does that frighten you? Tell me it frightens you!" It cackled madly through her own mouth, and Letitia faded away, unable to face herself in the mirror.

Don't...Letitia couldn't imagine it, her child gone. The growing emptiness of her womb was replaced with the *wriggling sensation of the spawn's life. It was building her back up from the inside, readying her again to bear its evil unto the world.*

"No!" She screamed it, forcing the words through the thing's control. "You can't have me!"

It jerked her about, slapped her face with her own hand, but in the mirror, her eyes were brown once more, if only for a second.

"Foolish girl!" it snapped, but Letitia wrested control from it, her rage pouring into her body like liquid that burned, hotter than the sun, warmer than a desert wind. It scorched away the presence, turning it into ash, and as it went Letitia was filled with a kind of fiery power that would turn her soul to ash.

Wracked with pain, she fell back to the table, doubling over as the creature tried to force her to stand, but in the struggle, it didn't feel the blade the witch had used to cut herself in her macabre ritual.

Clutching it in her damaged hand, Letitia brought the blade down.

It sliced through her forearm.

Transferring the knife to her other hand, Letitia spread the last vestige of her power into slashing her other arm. The creature squealed as Letitia met its gaze in the mirror, still within her eyes.

"What is left of me for you to claim?" she whispered, watching the blood that fell from the cuts on her wrist to turn to liquid silver, her essence falling away like water from the wounds. The creature railed inside her, searing her with its writhing hatred, but it was too much.

She had lost too much blood.

Letitia laughed at the creature before she fell to the floor. The room spun, her eyelids fluttered—this would be her final moment.

Yet somehow, she was still there.

And so was the creature.

It came back, knitting the cuts to her arms, fixed her perfectly, hummed as it went.

It was going to make Letitia its own...

Letitia wretched bile onto the floor, spilling from her lips where she lay prone, body wracked with ghostly pain.

"No," she whispered, spitting out the taste of vomit. "You gave yourself away, Lynwood."

It was a dream, just as she'd done to him. He had tricked her and she'd fallen into the trap of her past, almost dying as she had done before. He'd used a memory she had not let herself dwell upon, and he forced her to relieve it, but she had taken herself out the other side through her own pain.

Letitia was calm. She was unafraid.

She could hear the rain, even see a little, enough to know she was back in the foyer.

Every breath was a blessing, every thud of her pulse in her ears was a perfect noise.

There was only Letitia and the specter.

He was simply the remains of a man, not a greater evil with prophetic intent and not a terrible darkness that would swallow the world. Merely the pathetic excuse of a depraved individual whose disgusting and abhorrent nature hadn't allowed him to pass the veil.

There was a flurry in the air above her, but it was growing weaker.

"You do like to hum, don't you?" She stared up at the swirling dark above her where she lay prone on the floor. "And you aren't nearly as powerful as the demon was—I am still here."

She could see the confusion as it darted above her, seeking any means to hurt her. She experienced a far darker pain than he had ever known. He'd only ever felt different, had enjoyed his indulgence, and the one time he'd been remotely afraid was when he'd pulled the trigger.

He'd feared the beyond.

Lynwood couldn't hold a candle to Letitia's fortitude.

"You never had a chance against me," she whispered to it, all the while a gloating smile stretched her cheeks, a dim echo of her past.

The shadow blurred in its frustration and ineptitude and she laughed at it. Her stomach ached and she couldn't stop the burble as she stared up at it, giving it a chance in her inattention.

The spirit reached a clawed hand above her and holding the letter opener that had been on the desk brought it rushing down to her abdomen. There was no time or room to move.

The blow fell to the side, and the creature screamed a high whistling noise of defiance.

She felt it gather and saw it move, but it was no longer focused on her but behind her.

Alasdair stood in the doorway to the kitchen, lantern in hand.

He'd come back for her.

"Letitia!" he cried, staring at her on the floor, the knife wedged in the floor beside her.

"Give me the lantern!" she cried, rolling onto her stomach as she flung away the knife. He rushed toward her but she held out her hand, snatching the light from him and shoving him away. "You have to leave now before he takes you like he did Calbright. You have to run!"

Not waiting for an answer, she fled down the stairs of the cave, skirt held aloft so she didn't trip. She knew the phantom would follow her. If her taunts had enraged him before, it did not compare to the tornado of darkness coming down the stairs. He didn't want the woman he couldn't overcome in his private sanctuary.

Step after hurried step had her crashing against walls, and she nearly tumbled down the stairs, knocking her knee so badly it locked. For a moment she slid down several stairs before momentum allowed her to find her feet again.

She sensed it behind her, the swirling storm just out of sight, and through the crackling air was his hum, the incessant sound that gave him comfort and drove her ever downward.

Careening to the bottom, Letitia tripped, nearly bringing the lantern smashing down onto the ground.

Wrenching her arm away, she brought the glass to within inches of the floor before she managed to stop it crashing. Ignoring the bruises and aches assaulting her body, Letitia drew her knees up underneath her and struggled to stand. She wasn't alone.

She attempted to turn, fearing it was Lynwood's spirit again, but the touch was different. It caressed her hair and patted her bleeding wounds with a soothing coolness. So many touches, tentatively helping her stand to face the final darkness.

Letitia scanned over her shoulder, wondering where the phantom was when the spirits of the girls blocked the bottom of the stairs. Like the spirit of Lynwood, the swirling figures had haunted her visions, ever seeking her attention but without malice. They were here now, for this had become their hell. Their domain as much as Lynwood's, they barred him entry now. The whirling cloud of wrath couldn't enter the cave. As quickly as the specter worked at fighting and shredding the other shadows, another was there to replace it, and it could not reach Letitia to stop her.

Letitia turned back to the wall of gruesome trophies, sickened as the hair glimmered in the light.

She knew what she needed to do.

Letitia held up the lantern, arm aching, and it suddenly slipped from her fingers. Only the crook of a finger held it in her hand. She couldn't fumble or the spirit would attack her again, and she wasn't sure how long the other spirits would last. Fatigue was crumbling her walls, but the fervent desperation of the girls' spirits pressed upon her, asking for freedom. Tears burned in her eyes as she gritted her teeth against the biting pain in her arm, but she brought it back in an arc and flung the lantern across the prized collection of body parts.

Screams reverberated from the walls of the cave.

So many voices, screeching, rose up around her, forcing her to slap her hands over her ears as they cried. The flames flickered, consuming the hair and leathery skin and filling the cave with choking smoke.

But she wasn't done.

Taking a fallen wooden pole, she grasped the end not aflame and, coughing through the smoke, set the bed that contained Lynwood's corpse on fire. The darkness grew, a wall of malevolent intent, but it was too late as the blaze gobbled the dry straw and emaciated frame of his body.

Nothing could touch her, even as the wind gusted about her, for his presence was fading faster than the flames licking up the remains of his corpse. She stayed to be sure it all burned, but the smoke grew too thick, and with nowhere for it to go she drew a hand over her mouth, refusing to think on the foul air she breathed and made her way toward the stairs.

Letitia stumbled, barely able to hold her head up. The stairs were there in front of her—she could see them. Her arm hurt, her knee didn't want to bend, and so she crawled, moving one aching limb after another. The fumes were choking her, but she went on, thinking of nothing but escaping as her palm landed on the first stone stair.

Her sole focus was set on pulling herself up one step at a time, but with every stair, Letitia's energy was depleting. Her muscles shaking, bones so brittle they felt as though they might snap, she still pushed on, if for nothing else than she didn't want to die in that cave.

"Letitia?" Alasdair was calling down the stairs. "There's smoke! Are you still down here?"

"I'm here," she tried to say but could barely cough the words out.

"Hold on," Alasdair shouted, and she could feel the vibrations as he pounded down the stairs.

"Here!" She called out when she saw the glow against the staircase's wall, and he was there, brighter than a desert sun, reaching down to wrap an arm around her waist. Alasdair held her tight to his chest as he scrambled through the narrow space, and although she must have been heavy, she felt weightless in his adrenaline-filled arms.

They spilled out into the reception area and bolted through the front door and away from the hotel.

Gentle rain cascaded around them, the sky a somber gray.

As he set her on her feet, she turned back to the old hotel.

Every window was lined with girls.

Gone was the evil specter of Robert Lynwood, and instead, sad faces stared out at her.

Letitia filled with regret as they each faded, one at a time, slipping away faster than she could track. Her eyes went to the front door of the hotel, and what might have been a shadow was nothing more than the angle of the door.

No eyes watched her, and nothing moved inside.

The hotel was still, the spirits gone.

"Let's go home," Alasdair said, his arm tight about her. He slid her into the passenger seat, and over her shoulder Finola slept soundly, oblivious to it all.

"I'm very tired," Letitia announced softly.

"You were incredible." He leaned over and kissed her temple. "I don't know what I'd have done without you."

And with his touch, the darkness within was cold no more but as warm as the rising sun.

Chapter 24

Steam wafted over the train station's platform.
In the twilight, it turned to yellow-gold clouds, and the pedestrians waiting to board became dark shadows, but Letitia was not afraid.

She stood next to her luggage, having already said her goodbyes to Mrs. Finch and Imogen. Letitia had told them she was coming back and had paid several months' rent, but both had acted as though she'd be gone forever. Letitia wanted to return, but she'd be glad to escape Los Angeles over the next few weeks.

Letitia had returned to her apartment a few days after ridding the world—and Finola—of the specter to find photographers waiting. They badgered her for juicy details of the events at the old hotel—and of the services she offered.

Andrews had told them and been subsequently dismissed from the police force.

But it hadn't stopped the publicity.

The police were convinced of Geoffrey Calbright's guilt in

murdering the missing girls thanks to Alasdair and Letitia's testament and by the discoveries of human remains in the lair. What closure could be given to the victims' families had been done, but not by Letitia.

Hundreds of letters had come to the Driscoll law office and Letitia suspected there had been some rather unsavory things written to her. There had been an entire bag of mail beside Alasdair's desk on one visit, but he gave Letitia only a handful of letters.

Letitia's hands tightened at the memory of his behavior.

His time with her was spent going over their stories for the police.

Letitia memorized the lie down to the finest detail.

She told the officers that Alasdair had taken her to see the hotel, they'd found the secret cave, and then they notified the police. But she'd become so frightened by the horrid display that she'd dropped her lantern, accidentally burning the remnants.

Rescuing Finola was not included in the story, since the girl herself was reclusive and disinclined to tolerate the presence of anyone except Abby, Alasdair, and Letitia. The ghastly affair was better not remembered of her person in any case.

The senior Mr. Calbright was in the hospital, having taken a bad turn, and wasn't expected to live much longer after having discovered what his son had done.

The hotel had been scoured clean of any remains of either Calbright or Lynwood.

The police believed their story, and while Letitia had to go over it several times, it had been easy to recount with Alasdair by her side.

He had been nothing but a gentleman after what happened in the cellar, but the familiarity that had developed between them was gone. The sidelong glances, chaste kisses, and everything else that had been arrogantly charming about Alasdair had not returned.

He was her lawyer and all disposition toward her faded, and

they didn't have many private moments together.

Letitia hadn't wished to pry since they were both swept up in the investigation and in caring for Finola. When he didn't speak of it, a silence had fallen between them. Letitia had no way of knowing if the entire event had made him change his mind about her.

Alasdair's protection of Letitia hadn't faded—he still maintained the façade that Letitia was his fiancée. At one point Letitia had believed he would do as he said. But while standing on the platform, waiting for him and the tickets to go to New York and sail to Scotland, Letitia became afraid.

It wasn't fair of her to criticize him. He'd been working with the police on the case and defending himself against any involvement regarding the old hotel as he was the actual owner. They had believed him, but the police had been meticulous in their investigation given the public outcry over the atrocity.

When everything had settled down, he'd asked her to take Finola to Scotland.

She'd accepted.

She'd already written to Old Mother Borrows, who'd replied that she'd be delighted to help Letitia again. Alasdair had booked the fare, paying for three tickets: Letitia, Finola, and Abby.

He was going to stay behind.

She'd found out yesterday that he wasn't coming when Abby had stopped by to give her the final itinerary.

Standing on the platform, she shifted from one foot to the other, wondering if she shouldn't confront him.

"There you are." The high, breathy voice of Abby turned Letitia about, who looked over her shoulder for Alasdair.

"Hullo," Letitia said, barely letting her smile slip when she saw that it was only Abby and Finola. Letitia broadened her grin when she locked eyes with Finola, and the girl smiled shyly back.

"I'm sorry we're a disappointment," she said. "Uncle is busy at the office today."

Letitia tried to hold her shoulders straight to ensure that

they didn't fall too far.

"We should get on board," she said. "I didn't have tickets and wasn't sure what you'd booked."

"First class, of course," Abby said, waving the tickets at a train attendant behind her with their luggage. "I thought you could have a cabin to yourself. For privacy."

"That's kind of you." Letitia stepped aside as her luggage was collected. A knot was building in her stomach, a host of unspoken words stuck in her throat as the party approached the train. Letitia was directed to her cabin and sat down to stare out the window. People scurried now as the minutes before the train left dwindled, and though she searched through the crowd with little expectation, her heart fell at seeing no sign of auburn hair and a determined expression.

He truly wasn't going to say goodbye.

Letitia was planning to come back, so it was by no means the end, but she felt as though she hadn't told him what he meant to her.

Perhaps she'd been foolish to believe that words and actions in the heat of the moment would mean anything in the cold light of day.

Had she misjudged him so?

Her head bent as she heard the whistle of the train. Tears spilled onto her gloved hands.

"Stupid," she whispered to herself. "You're being stupid again."

Angrily brushing her tears aside, her fingers caught in the veiled hat.

It was the one he'd given her.

"Damn you, Alasdair." Letitia got to her feet, and taking her impulse for what it was, she stepped out of the cabin as the conductor was about to lock her door.

"Ma'am," he said, "we're leaving. You can't disembark now."

"I have no intention of catching this train." She swept by to walk down the platform.

"Tisha!" Finola was shouting from the window, her hand reaching out to Letitia.

Letitia caught it. "I have to go back. I'll catch up to you before the boat sails from New York. I won't let you go alone."

Finola leaned out the window to hug Letitia as hard as she could. "He's an idiot for not coming," she said, "but he's worried. You're not stupid. He's the one being stupid, pushing you away because he thinks it'll make you safe."

Letitia laughed. "Then he's very silly, isn't he?"

"Go," Finola said, as Abby smiled behind Finola, waving her off as Letitia stepped back and the train started to move.

"I'll see you in New York!" she called, before turning and running for the taxi stand. A host of cars waited, and she picked the first and slid inside.

"Where to, ma'am?" the driver asked.

"Driscoll's Lawyers downtown," she directed.

The cab crawled through the streets, the evening traffic building.

A kind of excited fear crept over her skin, sending thrills up her arms and legs, almost making her dizzy.

What if Finola was wrong? But she couldn't be. Letitia wouldn't think about it or she'd lose what little courage she had left. Instead, she tried to remember every smile he'd given her, every little quip of his personality shown to her, every time he'd kissed her.

"Here you are, ma'am." The cab pulled up to the curb, and she took money out of her purse to give to him, not waiting for her change. Rushing to the door, she saw the office was mostly empty. There was only a young clerk at the desk filing paperwork.

"Is Mr. Driscoll in?" Letitia asked.

"He went out for dinner a few moments ago," he said, coming around to take Letitia's coat.

"No, thank you," Letitia said. "Did he go somewhere in particular?"

He shrugged, and Letitia didn't wait but turned to leave

the office. If he had gone for dinner, he would have headed along to the restaurants further down the street. She vaguely remembered him talking of a favorite place. She ran to catch him up, hurrying between people heading in the same direction. The crowd was thickening, and she couldn't see his broad shoulders anywhere.

She slowed her pace once she reached the restaurant district, checking in windows for his auburn curls.

Where would he go?

Uncertainty dogged her every step away from his office, and she doubled back several times before heading on, also checking side streets. People were glancing at her spinning around, but she ignored them all. She had no idea where he could be.

Letitia closed her eyes, willed her thrumming pulse to still, and reached for him with her gift.

She had needed a tie to find Finola, but Alasdair was different. She carried a part of him within her, and from the cellar so too did he have a piece of her.

She thought of the sand and the heat of the desert.

His face when she'd first seen him.

When he'd first brushed his bare skin against hers.

She opened her eyes with a snap. *There.*

Letitia went further along the street, tendrils pulling her along, her instinct stronger and surer than ever as she arrived at the place where he ought to be.

But when she got there the sensation was gone. She was standing outside a little bar full of cursing workmen. Memory came springing back of a disreputable pub he liked to frequent. As small as it was, she could not see him in the throng of people, nor would she guess that he'd come here.

The smell of fat and beer filled the air, and her stomach turned in flip-flops as she looked about helplessly.

"Are you lost, Ms. Hawking?" a voice said from the balcony above the pub. "The train station is entirely in the other direction."

Letitia glanced up. Alasdair stood with his hands on the balustrade, a frown on his face and the light behind him casting harsh shadows on his countenance.

"I came to—" her voice died off, intimidated by his dark look at the glances that were being sent their way.

"To what?" he drawled down at her, and Letitia wondered if Finola was wrong.

"I-I came to see you," she said, staring up at him, wondering for all the world if this hadn't been a terrible decision. He might have cared for her once, but she'd saved his daughter, done what he had wanted her to. Perhaps what she believed had never been true at all.

"Stay there," he told her and disappeared.

Letitia debated following his instruction but wasn't sure how annoyed he might be if she left. She clutched her purse, ready to step away and back into the throng of people to let it carry her where it willed.

But then he was there, stepping through the low doorway. Alasdair didn't say a word but simply grasped her under one arm and escorted her into the pub. He was careful not to touch her skin, but she let his personality, a swirling sandstorm, scorch her. She regretted coming, but there was no escape now.

People made way for him, nodded as he passed, and shot a few curious glances her way.

Smoke assailed her nose, the reek of Guinness thick in the moist air, the warmth of those around her beading sweat under her coat. The sudden heat compared to the cool wind outside made her shiver, and Alasdair's hand tightened on her arm as he directed her to a narrow back stair.

At the top, there was a waiter, who merely nodded as Alasdair led her to a private dining room. It was tiny, with only space enough for two to sit at the dining table, though the place was set for one. A pair of doors opened onto the veranda where two leather chairs sat, partitioned from the other private dining rooms.

As he released her arm, Letitia stepped away from Alasdair, wanting to put as much distance between them as she could.

Her fluttering heart wouldn't slow enough to let her breathe. He crowded the small room, leaning against the now-closed door. She couldn't run, and so she wouldn't be able to escape the kind of tongue lashing she was expecting. To hear she was right all along, and that this would devolve once more into a fiscal relationship, would dismay her.

"Why did you leave my daughter?" he asked, voice soft, but the nuance of wrath already denoted by his behavior rendered her confession mute.

"I'm not sure," Letitia evaded, studying the room. Anywhere but at him.

"You might be able to afford tickets on first-class trains," he said, "but I'm not in the habit of buying them for others only to have them wasted."

"Oh!" Letitia said, whirling to face him. "It's always about money with you, isn't it?"

He raised a brow at her, mocking her. "What else is there in the world, Ms. Hawking?"

After all, they'd endured together, that it was coming down to the argument that they'd started with made her furious.

"How about compassion, sympathy, and kindness?" she retorted. "What about I—"

The word died on her tongue, but he was standing up straight now, gaze fixed on hers.

"I didn't quite catch that, Ms. Hawking," he whispered, taking a step toward her.

Letitia took one back, not sure if the dark look in his eyes was angry or predatory. She shook her head, tongue stuck behind her clenched teeth.

"Why did you leave the train?" he pressed, and she shrugged.

"Because you weren't there," she said, not able to lie, at least not about that—it was self-evident from the fact that she was here. Letitia would be damned if she'd say more while he bore such irritation.

"I thought I made myself plain before," he said, moving to the table to collect his wine glass, an amused curl on his lips when she flinched a little. "I was going to stay here and trust you would safely see to Finola's tuition in your arts."

"They aren't my anything," Letitia snapped, "and that could take months!"

"And should it prove necessary," he said, "I'd join you when things here have settled down."

There was an undertone that wasn't quite a threat, but Letitia sensed the fingers of something darker. She remembered how insistent he was that Letitia go with Finola. His suggestion had come about almost immediately after the investigation was over but, given Finola's ability, Letitia had thought nothing of it. Not when they both shared concerns over Finola's behavior after the event.

Often the girl had gotten her own way in matters of importance, and at the start, it had been because everyone thought her fragile. She'd wanted a party that was less about ribbons and other girls and more about grown-up frocks and subtly using her powers on unwitting guests. Finola wanted to go out to the theater and restaurants, frequently escaping her tutor to surprise Letitia in the city.

Letitia wasn't sure what drove Finola. A part of her had become hard as ice and indifferent to the advice of those older than herself. But she listened to Letitia.

"This wasn't only about Finola," Letitia said, watching him.

"It doesn't matter what it's about," he said.

"Then why are you pushing me away?" she asked, suddenly confused.

"This may be America," he said, "but they have certainly not abandoned their religion or their practices of casting out or even killing witches. I did not want you the victim of a mob or some other vile crime before I knew you were safely out of the country, and I didn't wish to speculate on what could have happened if we failed to prove Calbright's guilt. I had to be sure no suspicion would fall on you, I had to show that I was to blame for the bullet in his chest, or did you forget about that?"

In all that had happened, Letitia hadn't thought about the manner of Calbright's death. Alasdair sighed and put down his glass.

"Which is why you should have caught the train." He went on. "So, care to tell me why it was imperative for you to come seek me out?"

Finola's words came back to Letitia. *He's being stupid, pushing you away because he thinks it'll make you safe.*

"I thought..." she gulped and plowed on with eyes clenched shut. "Doesn't what we went through matter more than that?"

There was silence, and when she dared open her eyes he had gone quite still.

"You wanted to keep me safe," she said, the slow realization making her feel stupid. "Because you didn't before. In the old hotel. In the cellar and when I fought Lynwood. You couldn't help me, so you put distance between the case and me. You did it to protect me."

His head snapped up.

Finola had been right.

"Did you think my staying mattered so little, and that I was simply there to contain Finola's growing gift?" she asked, and he scowled, a flush coming to his cheeks. "Or was it because in the cellar you were naked, not of clothes but of showing your true self, and I saw every part of you and was not afraid."

"I did the unforgivable—"

"Stop pretending!" she shouted, before lowering her voice. "I've not been brave about so many things, but I didn't do all of that for you or for money or because of Finola. I'm tainted, and it doesn't matter as long as I can stop it happening to other people."

"I know now you were never motivated by money to give aid," he whispered. "But...no matter what you say, it didn't make me worthy of you."

She stared at him, and when he wouldn't meet her gaze, she took hesitating steps to stand before him.

"In all the times I've ever been afraid," she said, "and there were many, I've never been scared of you. Only *for* you."

"I simply...I wanted you to be safe," he said. "And I didn't do that at the old hotel."

She tugged off her veil, dropping it along with her purse and gloves on his chair.

"Look at me," she said. "I mean really look. I can't walk away from the marks it left on me, nor do I want to live a lonely and isolated life hidden away from the world. You came and showed me that I was still worthy of being someone's wife, that I could come to love again, and if that means one of us not being an impertinent ass for a moment, then it will have been as I've always known it to be with you."

"And how's that, Tisha?" he said, standing with his hands loosely at his side, but she sensed the coiled spring within him, the tension in his jaw as he spoke, the narrowed gaze.

"That once again, I'm here, I'm not running away, and you will not dissuade me from my convictions." She lifted her hand, placing the lightest of touches on his jaw. "I can be brave enough for both of us."

"Do you mean it?" he said, and she watched his chest rise and fall in quick breaths. "You really—you want to stay with me?"

Letitia smiled through growing tears. "Yes, because you made me worthwhile. You helped me be brave."

He seized her, wrapping her up in his arms, pressing her against him, cradling her head under his chin. She breathed in his scent, let the heat of the desert rush through her, and she knew that it would banish the stain and set her free.

"Oh, Tisha," he whispered in her ear. "I was afraid. I never wanted another bad thing to happen to you. I just wanted to wrap you in safety, to give you peace after all you've triumphed over."

"I don't feel that way," she said, relief warring with nerves. "I don't know what to do or say."

He cupped her chin with one hand, looking down at her lovingly. "I promise you it won't matter, none of it will. You've opened my eyes, over and over, and the only thing more admirable than your abilities is your courage. I've never felt weak until I saw how strong you are."

Letitia couldn't say a word, as his lips fell on hers and he kissed her with care, banishing the pain of the past.

They spent the next hours talking and eating and making plans for the future—to get married in Ireland by the sea, to travel the world with Finola—all of it lovers' talk.

By the end, Letitia's head was spinning with Irish whiskey and Alasdair's ceaseless kisses.

About the Author

E. J. Dawson both credits and blames her mother—by reading The Lord of the Rings by J. R. R. Tolkien aloud to E. J. twice—for her complete absorption with the world of fiction. Growing up in a haunted mansion sandwiched between an abandoned mine and an endless pine plantation should have been all the fuel E. J.'s imagination needed, but her parents filled her life with stories: about themselves, their lives, and the ones they found in the pages of books.

Writing all through her early years and completing her first book at the age of sixteen, E. J. let a wonderful pastime fall into a vague hobby. When she turned thirty, and doctors told E. J. she might not be able to have children, she had to find meaning in life again. Her sole focus turned to the one thing that made her happy: writing.

When E. J. is not writing or working in a small country town on council permits in Australia, she's walking her two rescue special needs dogs, spending time with her husband, or curled up with a book.

You can connect with her at www.ejdawson.com and on Twitter @ejdawsonauthor.

Content Warning

This book contains adult themes including miscarriage, suicide, pedophilia, death, murder, rape, and possession.

Printed in Australia
AUHW020830090721
348426AU00004B/8